UNTIL WE BREAK

MATTHEW DAWKINS

wattpad books

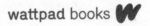

wattpad books

An imprint of Wattpad WEBTOON Book Group

Copyright © 2022 Matthew Dawkins

Content Warning: suicidal themes, death, mild swearing

All rights reserved.

Published in Canada by Wattpad WEBTOON Book Group, a division of Wattpad Corp.

36 Wellington Street E., Suite 200, Toronto, ON M5E 1C7 Canada

www.wattpad.com

First Wattpad Books edition: September 2022
ISBN 978-1-98936-587-8 (Trade Paper edition)
ISBN 978-1-99025-969-2 (Hardcover edition)
ISBN 978-1-98936-588-5 (eBook edition)

Library and Archives Canada Cataloguing in Publication information is available upon request.

Printed and bound in Canada

1 3 5 7 9 10 8 6 4 2

Cover design by Lesley Worrell

UNTIL WE BREAK

UNTIL WE BREAK

PROLOGUE

The girls were determined to watch the sun rise. It was Jessica's idea. She desperately wanted to do something that felt normal—an activity that other teenagers often wasted their time on during their long weekends, or days off, or summer holidays. Time at their age was brief and selfish, Jessica had told Naomi. Even briefer was their time away from the Riverside Dance Academy. Before they knew it they'd have to go back into the dance studio in order to bend and twist themselves into shape for their next dance competition. Right now was their only time to feel free. She said it, and to Naomi's ears it already began to sound liberating.

It was why in response Naomi suggested they lie on the carpeted floor tonight instead of on her bed. As she was explaining it to her best friend, Naomi wasn't sure if this was the once-in-a-lifetime type of freedom Jessica had in mind, but the other girl did not hesitate to collapse on the floor. Jessica asked Naomi for the blanket off her bed and Naomi quickly grabbed it for her. Maybe Naomi was onto something after all. She dropped right next to Jessica on the carpet and threw the blanket across their bodies. Comfortable now, she turned on her back to watch her ceiling fan.

"Have you ever seen the sunrises in Riverside?" Jessica asked.

"Well, I've been awake at sunrise but never actually stopped to watch it. Why?"

Jessica tutted. "You have to pause to pay attention to these things, Naomi." She looked over at her. "You're going to love it. It's like a sunset but better. Instead of everything turning black, everything turns into color. For a moment you forget the sky is supposed to be blue. That's how much color you can see."

Naomi turned to look at her and asked, "How often do you watch sunrises?" It was hard to imagine Jessica regularly waking up at that hour just to watch the sun come over the horizon. Usually, she didn't even want to wake up for their 8 a.m. rehearsals.

Shrugging, Jessica answered, "I've only done it once." Naomi raised her eyebrows. "But that one time was enough, you know? Like, I can still remember it. How often do you need to experience something beautiful to know how amazing it is?" They remained on the floor long thereafter. They moved on from talking about sunrises to sunsets, which Jessica insisted were worse in a lot of ways. *Sadder* was the word she used. Then they talked about Naomi's dad's promotion. The new burger place that was opening downtown. How, perhaps if they weren't homeschooled, their friend group wouldn't be just them in Naomi's bedroom at five in the morning.

Cutting herself off midsentence, Naomi sat up. "Speaking of burgers, I'm hungry. Should I grab us some snacks?"

Jessica leaped up. "I was just about to say that! Do you think there are any leftovers from dinner?"

"Probably. But Mom would say we shouldn't eat pork this early in the morning." Naomi's head fell. She was just about to suggest making a sandwich as an alternative when she looked up and saw Jessica grinning at her. Naomi laughed. "What?"

Jessica pushed her. "So we don't ask her! She's probably gone to sleep by now, anyway!"

Naomi laughed again, her grin matching her best friend's this time. She nodded. "All right, let's do it."

Slowly tiptoeing down the staircase and taking extended, far-reaching steps all the way to the kitchen, Jessica and Naomi gripped each other by the arm, snickering. Naomi tried her hardest to not bust out laughing when Jessica gently opened the fridge and asked if they should grab the tub of potato salad to go.

Now Naomi wasn't sure if *wasting* was the right word. Maybe other people their age would waste their free time on whatever felt easiest, but being out here did not feel like a waste at all. After all, Naomi was with Jessica, they were holding in laughter (which only made them want to laugh more), and the sun was about to come up. It didn't feel fair to describe such a good thing as if it was something meant to be discarded. Naomi couldn't offer an alternative to describe what they were spending their time doing instead of dancing, but it definitely did not feel like a waste. It felt, actually, like the opposite.

Milliseconds before the timer on the microwave hit zero, Jessica stopped it. She spun to Naomi. "I almost forgot!" If the microwave had beeped, Naomi's parents probably wouldn't have heard it anyway from all the way upstairs. Naomi decided against reminding Jessica about that, though.

Instead, she pushed her cold plate into Jessica's arms. "Do mine! Do mine!"

Jessica grabbed it and replaced the plate in the microwave. They inhaled the aroma of the steaming jerk pork with rice and peas. Jessica turned to Naomi and soberly told her, "This. This, Naomi Morgan, is heaven." Naomi fought back the urge to ask what kind of heaven then deserved to be called a waste.

When both plates of food were finished heating, the girls scurried back up to Naomi's room. They gently took the steps two at a time, shutting off all the lights they had needed to turn on, and finally locked the bedroom door behind them. Naomi plopped down on the floor. "You know, I'm starting to think you're only my friend for my mom's cooking."

Jessica had already dug in. "Fair observation," she said between bites, opening the potato salad she had decided on bringing after all. "But I would also like to posit that we have a number of things in common. See example A: our shared suffering in the academy."

Naomi was spooning rice into her mouth now too. "As a rebuttal, I would like the jury to take a look at example B: Jessica Kingsley refusing to even swallow her food before speaking."

Jessica smacked her lips. "The oxygen helps the food oxidize. Better for flavor."

Naomi let out a howl. "That's gross, and it doesn't even make sense!"

Jessica shrugged, on to the next forkful.

They sat in silence for a moment, Naomi watching the other girl continue to eat. She spun her fork aimlessly in the rice. "I still can't believe Prix is this summer."

Jessica groaned. "I don't want to think about it. This is our break, please. We get two weeks for ourselves out of the whole year and this time, I'm determined to take *full* advantage of it."

Naomi wasn't sure how Jessica could not think about the Youth America Grand Prix. For the past few weeks Naomi had been watching documentary after documentary and thinking of the best ways to structure her days to get more dancing in. "I know, but isn't it scary to think about?"

"Only if you let it scare you, Naomi."

It was easy for her to say. Jessica Kingsley always got solos. Naomi had seen the back of her curly head of hair as she glided across the studio floors so often at this point that she could probably draw it from memory alone.

Watching Naomi sink into herself, Jessica dropped her fork and put her plate down. "I'm sorry. I didn't mean to sound insensitive. But, Naomi, you're a talented dancer. I know it. Valentino knows it. Everyone at the academy knows it. If you keep overthinking, you'll psych yourself out."

"Thanks, so are you. I just don't know how you're so calm about it. You know our odds."

Jessica took up her plate again. "I'll stress about it when I set foot back in the theater. But right now, I just—I just want these two weeks, outside of that *cage*, to be ours. Our time. No dance academy. No Valentino. No Prix. And definitely no New York City Ballet. Just us. Right now." Her mouth was beginning to turn up at the sides, the tips of her teeth appearing.

Naomi had been rehearsing herself out of breath for ballet for so much of her life that now, every time Jessica mentioned relaxing, it felt like a sinful idea. Jessica had been a worrier once, too, but in the past few years her strict shell had eroded. She didn't stay up late rehearsing. When they got to crosswalks, she didn't practice her stances while waiting for her turn to walk. Jessica didn't even talk about ballet all that much anymore. Yet it never stopped her from being one of the top dancers at the academy. Naomi, however, was sure the moment she began to relax in the same way all her success would slip from her fingers, like slick oil. Dread bubbled in the pit of her stomach just thinking about it. She was about to ask Jessica how she managed to dance so well without taking ballet that seriously anymore when Jessica glanced over her head, shock replacing her grin.

Jessica sat up. "The sun's coming up! It's happening!"

She took Naomi's arm and pulled her up. Naomi let out a laugh. "Where are we going now?"

Her best friend spun, glancing at her in astonishment. "Outside! We can't watch the sunrise from your bedroom window, are you mad?" Giggling, the girls ran out the door this time, not caring how loud they were. The whole neighborhood could wake up and it wouldn't matter. Maybe they should have been waking up for this. Maybe this was something everyone ought to see. Jessica surely thought so. Outside, the sky had only just begun changing color. White clouds were swimming in pink and the orange sun was starting to appear over nearby houses.

Naomi shrugged. "Maybe we should have watched it from the roof."

"This works!" Jessica shouted, still running across their lawn. "Come on, let's get closer! These houses are in the way!" Naomi laughed.

She went after Jessica, set to waste more of their free time together or whatever it was that meant being able to feel the fresh sun on their faces in a quiet, lonely neighborhood; but Jessica was already out on the road by now, still running in her long summer dress. She was far ahead of Naomi and too far into the road itself to notice the brief honk of a car. By the time she turned, the car and Jessica had left Naomi's field of vision. Naomi ran out after them, her heart slamming against her chest. Peering down the street, she saw that the car was only a few feet away. Jessica's body, however, was a block down. And she wasn't moving. Naomi screamed.

ACT
ONE

CHAPTER ONE

Everything breaks—that's what the metal barre was for in the Riverside Dance Academy. Young dancers new to pointe shoes and rubbing Tiger Balm onto their ankles at first use the barre to help keep their balance. But after a few years, when they've broken enough pointe shoes and their bodies have begun to ache, they realize that bones break far too easily, and these horizontal waist-high metallic barres drilled into either wall of the dance studio are really there because dancers often need something to squeeze.

However, on a stage where they need it most, there are no barres. There is only the open floor.

The entire Riverside Dance Academy was holding on to the barres now. For the past four minutes they had been lined off in an unmoving, low plié. Their bodies were still as concrete—hushed. The only sound was that of Valentino's quick, barefooted pacing across the Marley floor. It was his instruction that was keeping them there. Punishment, he called it, after hours of abysmal dancing.

Naomi supposed punishment was the right word. Her legs were burning now and her outstretched arm felt more and more like it was just begging for permission to go limp. But she also knew that from the pain she would emerge a much better dancer. The agony of what a proper low plié felt like would be seared into her muscle memory and she would be that much closer to perfection next time.

The dance studio had one barre bolted into each wall on the right and left sides of the room. Unless Valentino made the decision to rearrange them, the same girls always took the places on the barre that were closest to the front of the room in order to self-correct themselves more accurately in the mirrored wall ahead. The few boys in the academy were scattered between the middle and the back, not because they didn't care for their own correction but because the odds of a girl getting into an academy were three times slimmer than theirs. They would have to wrestle and bicker to secure a spot that close to the front over a girl whose career was already closing in on her. The students watched as their instructor moved individual dancers, slapping and twisting their postures into place. He pulled faces down and snapped gazes into their correct directions. *Wherever the eyes look, the body follows* was what he often told them.

Naomi's eyes were trained on Valentino from across the room. Each time he adjusted a dancer, Naomi mirrored the correction herself. Wrists higher, but not too high. Back straight, but not stiff. At times like this, Naomi saw clearly her requirements.

Valentino Beaumont had created the Riverside Dance Academy a little under a decade ago, but he couldn't quite afford a building of his own just yet. In fact, his classes currently resided in the basement of the Riverside Performing Arts Theater, so chipped walls and chilly air-conditioning were the norm. None of that, however, stopped the twenty-something dancers from paying the slightly outrageous class fee to receive his instruction. Because in ballet, you pay for art, not facilities, and here in the run-down building sitting awkwardly in Downtown Riverside, the art was taught by Valentino Beaumont who in turn had been taught by George Balanchine. That type of art that was priceless. The dancers knew it too. A man as talented as Valentino deserved better recognition for his craft than what the little Riverside community was able to give him—it was partly the reason all the dancers were holding their breath around him now.

Finished setting them into place, Valentino backed away. With his back flush against the mirrored wall and the dancers arranged in his field of vision, he snapped his fingers at his latest intern and the teenage boy bolted upright. The dancers watched him clumsily shove his phone into his pocket and, from his corner in the studio, set his fingers to the piano. Valentino said, "The routine. Again." Then, over the tune of the music beginning, he counted them off.

Naomi brought to life all the corrections she'd observed. Her head smoothly traveled with her arm, her movements were precise, and she maintained her pointe perfectly throughout. She could feel her body singing with the music, her muscles twisting in harmony. But out of the corner of her eye, she caught Valentino turning to the opposite side of the room. He was still cranking arms to where they belonged and under his breath critiquing the same dancers that he'd shouted at only seconds ago. He spun around to the entire class and loudly said, "If this is how you intend to dance at the Youth America Grand Prix this summer, save yourselves the humiliation and do not bother signing up."

She was sure she was executing the barre routine elegantly, even after their full eight-hour class. Naomi waited for him to look at her.

Valentino continued speaking over the music. "This is an international competition, meaning the best dancers from across the world will be there. I guarantee you that each and every one of them wants your spot in your dream company." In front of Naomi, Bethany could hardly extend her right leg, and Naomi was sure the shaking barre was thanks to Samantha trembling two spots behind her. Sandwiched between them, Naomi knew her movements looked even sharper. She waited for Valentino to notice even that fact.

"Here is your reality check, ladies and gentlemen. Dancing is beautiful, yes. The best dancers make what we do look magnificent, even pleasurable." Valentino's tone darkened. "But when every other dancer in the room looks magnificent, where does that leave you? Hard work, dedication, and struggle is what separates the best of us from the worst."

Naomi made sure all her limbs were extended. She pushed herself upright. Checked the angle of her feet.

The class silently watched Valentino retrieve his discarded bag and shoes from the front of the room despite the ongoing music. Many of them froze in place or came off pointe completely. Walking out with his back to them, he said, "Grand Prix is only two months away. Come ready on Monday with a routine of your choosing, and we'll be getting to work. I'm in need of some serious impressing." He turned around a final time to face their eager expressions. "There is only one dancer in here right now who I think stands a shred of a chance." Valentino's eyes, followed by everyone else's, landed directly on Naomi. They lingered for a moment and there was a flicker of something agreeable that passed over the man's expression. Then Valentino spun and exited the dance studio. The piano music abruptly stopped. Valentino's intern quickly collected his things from around his spot at the piano and stumbled out after him.

The academy let out a collective exhale. Murmuring and distancing themselves from the barre, some dancers pulled off their pointe shoes, while others simply went out the door. Naomi was smiling. It happened so suddenly, really. She was only exhaling like everyone else when the grin managed to quickly escape onto her face. She knew it was only a barre routine, but Valentino's affirmation meant that she must be getting closer to perfection. When she finally wrestled her smile down and lifted her chin again, there were eyes staring back at her in the mirrored wall. Only briefly. Then they scattered. She didn't catch a specific face; it just felt as if they were all one person.

"There she is." Suddenly, Jessica was standing directly in front of her. Her hands reached out to grab Naomi's shoulder and a huge smile was on her face. "Good job today."

Naomi nodded but she couldn't help notice how much Jessica looked like one of them here. One of the one person. Jessica could pull off the ballet-pink tights just like they could, and in the mirrored walls she never stuck out like a dark bruise on white paper. She supposed that quality—of sameness and uniformity—transferred into Jessica's effortless dancing.

Naomi could not help but wonder which of her own qualities transferred into her own dancing.

"I'm proud of you," Jessica continued.

Naomi's head cocked. "Really? You don't have any notes?"

As if she didn't want to say anything at first, but since Naomi had asked, she might as well be up front about it, Jessica told her, "Well, it isn't how I'd do it. Of course, your extension was uneven and sometimes you came out of the plié too late but you did great nonetheless." She smirked. "Everyone else seems to think so. Didn't you see the look on their faces when Valentino said you were better than them?" Jessica crouched on the floor and began stretching. "They were practically steaming."

Naomi joined her best friend on the floor. "He didn't say that." Jessica was twisting her body into the stretches, not the slightest strain on her face while Naomi pressed her legs against the floor and slowly took her toes into her palms. A sharp snap cracked from the tendons in her ankle. She clenched her teeth.

Jessica responded, "Of course he did. Didn't you see his face? I'm sure I saw an almost smile when he looked at you."

Briefly looking up into Jessica's green eyes, Naomi nodded before returning her eyes to her ankle again. She tried bending it back and forth in search of the pain that had settled somewhere beneath her skin.

Jessica followed Naomi's concerned gaze. "I'm sure that happens to every dancer in the top companies. That just means you're on the right track." When Naomi didn't take her eyes off her ankle, Jessica added, "The School of American Ballet will be at Prix this year, you know."

"I know."

"You'll impress them, I know it. You'll get into their program and then from there you'll get scouted to dance in the New York City Ballet. It will take work, but we'll get there. I believe that."

Her tone was flat, dark even. But Naomi swore there was also a light breaking out from it, warming and brightening their conversation. "It's been our dream since we were little," Naomi said out loud. The few dancers still idling in the studio spun around. They exchanged glances and hushed murmurs.

"And we'll get there," Jessica affirmed.

Naomi smiled widely at that. She set her palms on the floor behind her and looked through the stained studio windows touching the ceiling. The view was barely visible, but every now and then she saw a car drive by. Naomi muttered thoughtfully, "Can you imagine us leaving Riverside? This place feels endless."

"Tell me about it. There won't be any good dancers left."

Naomi chuckled sheepishly.

"I'm serious. Look, Samantha was trembling! She cannot keep up!"

Naomi sprung forward, her mouth agape. A contagious laugh erupted from the both of them—one that had a few heads in the studio turning.

If Naomi was being honest, she wasn't sure how she would survive if her best friend didn't go to the New York City Ballet with her. Where she was the routine, Jessica was the music. And everyone knew a routine without music was meaningless.

It wasn't too dark on the walk home. There was still a bit of sunlight peeking out from the horizon between homes, and anyway, the girls had each other. Even if there were no lights in the sky or on the streets and it was pitch-black the whole way, they were still two halves of something bright when together. During their walk to Naomi's house, they were organizing the itinerary for their departure from Riverside and preparing for their future dancing with the New York City Ballet. They had decided that Jessica would dance both swans in *Swan Lake* and Naomi would be Giselle in *Giselle* every time they performed those ballets, but no matter who the lead was, they would share each other's dressing rooms. Then they went on a tangent about sharing everything, except tights. Jessica told Naomi that her dad would give her his car so she could pick Naomi up one summer evening and the pair of them would drive straight to New York together for their first day. Road trip music was to be strictly pop, nothing slow. Windows would be down all the way, even at night, and whenever they got cold, they would use the blankets in the backseat. Wasn't it usually cold in New York? They would have to go shopping the next day for warmer attire when it inevitably snowed. These conversations always seemed so far away and imaginary at first, but with each added detail their hypothetical future began to feel more and more like a sure present.

Their conversation had trailed off into silence by the time they arrived at the front door of Naomi's house. Naomi undid the laces of her sneakers on the front porch and stepped inside with Jessica behind her. The house was silent even though it was barely seven in the evening, but on Fridays, Naomi knew, her mother was in the living room. The girls made their way there together and as expected, the entire space was littered with dental floss and shiny fabrics. Naomi's mother sat in the midst of it, oblivious and hard at work.

Naomi cleared her throat over the noise of her mother muttering to herself. Aja Morgan looked up and saw her daughter in the doorway. "Oh good, you're home. I'm done with these but I think I might save those for Monday, how's that sound?" Aja pointed across the floor covered with loose newspaper sheets to a pair of freshly dyed dark-brown tights, then to a pair of untouched light "flesh-colored" tights.

Naomi smiled. "That's fine, Mom. Thanks."

"Are you sure?"

Briefly, Naomi wondered what the girls' mothers who didn't have to dye their daughter's tights did on a Friday evening. Watch television, maybe? "Positive," she answered.

Aja began collecting the undyed tights and folding them into a nearby bag. "How was ballet?"

"Good," was Naomi's usual answer, despite whatever had happened that day. It came so naturally now, the lying. The first and only time Naomi had answered with something true, her mother had sat up with her all night to watch her practice the Sugar Plum Fairy variation from *The Nutcracker* in her standing mirror until it was perfect. Aja told her no matter what, they would get the variation right. She had spent too much money, too much time, too much effort for Naomi to be anything less than perfect. Looking back, Naomi wasn't sure if they ever got to perfection, but she distinctly remembered the sound of her mother's miscounts at around three in the morning.

Jessica nudged Naomi in her side. She gave Naomi a look

then nodded at Aja. Then it dawned on her. Naomi cleared her throat. "Valentino said I have a shot at Prix, I think."

"He did?!" Aja stood up and skipped over the fabrics on the floor. She embraced her daughter in a tight hug. "Oh, you're going to do so well!"

Naomi nodded. This, too, was beginning to feel like more of a sure present. She continued, "Well, he said something like that."

Aja squeezed harder. "I'm so proud of you, Naomi." Then, slowly, she disengaged from her daughter and held her face, searching her eyes. "But you know if you didn't do well this year I'd understand, right?"

Naomi blinked. "What do you mean?"

Aja closed her mouth. She was thinking. Naomi could see the thoughts swirling in her eyes. Her mother said to her, "Losing a friend at this age can be hard, Naomi. You don't have to put any more pressure on yourself."

The walls of their large living room began caving inward. Naomi must have pulled a lever or accidentally brushed against a hidden red button because her mother's hands clutching her face now felt like a trap. Naomi looked to her right, to the spot where Jessica had been just a moment ago, but there was no one there.

She licked her lips, lying quickly, "I'm doing fine." The walls stopped moving.

Aja embraced her again. "But if you ever need to talk, I'm here. Jessica would be so proud of you, Naomi."

Slowly, Naomi placed her hands around her mother to seal their hug. She waited for the walls to recede but they didn't move. Pulling back again, Aja told Naomi she was going to make dinner and it would be ready soon. Naomi nodded, thanked her, and went up to her room alone. She closed the door behind her and dropped her bags to the floor.

Two weeks ago, after the funeral, Jessica had come back to help Naomi reorganize this space. The television was no longer on the wall because dancers didn't have time to watch movies. The carpet was rolled into a cylinder in the corner because how was she supposed to practice on a carpeted floor? Jessica even told her to bring the standing mirror from the living room in here so she could sit up with her every night and count her variations, like her mother used to. Jessica never miscounted.

"Don't listen to her."

"I won't."

"You know I'm with you, right? I'll always be right here with you."

Naomi looked up and there she was, really. Jessica was standing right there in the corner of her bedroom. Where else would she be? They were supposed to dance in the New York City Ballet together. Drive there with the windows down listening to pop music. Be the music to Naomi's routine. None of that could happen if Jessica was dead.

CHAPTER TWO

Jessica was around a lot these days. The following morning, for example, she shook Naomi awake and reminded her of her outgrown toenails. Terrible for dancing—especially with rehearsals for Grand Prix beginning on Monday. So the first thing the girls did on Saturday involved Jessica holding Naomi firmly by the shoulders as Naomi snipped her toenails down to the line. The activities that followed were different types of cuttings.

For breakfast, Jessica divided Naomi's portions. Then it was dancing straight into the afternoon, while Jessica watched and corrected Naomi in the standing mirror. Lunch was the same. The evening was the same. Dinner was the same. The night was the same. The girls were, more than they had been in the past two weeks, attached. Where one was, there was the other, and for it to have been any other way would have meant that too many things, like the toenails, would eventually be outgrown.

Before Naomi slept, Jessica made clear that the bedroom's floor space was insufficient as well. If they were serious about getting into the New York City Ballet one day, and they were, Naomi would need a real studio with a metal barre and flooring and all the other unmalleable things a dance studio offered. In other words, they needed the Riverside Performing Arts Theater. Jessica was, Naomi knew, right. So she packed her tights and all her equipment and set her alarm for eight the next day.

Jessica woke her at seven.

She explained that more time awake really meant more time to rehearse. Which meant that Naomi could make her routine tighter, which ultimately meant that the earlier she woke up, the higher her chances would be of getting accepted into the New York City Ballet. Naomi quickly showered, changed, and leaped down the stairs. When she got to the landing, she noticed how quiet the rest of the house was. It was a Sunday morning so she knew she'd be the only one up. In fact, she counted on it. Except that when she got to the living room on her way out, she heard snoring coming from the couch.

She had assumed initially that it was her father. She didn't know why—she'd never seen him sleep on the couch before—but somehow it felt like the right conclusion. But when she got closer, Naomi saw it was her mom lying there. Fast asleep with a blanket lazily covering her midsection. Next, she noticed an open bottle of wine on the coffee table and its accompanying half-full glass. Naomi walked around the couch and fixed the blanket over her mother. She'd never seen her mom out here drinking wine before, and she wasn't sure what to make of it.

But she wasn't sure she had the time to think about it either. Jessica was already urging her to hurry. "We have to get going! You need to rehearse!"

Naomi gathered herself.

Scurrying out the door, she convinced herself that a lot of adults drank wine on Saturday evenings; her mother was no different. If anything, her mother was the same, and she could drink as much wine on as many Saturdays as she'd like.

On their walk to the theater, the girls brainstormed the best routine to impress the judges from the School of American Ballet at Grand Prix. They figured if George Balanchine had founded the New York City Ballet, the School of American Ballet, and taught Valentino, then the most effective strategy for demonstrating Naomi's commitment to all three would be to perform a piece from one of Balanchine's own ballets, *The Nutcracker*.

Jessica warned Naomi that the ballet was a bit juvenile, but eventually the girls decided to use that to their advantage. At Naomi's level she could make the moves she'd been practicing since she was twelve look flawless. The Dance of the Sugar Plum Fairy would come especially easy for her, given how often she had rehearsed it in her standing mirror. At home, the pain had made the ballet memorable. Onstage, the pain would make the ballet perfect.

The Riverside Performing Arts Theater was usually dark and closed off on Sundays since the dance academy wasn't there to bring it to life with their practicing. But every other Sunday, like today, the building opened up for the community choir. They came here for a few hours a day to rehearse songs and hymns, but for Naomi, it also meant that the theater was open for anyone else to use. Namely, her.

Naomi and Jessica went up the main entrance steps, where they pushed the double doors wide open. The choir was already there. They had taken up the entirety of the main stage and had mics, speakers, and instruments scattered across the raised platform. Some members were walking idly about, others were seated. They weren't even wearing matching gowns like Naomi had expected them to, but despite this inconsistency, their harmonies were flawless. Their voices layered on top of one another and wrapped high into the air. Naomi wondered how they could possibly know to match their voices that well when they couldn't even match their clothes. The dance academy relied on that kind of sameness.

Jessica grabbed Naomi's hand, insisting that they didn't have time to listen. She pulled her past the rows of seats and circled backstage where they descended the staircase and went into the tunnel that fed to the girls' dressing room. Walking inside, Naomi exhaled heavily and found an ottoman to plop down on. She hadn't realized they'd both been running.

The dark dressing room wasn't ready for them. There was spilled makeup on the vanities, and the chairs were all out of place. It was clear that the janitor hadn't come by yet. But now that they were here, the melodies from the choir were silenced. Behind all this concrete in a small room of the enclosed basement, hardly any sound penetrated. All Naomi could hear was her own breathing and Jessica pacing nearby.

Naomi fished her phone out and checked the time. Eight o'clock.

"You know, I hear at NYCB all the dancers turn their phones off the moment they set foot in the building."

Naomi turned around. "Oh, I wasn't—" But Jessica was ready.

"It keeps them focused and professional. That's what I hear, anyway."

Naomi switched her phone off and slipped it into her bag. "How do they get calls and texts then?"

Nonchalantly, Jessica told her, "They don't. Not when they're dancing."

Naomi nodded. It made sense. "Dance, above everything else" seemed like a mantra that dancers from the New York City Ballet would repeat to themselves before they went to bed at night. Opening her bag, she exchanged her sweats for tights and then sat on the floor. She tucked both knees in to get a better look at her toes. The big one was the darkest this time. Once, Naomi used to wish that she had squared feet like some of the other girls in the academy; then at least the pain would be equal across all her toes. But now she'd come to realize that maybe having all the pain in one place wasn't so bad as long as her other four toes could make up for what the big one couldn't anymore. Corns swelled on the sides of her pinky toe, and there was a new blister on her metatarsal.

Digging through her bag, Naomi uncapped her tube of Tiger Balm and rubbed the numbing gel into her ankles where swellings were prone. Then she tore off strips of athletic tape with her teeth and wrapped her toes individually to cover all the freshest scars. She made sure her pointe was still flexible and the tape wasn't too tight. Then she covered the damaged feet with soft lambswool and finally pushed them into her pointe shoes.

"Perfect," Jessica commented. Then she called, "Let's go."

Naomi had danced this ballet numerous times before, so she knew the entirety of *The Nutcracker* by heart. She could easily run through it twice from memory alone but her technique, it seemed, was not as effortless. Jessica made that apparent. She was standing in the spot Valentino usually occupied during classes to instruct. But there were more corrections than anything else, mostly to do with Naomi's posture and the extension of her legs. Throughout the day, as Naomi tried to fix herself, her right ankle kept resisting. She stretched the joint a little more and occasionally paused to roll her heel out of the discomfort. None of it helped.

Close to the end of the variation, she wobbled. Jessica warned her, "Don't stop, Naomi."

Naomi drew a breath and glanced down at her ankle before she took her next turn.

"Chin up," Jessica commanded.

Then into Naomi's turn Jessica said, "Faster."

The rigidity in her ankle, however, would not let up. Neither would Jessica. The pair of them fought one another at accelerated counts until Naomi's pointe finally slipped. Her entire body weight crashed down onto her ankle right before she just barely caught, steadied, and froze herself.

Jessica's voice sank into a rumbling vibrato. "Keep going!"

The tone of the outcry was dark and unfamiliar. When Naomi turned to look at her best friend, she realized Jessica's voice wasn't the only thing that was unrecognizable. There was something different in Jessica's expression. Something angry. It seemed, to Naomi, that although she herself had stopped spinning and her ankle had finally gotten to rest, Jessica was still baring teeth.

But like power resurging through a dark house, concern glazed Jessica's face, and she ran over to inspect Naomi's foot.

She held her ankle gently, inspecting it with narrowed eyes. Tutting, Jessica stood up straight, declaring that Naomi's pointe shoes were the source of the problem between Naomi's ankle and herself. She declared this pair of pointe shoes dead.

Naomi had only danced in them for three days.

Jessica then took her arm and quickly suggested they go home and break in one of her unused spares. Naomi nodded. She tried not to flinch when her best friend looped her arm through hers. Pointe shoes were fragile, unreliable things. This wouldn't be the first time they caused more harm than good. Perhaps that pair simply could not keep up with her and her best friend. Briefly, Naomi glanced at Jessica.

Feeling her eyes on her, Jessica turned. "What's wrong?"

Naomi swallowed. "Nothing. I'm just glad you're here."

Grinning, Jessica doubled down. "Glad to be here."

When Naomi and Jessica stepped into the dressing room at the theater on Monday morning, the other girls were already there. Naomi had hoped that no one else would come this early. That way, she could undo and redo herself in preparation for her first rehearsal for the Grand Prix. If only for the peace and quiet, at least. But the other girls, it seemed, had had similar ideas, and now Naomi was staring into the sea of them occupying the space.

Jessica suggested tomorrow she set her alarm even earlier. Six in the morning should be good.

Naomi shouldered her way inside the dressing room. She

lowered her chin as she went, but no one was about to stop her to hold a conversation, and she knew that already. Not a single dancer in the Riverside Dance Academy, besides Jessica, had made a point of speaking to Naomi. At first she thought it was because they didn't have anything in common, or they were just as shy as she was. But the years went by regardless; so, in the end, it didn't really matter.

Naomi found her seat on a bench in the corner and opened her bag to get changed. She told herself she didn't have time for their gossip anyway. She knew that she needed to focus on what was to come for the next two months instead: early mornings, late evenings, more drastic forms of cutting. She didn't need other girls to get her through that. She didn't need them at all.

Naomi looked over her shoulder toward a vanity where the other girls were sharing numbing gels and passing out tiny pills that they all swallowed without water. At another table, girls were rolling out the bottoms of their feet on a communal tennis ball. In the corner, some others were placing themselves on the scales Valentino kept propped there. Everyone had to discover their own unique way of making their body bend in ways it was not meant to in order to dance. In here it was obvious, like swallowing capsules of ibuprofen to kill the pain and rubbing Preparation H—a hemorrhoid cream—all over their toes for the anesthetic relief. But onstage, no one could tell. So long as their makeup was bright and they were all able to stand on pointe, it did not matter what they did back here.

"Competition. That's how you better start seeing them," Jessica told her. "In fact, it's probably how they already see you."

Staring into the sea of girls in the dressing room Naomi asked, "You think so?"

"Definitely," Jessica said quickly. "And if not already, then soon. In that case, better to have a head start." Naomi examined them—the other girls. Valentino's classes were famous, after all, because under his instruction dancers became exemplary. Sharp. When his dancers entered the Grand Prix, they were all the other girls could whisper about. And Naomi wanted that. They all did, even if secretly.

In that way, it made sense for Naomi to not be too friendly to the other girls in the academy. What was the point of being nice in here only to do everything in your power to be better out there? They would be lying to each other, and they would know it. The thought made Naomi's stomach knot. Jessica was different, of course. She didn't care about the competition or being the best. She danced because she liked it. In here, that was rare.

Realizing that, Naomi turned to her best friend as she was eyeing the other girls and gave her a quizzical look. Jessica, usually, couldn't care less about who was competition and who was not. Those things had never meant anything to her before. But as her best friend turned to give her a knowing look, Naomi grasped the fact that it clearly meant something now, and for good reason. The stakes were higher—this was her career. And these girls *were* in fact her competition. If Jessica was taking it this seriously, maybe Naomi should too.

Naomi was out of the dressing room and in the dance studio in under ten minutes. There, she realized, she was in first position. There were no other dancers here. Just her, Valentino, and his intern. Naomi thought back briefly to what her best friend had said about having a head start and exhaled.

Valentino turned at the sound of the door shutting on its own. "Naomi." His voice bounced off the walls when he saw her. "You're early."

She nodded proudly, stepping farther inside.

"How do you feel?"

Jessica gripped her hand. Naomi answered, "Ready."

Valentino smiled. "Okay, well, since you're here, why don't we go ahead and fill out the Grand Prix application form?" He retrieved the piece of paper and a pen from his intern and walked back over. He asked her the simple questions first, name, age, address, weight. Then came the only question Naomi cared for: "Which schools are you interested in?"

It was a procedural question. At the Youth America Grand Prix, ballet schools from across the country came to judge new talent and offer them scholarships to attend their schools. Dancers also got the chance to pick which schools they were interested in. Usually, dancers put down their top three. But for Naomi, there was only one option. The School of American Ballet. Because of its ties, almost every dancer who did well there ended up dancing for the New York City Ballet. This was the single path that made sense for her. And so she said that.

"That's it? One school?" Valentino asked.

She nodded. It didn't matter which other schools gave her scholarship offers. She would just turn them down anyway. This, the School of American Ballet for two years, then straight to the New York City Ballet, was what she wanted. All she wanted. The application form should reflect that.

Naomi looked up at Valentino and smiled. Together, the girls said, "Yes. One school."

Worry flashed across Valentino's face. "Are you sure about that, Naomi? You do realize that putting at least three schools makes you a more competitive prospect, and it's never a good idea to put all your eggs in one basket."

It was all Naomi this time when she answered. "I'll be competitive anyway. They'll see that onstage."

Valentino watched her carefully. But she only moved to the barre where she began her stretches. Still, even then, he waited. He waited when the other dancers began to file in, during rehearsal, and after it ended. Valentino Beaumont finally wrote down the School of American Ballet as Naomi's only option when it was nighttime in his office, and all the dancers had left, and Naomi still hadn't found him to reconsider.

Arriving home, Naomi saw the newspapers and the assorted fabrics on the floor but her mother wasn't among them. She must have been in the kitchen. When Naomi got there, however, the stove was on and the pots were steaming, but it wasn't because of her mom at all. "You're cooking?"

Ethan Morgan looked up at his daughter and laughed. It was an embarrassed one, with clenched teeth and high shoulders. "Yes, I am cooking," he said. "Your mother ran out to get some stuff from the store so she asked me to go ahead and start dinner." A silence hung in the air before he added, "Relax, it's mostly leftovers."

Ethan Morgan was California born and raised; he even claimed to have been a surfer at one point. So it was somewhat unusual for him to cook, especially when Aja had been born with whatever culinary magic people were born with in Jamaica and had brought that into their family kitchen.

"How was your day?" he asked.

Stepping farther into the smoky room, Naomi wondered if her father even knew that she had started rehearsing for Grand Prix today. Had she told him? Did her mother tell him? If he did know, surely he would have said something? Or did he just not care? And this was often the problem with silence. You never knew where it started or stopped; you only knew that it existed.

"It was fine," was what she ultimately decided on. "Yours?"

"Good," Ethan answered. "Filled two cavities back-to-back today, and that's about as interesting as it got for me." He laughed at himself, stirring the pot on the stove thoroughly and giving Naomi a smile over his shoulder.

Jessica pointed to Ethan's attire—a button-up and dress pants—and folded her arms. She said, "Doesn't your dad get off at five?" Then she pointed to the clock up on the wall. It read eight.

Naomi glanced back at her father. Looking away she asked, "Did you just get home from work?"

Ethan nodded, setting down the kitchen towel and turning down the gas. "Yeah, I had some extra patients that took me pretty late today but don't worry, dinner won't be long. I promise." He wasn't facing her.

Naomi stayed silent.

Her father was the one who spoke again. He turned the burners off completely then moved to open the cupboard and gather plates. "Actually, why don't you set the table, Naomi?"

She nodded and filled one arm with three porcelain plates and utensils and the other with three place mats and quickly went to distribute them on the dining table. Jessica followed her as she set each of them down, and when she pulled out a chair to sit, Jessica did the same. Across the table from each other, they sat in silence. Naomi went to take out her phone from her pocket and Jessica kicked her under the table.

Naomi pulled her arm back. Maybe dancers at the New York City Ballet didn't use their phones at the dinner table either. Maybe they used the time waiting for food to mentally rehearse instead. Under the table, her feet began to perform. Jessica smiled. Naomi kept her eyes on the place mats.

Her dad brought over the plates of food shortly thereafter. Mountains of steaming rice were toppling over into the curry chicken, and the aroma quickly filled up the dining room. Aja had established long ago that these were the portions that were served in her house. She often told Naomi that this was what a real meal looked like, and that the rest of the United States had gotten it all wrong. But Naomi knew, especially with Jessica looking at her, that she couldn't eat all of this. Ballet costumes stopped after a certain size.

Ethan set Naomi's plate down before his own. As he grabbed the hot sauce and took a seat, he asked, "How was class?"

It wasn't class, she wanted to say. *It was rehearsal. For Grand Prix. How don't you know that?* "It was good."

Naomi watched her father obliviously nod in response and wondered how skilled she had become at acting. Onstage, she faked everything, just as she was supposed to. All the highs and lows of her performances were cued, counted, and rehearsed so she could bring to life someone who was not her. But this dining table wasn't a stage. This building was a home, not a theater, and yet she found the lights a little too bright as she fought to suppress her own emotions long enough to perform whatever feeling would give her the most approval from a crowd. Right now, that was a hesitant father and a hypercritical best friend.

Ethan looked up and, still chewing, asked, "How're you holding up?"

The easier answer slipped out again. "Good."

A few beats passed between them. Ethan swallowed and rested his fork on his plate. "You know," he began. "You don't have to practice every day. If you're not up for it, you can stay home. I'm sure everyone would understand, Naomi."

The walls began to shift but Naomi kept her eyes on her plate. Who was "everyone"? Surely not Valentino, who she was sure would punish her the moment she stepped in the studio again. Definitely not the other girls, who would smirk confidently to themselves, knowing she was weaker than they were. Didn't he know dancers didn't take days off?

"I'm fine."

Her father watched her momentarily. "No one would blame you if you wanted to take a break, Naomi."

Jessica scoffed.

"I already told you, Dad. I'm fine." Then Naomi looked at him and added, "I promise."

Ethan looked as if he was about to say more before he sank back into himself and whatever words he was going to utter dissolved in his mouth. He cleared his throat and picked up his fork. It had been like this a lot since the funeral. Her father would attempt to connect with her but he'd always come up just short of being able to scale the wall Naomi had put up. Really, it was years in the making. Before ballet, Ethan had been the parent Naomi went to about everything. But over the years,

Aja had invested more time into ballet with Naomi, and after a few years of the Riverside Dance Academy, Naomi became synonymous with ballet. As a result, everything between her and her father eroded. These were the types of interactions that were left.

They sat and ate in silence for a few more minutes, and when that became too unbearable, Ethan took out his phone and began to scroll through it. For the remaining thirty minutes, dinner was just Naomi, Ethan, and Jessica sitting around the wooden dining table in the quiet.

Before bed, Naomi was using a pair of scissors to etch the bottom of her pointe shoes in order to give them extra friction, while Jessica stood in the corner. She was suggesting ideas for how Naomi could impress the judges from the School of American Ballet.

Then, suddenly, she said, "Do you think you make him proud?"

"Who?" Naomi asked, cutting into the bottom of her pointe shoes.

"Your father. If he was proud of you don't you think he would have remembered that today was your first rehearsal for Prix?"

"I'm sure he just has a lot on his mind."

"Naomi, you're his daughter. He should have known. Unless he doesn't care because he doesn't think you're good enough."

Naomi chewed her bottom lip.

"Are you?"

Naomi blinked. "Am I what?"

Jessica stepped forward once. "Good enough."

Naomi sputtered. "I—I am. Valentino said I had a chance at Prix."

"Yeah, well, I'm not convinced. And neither is your dad, apparently. And everyone else woke up earlier than you today." Jessica leaped up. "It's that stupid phone. It's distracting you too much." Jessica took the cell phone off the nightstand where Naomi had left it and threw it into the last of her dresser drawers.

"Jessica, wait!"

"Come on, you need to practice." She grabbed Naomi by the elbow and dragged her up. Naomi's grip on the pointe shoes slipped. The sharpened edge of the scissors dug into her skin. It birthed red against her palm.

Naomi flinched. "Jessi—"

Her best friend shushed her. "Principal dancers get hurt every day. Do you want this or not?" Jessica's fingernails were carving crescent moons into Naomi's skin. Naomi couldn't say no. She didn't want to. Her hand dripped velvet as tears dared her eyes but never got the courage to fall. She told herself it didn't hurt. She told herself it didn't hurt. She told herself it didn't hurt.

Jessica said, "Good. Let's start stretching."

CHAPTER THREE

A light whisper would have woken Naomi without much trouble but Jessica had given her a hefty shake instead. Naomi's phone was gone, and with it all her alarms, so Jessica had taken the responsibility of being Naomi's wake-up call. It was barely sunrise. *Just to be sure*, Jessica had explained when Naomi's eyes finally opened. Before either Aja or Ethan had a chance to stir themselves awake, Naomi was already stretching out her limbs in her standing mirror. Today, it felt a little more like torture.

Naomi could still feel the sting of the gash in her palm each time she held on to anything. In every push, pull, and stretch, pain like fire crackled in her hand. After she had danced long enough to satisfy Jessica last night, Naomi had hurriedly gotten her first aid kit from her bathroom and tended to the wound. She cleaned it with iodine and gauze, then wrapped her hand tightly in a bandage, clipping a safety pin at the end to keep everything safe. It did nothing; the pain was persistent. Jessica congratulated her, though. She said Naomi was beginning to behave like a true principal dancer now. Staying up all night, tending to wounds. *Practice for the real thing*, Jessica dubbed it.

In any case, the cut was on her hand and not her feet, so Naomi thought it was inconsequential. As long as she could still dance, that was all that mattered.

Today was the second day of rehearsal for Prix, and over the years, Naomi had grown accustomed to the nervous feelings that accompanied the first few weeks of preparing for a competition. The Riverside Dance Academy had put on numerous shows year after year, so Naomi expected the churn in her stomach by now. It meant, she knew, that she was concerned about the right things. However, there was a time when messing up or underperforming hadn't been Naomi's biggest fears. Not even close.

When she was younger and moving between different dance schools, each time Naomi entered a new studio she could feel herself standing out. Even as a toddler she wasn't blind to the looks everyone gave her. It didn't matter that her tutu was pink, just like every other girl's, or that with everything inside her she loved to dance. None of that was enough. The gazes of all the adults went deeper than the way she was dressed, but not far enough to see her heart. They only stuck to the surface of her skin.

Naomi's first ballet instructor was tentative about teaching her for that same reason. *She's afraid you'll be too strong*, was what her mother had told her. Naomi responded, *But I want to be strong*. Her mother didn't smile back. She knew the color of Naomi's skin and the baggage everyone thought came with it would always set her apart from the other girls. It was this that Aja had asked Naomi if she truly understood when she sat her down at the age of ten years old and said, "Do you love ballet?" Even then, the conviction came easy to Naomi. Her mother asked again, slower, and looked deep into Naomi's brown eyes. Naomi's answer didn't change.

That same week Aja started working part-time at a law firm. She spent all her extra hours at home thereafter breaking, remaking, and repainting Naomi's costumes and tights to match her skin tone. She enrolled Naomi in the Riverside Dance Academy, a new environment with an instructor she trusted, and began homeschooling Naomi so she would have more time to dance. Aja located another supplier of pointe shoes, one that considered Black skin as flesh colored, never mind the higher price. For every Black girl, Naomi supposed, this was what they had to do in order to dance ballet. Rebel and dance. Dance and rebel. Their very existence was in opposition.

But later that year, Naomi met Jessica at the academy. Finally, a girl who looked like her. But the relief was short-lived when Naomi came to realize there was no rebellion from Jessica. She didn't have to. No one looked at Jessica strangely. Her curly hair was easier to get in a bun. She never had to change the color of her costumes or pointe shoes because the pinkish tan matched her natural complexion closely enough. And that was when Naomi knew things would always be a little different for her here. A little worse.

Yesterday Naomi had been late, so today Jessica had made sure they woke up earlier. It paid off too. The girls arrived at the theater when it was still locked and the sky was dark. The building, like everything else around it, seemed to be asleep. Naomi looked at it and found it a little terrifying, like a bear at rest. She thought twice about walking up to it and waking it from its rest. But Jessica was already hammering on the front doors.

They didn't budge.

"Locked," Jessica finally announced. "We'll have to try the back." Jessica grabbed Naomi's arm and led her around the building.

Riverside was chilly at this hour and a breeze blew Naomi's flat-ironed hair up and up and over her head to the sky. The back door was sometimes left open during the week for emergencies and to accommodate the different artists who spent sleepless nights inside the building, but this area of the academy was nothing like the front. Guests and audience members didn't use the back entrance. It opened onto an empty lot with graffiti on an adjacent wall and a narrow alleyway into downtown. So performers who needed to smoke used the back entrance. Dancers who needed another dose of ibuprofen or something stronger used the back entrance. Naomi was certain that it never once occurred to many visitors to the Riverside Performing Arts Theater that there was a dingier, lonelier, more commonly used entrance at the back.

Naomi gritted her teeth against the cold and pulled at the theater's back door. Thankfully, it was unlocked. Inside, she saw that the stage was empty and the faint light coming in through the windows was barely enough to illuminate the theater much less herself. Naomi didn't mind it, though. When she finished changing in the dim changing room, humming the melody to *The Nutcracker*, she moved directly into the dance studio. Without switching on the lights, she sat down in the center of the floor and began warming up. She dedicated the next fifteen minutes to the complete submission of her muscles.

Aspen Letterman was next to arrive. She came in with a padded step due to her warm-up booties, and echoed the slam of the studio door. She looked up, realized all the lights were off, and kept walking anyway. Naomi and Jessica watched as she made her way to the other side of the room, ignoring them completely, and set down her water bottle.

Then she grabbed the barre and attacked her stretches. Her slim physique moved with such power Naomi worried that at any moment Aspen might just snap in two. She supposed that was the quality that made Aspen's dancing so special. Watching a brittle girl move with so much strength across a huge stage. It was compelling to watch, Naomi admitted, even if the allure was danger.

Aspen hadn't always been like that. There was a time when Aspen couldn't jump because her weight had held her back. There were days when her size would cost her roles, and the other girls had nasty insults on their tongues. Then one day Aspen stepped into the studio, and she was thin as a pencil. That day, she became a force to be reckoned with. And everyone in the Riverside Dance Academy forgot all about the plumper Aspen, especially Aspen.

"Ready for today?" Aspen asked.

Naomi's eyes flicked up from Aspen's thin legs to her face. "Yeah. Yes. I'm ready."

Aspen smiled. Naomi wanted to smile back but she wasn't too sure if she was invited on the other end of the smiling matter. Instead, she said, "You can turn on the lights, if you want."

The other girl shook her head. "No, I don't mind. I like it better like this, actually." Then, almost immediately, she asked, "What happened to your hand?"

Naomi looked down at it. She wasn't sure when Aspen had looked at her long enough to notice the tight bandages. She thought for a moment, then told her, "I cut myself," because she wasn't yet sure if she could lie to Aspen and make it believable.

Aspen paused her stretching and turned around. "Is everything okay?"

"Yeah, it was just an accident. Etching my pointe shoes."

The blond girl gave a hum. She grabbed the barre again. "Does it hurt?"

"Not enough to be anything serious." Before the silence got too comfortable, Naomi continued, "How about you? How do you feel about today?"

Aspen firmly pressed her blond hair down into her scalp, despite there not being any strands out of place to begin with. Many dancers here were like that: fixing things that didn't need to be fixed. "Oh, I'm excited," she said confidently. And in her presence Naomi forgot she was supposed to feel confident too for a moment.

She said quickly, "Me too."

"I can imagine. Valentino can hardly take his eyes off you. That must be exciting." Aspen had stopped looking at Naomi by now. Instead, she was staring at the wall straight ahead. To Naomi, she seemed to be in deep concentration.

"You think so? I feel like he barely sees me."

"Well, he did basically say you'd do the best at Prix." She

looked expressionless but there was still something soft and moving in her features.

Naomi started, "Well, I wouldn't say that. If anything, it was more pressure . . ."

"More pressure," Aspen echoed. "Well, then, I guess it's a good thing he's not a judge at Prix. Too much pressure." The studio went still.

The doors opened wide to usher in Valentino. His intern and a few other dancers followed him, filling the space between the girls. "Good morning, ladies." He slipped off his shoes. "Ready to dance, I see."

The girls stood upright as the room filled. There was a shift. Naomi couldn't see Aspen anymore through the passing dancers' bodies, and she guessed the dancers were now acting as a buffer—the kind that stopped two things from smashing into each other and breaking loudly. Naomi turned around to find Aspen, but she found Jessica, who was looking directly at her, first.

Naomi turned, straightened her back, and put her chin up.

Valentino cleared his throat at the whispering dancers finding their places in the studio. As they quieted, he said, "I've spent last night considering you all." There was only twenty of them, so Naomi couldn't imagine there was much consideration. "And I know I usually allow you to pick your routines for Prix, but I wanted to try something different this year. I will be giving you your routines instead. Routines that I think suit your dancing well, and we'll work from there."

One of the few boys, Josiah, said, "But I've rehearsing Don Quixote for days."

Valentino said, "And you would have made a fine Don

Quixote, but remember that what I see, the judges see, Josiah. And we want to make sure that whatever the judges see, they like, no?"

No one said anything. The dancers simply traded glances among themselves.

Valentino took that as a clear agreement. He quickly began listing out who he thought would be good in which roles, and Naomi could admit that most of them seemed accurate. Luke as Prince Désiré. Aspen as Queen of the Wilis. Samantha as the Sugar Plum Fairy. The other dancers generally didn't seem to mind too much either. Maybe this wasn't such a bad idea.

"Naomi," Valentino called, "I want you dancing Odette's variation, from *Swan Lake*. Right before the end of the second act when the White Swan realizes she is doomed because of her love. Think you can handle it?"

Immediately, Naomi thought of Jessica. The pair of best friends had already made a pact that Jessica would always be the one to dance the lead in *Swan Lake*. Naomi spun to look at her paling best friend.

Not really waiting for an answer, Valentino said, "Perfect." Then he called on another dancer.

He was oblivious to the fact that he had just robbed a routine from a girl. A girl whose eyes were dark with vengeance and staring right at Naomi. Naomi sank. Jessica grew tall. They spent the rest of rehearsal like this as Valentino taught Naomi the variation for the White Swan.

It was out of the question, of course. Naomi would never steal her best friend's role. The one they'd agreed on since what felt like the beginning of their friendship. It would break them both.

At the end of the day's rehearsals, she went to find Valentino in his office.

She knocked on his door, but it was already ajar and slowly swung open of its own accord. At the far end of the room, Valentino was sitting at his cluttered desk with a pen in his hand. Naomi hadn't been in here for years, but she was sure it hadn't always looked like this. Cabinets were half closed. Papers and tights were strewn over the floor. Naomi looked at him; his shirt half unbuttoned. "I'm sorry, should I come back another time?"

"No, Naomi. Come in, please. And close the door behind you." Naomi did just that. She couldn't help but notice how much hotter it was in here than it was outside, and there was an odor she couldn't quite trace. Valentino set his pen down on some papers that were sliding out of a loose folder on his desk. "What's on your mind, Naomi?"

"Well, I was just wondering if I could dance something else. I've never danced the White Swan before, and I don't think I'll be quite good at it anyway, so I think, well, I was wondering if I could dance something else."

"Anything else," added Jessica.

Naomi added, "Anything else."

Valentino exhaled. "I'll tell you something, Naomi. Your technique is great. I think you have the dedication and drive to be a brilliant dancer." Naomi smiled. "But dancing is more than that. People come to the theater not for the technique per se, but to witness a performance. To see love, drama, pain, flash across the stage. That's how dance connects people, really. But I haven't been getting any of those emotions from you lately, Naomi. I want to see you feel again."

Noticing her expectant, confused gaze, Valentino sighed. "Tell me, Naomi, what is *Swan Lake* about?"

She recited, "Well, it's a love story where Odette falls in love with the prince but then she's turned into a white swan. Odile, the Black Swan, marries the prince while disguised as Odette, and the White Swan lives in despair on the lake—"

Valentino cut her off. "Right there. Pain. Helplessness. Despair. We can all relate to those feelings, don't you think?"

Naomi didn't say anything. She could feel the narrow walls of his office ready to close in on her.

Valentino continued, "I think you can really do that performance justice, Naomi."

Her mouth went dry. "I don't understand." She paused. "What does that have to do with me dancing the part?"

"Naomi, given everything that has happened to you, I think this performance can really be a healthy outlet. A chance for you to express yourself in a way you know." Watching her for a few seconds, he pointed at her and said, "I can see it now. It's in your eyes. Maybe if you put some of that pain and grief—" Jessica had gone by now.

Valentino stopped himself and rethought his words. "Look, as dancers, more often than not we have to take the bad things that happen to us and dance them out. It can be our closure in a sense."

"I don't need closure." Jessica reappeared. This time behind Valentino. But it wasn't the Jessica that Naomi had been seeing recently. The girl looking at her was different, original. She was in a tattered summer dress, hugging her elbows and watching Naomi sadly. In an instant, she disappeared again.

"Are you sure?" The office space became smaller. The words came slowly, carefully, out of Valentino's mouth when he said, "Naomi, what happened to your hand?" Naomi glanced down at the bandaged cut from last night.

She moved her arms behind her and twisted the fabric of her tights on her index finger. Hunching her shoulders to accommodate the gradually decreasing space she told him, "I'm fine."

Valentino's eyes narrowed. His gaze felt thick and heavy when he said, "I don't believe you, Naomi. I really think dancing as Odette could be good for you."

Briefly, she thought it didn't matter whether Valentino believed her, it was true. Naomi compared it with other things she considered to be true, like her best friend, her passions, and the moving walls. But it quickly began to feel as if she was pulling on a loose string, quick to get to the end before realizing too late that there were many things it was keeping together. Now, like buttons on an old sweater, everything was beginning to fall away.

Valentino spun in his chair. "When I danced, I had something similar happen to me. It might seem like a long time ago, but the struggle of a dancer is unchanging. Eventually we have to lean into our performance for solace." As he looked off into the distance, Naomi could see something wash over him. He stood up and fully turned his back to her. "Trust me," he said, "there's strength in giving in."

Naomi didn't hear a word of what he said afterward. She

was much too preoccupied eyeing Jessica, the one she was too familiar with now, appear right next to him. The girl glared darkly at Naomi. Jessica's gaze flashed down to Valentino's unattended desk. Sitting atop all the paper was his lanyard holding the key to the theater. Smirking, Jessica reached for it. Naomi shook her head. *Don't.*

Valentino turned around. "I'm worried about you, Naomi. I've seen too many dancers listen to their mind over their body and their heart. Your head might say one thing, but listen to your body and your heart. They have something to say too. I won't give you a different variation because I want you to at least try this one. Can you promise me that you'll give it a go before you back out?"

Naomi took two steps back. She muttered the first sort of apology she could manage. "Yes, I'll try my best. Thank you, Valentino." Her back brushed against the door, and she spun around to open it. Naomi didn't look back at her instructor because in her peripheral vision she could still see the demented contortion of her best friend glaring at her. Naomi opened the door and left.

Out in the hallway, Jessica was beside her again.

"Let's go home," she said, jingling Valentino's set of keys in front of Naomi's face. "We need to rehearse."

Looking at the floor, Naomi asked, "Why did you take those?"

Shocked, Jessica answered, "Because you need more hours in the studio. No more hoping the theater doors are open or dancing at home." Then, as if it was obvious, she added, "Naomi, how else do you think you'll be good enough?"

CHAPTER FOUR

The moonlight came in streams through Naomi's blinds. It wasn't much light, but it was light all the same and that was enough. Naomi stared back at the expanse of the night sky. Under different circumstances, the peace would have lulled her to sleep. But these days, Naomi was beginning to realize that silence didn't necessarily mean peace. Some silences were wars. She thought back to a few nights earlier when she and her father had been sitting around the dining table, quietly pretending to have dinner together. She wasn't mad at him, per se, but it still felt like they were fighting. He hadn't done anything wrong. In fact, Ethan was constantly asking how she was doing. But maybe that was the problem. Naomi didn't want to feel as though she was a fragile object he had to tiptoe around. If he really cared about her still, perhaps he should come to the studio and watch her dance or know the differ-ence between *class* and *rehearsal*. And this was only one of the many silent wars Naomi was battling. Naomi held her breath and glanced at the spot next to her. Jessica was asleep.

Slowly, Naomi's thoughts resurfaced from the depths of her mind, daring to be confronted. Unsheathed. They had been eating away at her all day, but she couldn't dwell on them for too long or Jessica would know. And she would never allow it. So Naomi had submerged them until this point, when sleep finally claimed her best friend. Naomi carefully readjusted to look out at the moon again. Everything felt easier under its gaze.

I can see it now. It's in your eyes. Maybe if you put some of that pain and grief—

Grief. The idea of such a thing felt so distant, further than the funeral even. Those things were buried so deep it was as if they hardly existed at all. Everything about the funeral, and what she had felt during that time, felt so far removed from the here and now: the current Naomi staring into the night with the Youth America Grand Prix only months away. Because what did feel real and pressing was Naomi's career. The one she had been homeschooled to accommodate. The one she had been working toward since she was a toddler. The one her mother gave up her livelihood for.

It seemed obvious. Practice over pain. Only one of those things came with all the rewards, glory, and pride she had worked so hard for.

But then why did Naomi still feel like she was losing?

"Ignore it," Jessica said next to her.

Naomi spun. Jessica's eyes were on her, as if she hadn't been asleep all along.

Naomi bit her bottom lip. "I'm trying."

Jessica quickly sat up and grabbed Naomi's hand.

This, too, was another thought that persisted within Naomi. The Jessica she had seen in Valentino's office was familiar. More so than the one in front of her now, coldly holding her hand with a heavy seriousness in her eye. Jessica was never this serious, was she? Naomi pushed the thought back down.

The girl looking at Naomi said, "Maybe he didn't mean that last bit. Maybe he just wants to see you portray a little more love. The White Swan was in love."

Naomi crossed her legs on the bed. "Jessica"—her voice trembled—"he said grie—"

"Well, you don't have any grief," the other girl snapped. "Why would you be grieving?"

Naomi toyed with the fabric of her sheets. The walls crept a little closer. The moon and all its light felt blown out.

Jessica pulled Naomi off the bed and picked up her bag, pushing it into Naomi's chest.

Naomi looked at her blankly. "Where are we going?"

"The theater. We have the keys, remember?" Naomi opened her mouth to ask why, but Jessica was, as usual, two steps ahead of her. Picking up Naomi's pointe shoes and tights, she said, "You should be dancing right now. You need to get out of this room. Too many bad thoughts. You'll rot in here."

"Jessica." Naomi used her free hand to pull her back. She looked up desperately at her friend. "I don't think the room has anything to do with what's rotting. No matter where we go, everything feels just as dilapidated. Nowhere feels steady anymore."

Jessica brushed her off. "Don't be ridiculous. The theater is steady."

No, Naomi wanted to say, *it's not.*

Jessica dropped the pointe shoes and the pair of tights she was holding on the floor. She scowled.

"So, that's it then? You take my role, and then you complain, and now what? You don't want to dance at all anymore?"

"I want to dance it's just . . . I'm not sure I want to dance like this. As if I'm running. As if I'm being chased all the time. Dancing shouldn't feel like that." Naomi wasn't even positive those were the words that accurately described what she was feeling. It felt like her vocabulary couldn't capture such a thing.

Jessica wriggled her arm out of Naomi's grip. "If I don't chase you, Naomi, who will? If I'm not here to remind you of where you need to be and what you have to lose, where will you end up? You need me. Isn't that how you've always seen me anyway? A reminder of everything you're not?"

Naomi's mouth opened and twisted, an attempt to form the words she desperately needed to respond with. *Of course not. You remind me of good things. I miss you.* Moments joined one another again and again in which Naomi's mind sped but her throat struggled and the words themselves never actually came. Eventually, her eyes slipped from Jessica's gaze all the way down her body and to the hard floor.

Jessica smiled. "Don't let Valentino get in your head. He was probably taking out his own problems on you. You don't need to be grieving to make a convincing White Swan, I would know." Jessica smiled and took Naomi's hand in hers. She squeezed it. It was a promise now.

When the girls arrived at the theater that night, Jessica handed Naomi Valentino's lanyard with the keys to open the front door. Naomi was startled to feel the cool metal land in her hand. She couldn't fully explain why, but a part of her had been hoping that the keys, just like Jessica, would appear and reappear when they felt like it. But no, they weren't going anywhere, and that reality was more frightening.

Naomi used the keys to unlock the theater, and the pair of them walked inside. Jessica had told Naomi that the main stage was closer than the dance studio and the dressing room in the basement, so it made more sense to dance there. This way, they could get straight to work. Waste less time. Naomi switched on the stage lights then launched herself up on the raised stage. She changed in the same spot, peeling off pajamas and replacing them with tights and pointe shoes and bravery. When she was done and she looked out into the dim, empty audience, Naomi felt brand-new. As though dancing, not necessarily for anyone in particular, would be a little more satisfying than any position she'd earned in a competition.

Jessica came up on the stage next to her. She whispered a word of encouragement then started to count her off into the variation. Naomi inhaled. In the darkness, she hoped she was tall and light enough on pointe in order to be lifted off her feet and carried away on Jessica's counts. But Naomi was neither tall nor light. Somewhere, regrettably, she knew that her pointe shoes weighed her down by the ton and there was no escape. Especially not into the large expanse of the sky. She was grounded, not because she was flightless, but because she was tied to her cage, like a bird being treated as if it was a dog.

The theater doors pushed open. A boy stood in the outline

of the open doors. Naomi stopped. His silhouette walked in and looked around—all around, as if he had expected someone, perhaps in the back row, to also be there.

Peering through the dim lighting, Naomi wondered if this was a boy from the academy. He didn't look familiar, though. Maybe the Riverside Choir? Or some other group that used the space? Naomi knew she was wrong when the boy asked loudly, "What are you doing here?" Anyone who used the theater regularly would have walked right past her because they would know exactly why another artist would be here at this time. They all had that much in common.

She answered, "Dancing. Who are you?"

He had walked far enough in now that she could distinguish him from the shadows. His complexion was dark, as dark as hers, and he had a head full of twists down to his shoulders. "At this hour?" he questioned.

"I'm a dancer," was her reply.

The boy stretched out his arms, indicating the large, empty theater. "How can you dance with no audience?"

Naomi blinked. "I—I don't always dance for an audience. Sometimes I dance alone. I don't really need anyone to watch me all the time." She looked over at where Jessica was standing, but the other girl was no longer there.

The boy laughed—so heavy and loud that it echoed throughout the entire building. "I'm just teasing. Are you always this serious?"

She wanted to say something like *I have to be*, or *Only when I need to be*. But looking down at him in the dark theater, all she could really manage was, "These days, yes."

As he walked farther into the theater, closer to the stage,

Naomi felt a very specific fear clutch her throat. The theater was dark and held only the two of them. Escape was behind him too. No one would be able to hear her if he was the type of boy to use and discard girls in dark, empty rooms. She took a step back. "What are you doing here?"

For a moment, Naomi was worried it came out too croaky. That, whoever this stranger was, he could sense her weakness, and it would embolden him to do whatever he had come here to do.

The boy stopped walking briefly. He raised his palms up into the air. "Hey, friendly face." He smiled brightly as if for proof. "I was just taking a walk and I saw the lights on. Not many places are open at this hour so I thought I'd check it out. My name's Saint. How about you?"

There was a certain innocence in his smile, and Naomi could now hear his voice pitch upward. She realized he must be close to her age, maybe even younger. After a few moments she answered, "Naomi."

"Nice to meet you, Naomi." Saint looked around at the theater again. "So do all dancers usually dance at three in the morning?"

Naomi knew he was joking, but she couldn't bring herself to laugh. "Some of us. Not all. Usually, though, we're here five days a week." She thought about her answer a little more and tried to consider how often she had seen someone from the Riverside Dance Academy stay back after class or arrive a little too early. She said, "We just dance until."

He put his hands in his pockets. "Until what?"

She shrugged. "Until we're perfect."

He gave a smile Naomi Morgan recognized all too well

then said, "Sounds like a tough way to think about art, like dancing."

She wanted to tell him that art and ballet were dissimilar in a lot of ways. Art was free and uncontainable but ballet had rules and structure, judges and competitions. It was art for some, sure, but for her it was work. Instead, Naomi opted to ask him a question this time. "What about you? Do you normally go for walks at three in the morning?"

"Oh, of course. Riverside is different at this hour. I've met some pretty interesting people." He looked at her as if he was just noticing she was in nonmatching tights and dirty pointe shoes. "And it just keeps getting better. What are you wearing?"

Naomi laughed. "I wasn't expecting visitors. Anyway, in ballet it doesn't matter what you wear to rehearsals."

He said to her, "I've never seen ballet before." He shrugged. "Can you show me something?"

Naomi looked down at herself. She had performed for crowds since she was a little girl. Yet, here in an empty theater except for herself and a stranger, she felt frozen in place. Her brain tried to think of a ballet. Should she perform one she already knew very well or should she dance the White Swan she had just been practicing? Would she be good enough? Would he even recognize whether she was good or not? There were no judges, no lights, no music, no cue. Naomi looked up at the boy. "Like what?"

Saint had already taken a seat in the second row. Legs crossed, he told her, "Anything you want. Whatever you were rehearsing before I got here."

Naomi waited for him to start laughing at her again. She could hear it already: *Are you always this serious?* But he never did. More precisely, he was nodding hopefully at her, egging her on. There was never any egging on in ballet. People expected you to be ready all the time and so they narrowed their eyes at you and watched for your faults. This, watching for your success, was new to her.

Naomi took her position and counted herself off. The White Swan came to life. Two long arms transformed into giant white wings, twisting and folding downward as she lowered her body to her extended feet. Then to her sides, they flapped and her sharp pirouettes lifted her up and up. Skybound, her chest lifted. There was no music, but something was singing. Naomi took across the stage diagonally, spinning as if each turn was a celebration of the last.

Saint waited until her performance was finished and she was frozen, her chest heaving before he stood up. His slow claps echoed throughout the theater. Naomi smiled back and bowed. She was grateful; her audiences were usually a lot harder to please than a single boy on his feet, cheering at her from the second row. "Wow, what was that?"

"Odette, the White Swan's variation in *Swan Lake*."

Saint jumped up on the stage to join her. "I'm impressed," he said. Naomi couldn't tell if he meant it. He was still grinning brightly at her, but he wasn't giving her any feedback either. Saint wasn't telling her how her pirouette was beautiful but could use a bit more grace on the descent. She had to ask him, "What did you think?"

Saint's eyes widened. "Incredible. I've never seen anything like that. You know, I thought ballet would be a lot slower. Even boring. But that was just . . . wow. And the way you danced it . . ."

She cocked her head. "Really? There wasn't anything you thought I could improve on or I should change?"

Saint thought for a moment. "No." He came up short. "To me, it was perfect the way you just did it."

Naomi's shoulders fell. She stretched that moment for as long as she could, replaying it over in her head again and again. She couldn't remember the last time she had danced for anyone who didn't have a critique for her. It reminded her of what it felt like to dance as a little girl, when her mother would clap and cheer regardless, and Valentino smiled a lot more. When she came back to herself Naomi was debating between asking Saint whether he was sure he didn't have any comments and performing for him again for a second dose of that smile.

A cell phone rang. Naomi thought it was hers at first, but then remembered Jessica had taken that away. Saint fished his phone out of his pocket and held it to his ear. "Are you okay?" was how he answered it. He turned and whispered the rest of the conversation under his breath. Naomi stared at Saint's twists as his back turned to her. They were full and thick. She wondered how the dance academy would react if she ever got such a thing. She tried to think of a single dancer, anywhere, in any academy, with anything other than straight hair.

Saint hung up his phone and turned back to her. "I have to go."

"Is everything okay?"

He nodded. It was the kind Naomi recognized as a lie. "Everything's fine." He jumped off the stage and glanced back with a smile. "But, if you dance the way you just did in that ballet you showed me, I'm sure you'll impress everyone. It goes hard."

Naomi fought back the urge to ask him not to go. It was clear he needed to leave, considering he was already halfway up the aisle, and anyway, she had only just met him. But it was because she knew the moment that he stepped out those doors everything would lock up behind him. She knew what she would have to go back to doing. Was that selfish of her?

Saint waved good-bye, and Naomi wished the doors would magically lock him inside. He used his shoulders to effortlessly push one of them open and left it to swing shut behind him. As it clicked with a lock, Naomi stood on pointe before Jessica appeared and had to tell her to do so.

"Finally," her best friend purred. "I couldn't wait for him to leave. Now, from the top."

CHAPTER FIVE

Nothing rested easy this side of Riverside. People on these sidewalks lay on top of strung-out cardboard boxes next to benches that had been redesigned to no longer accommodate them. Store owners took extra care to lock their livelihoods behind bars, convinced the weight of all their jingling keys was a necessary burden. Pedestrians passed with their shoulders high. Women looked behind them.

The outskirts of town were crawling with people waiting to take their helpings of whatever would satisfy them most with the least effort. Powders in tiny transparent plastic bags for the lonely, trash cans for the hungry—for Saint, whatever solace and inspiration the night sky could give to him.

He was strolling back home now, hands in his empty pockets as he crossed Oxford Street on the edge of Riverside. His head hung low, and although he should have been more vigilant, Saint knew everyone here recognized him. Most of them were harmless, too, once you got to know them, like Mr. Blythe near the park. All that man wanted was someone to heed his warnings that the sky above them was about to fall. The sky never moved, not one single day, and Mr. Blythe had probably been looking up for so long that he'd lost the true depth of the distance between himself and the big blue long ago. But Saint decided to believe him every day anyway. He thought it didn't really matter what the frail, grayed man was stuttering at him each time he walked into the park because he only wanted what everyone else not looking at the clouds wanted too: someone to believe in him.

Saint hadn't planned on walking this far tonight. He usually only went around the block, maybe stopped by a deserted bench on the sidewalk and searched for inspiration for his newest drawing. But his legs didn't stop this time. They kept him walking and walking. Maybe it was because he had already seen everything there was to see here. He had drawn the brick houses in his community and given them all lights, as if there was actual good life happening inside. He'd painted a pack of stray dogs set free and running, even Mr. Blythe with his tattered scarf in the wind. He had imagined and reimagined all their lives here so many times on paper that perhaps he had exhausted all their potential. Perhaps he had stretched them thin.

And that had led him away. Saint had left his neighborhood and kept walking, already determined that tonight he would keep going until he discovered something new to draw in this town. When he stumbled upon the Riverside Performing Arts Theater, he didn't expect much from it either.

Close up it seemed like just another sad building he was tired of giving life to, and considering the time of morning, and the fact that its lights appeared dim, he was about to walk away. Then he heard an echoed voice coming from within. The idea of performance, in whatever form it took, happening on a stage excited him enough to try the doors. Already unlocked, they pushed open easily. There, he saw her.

In the dim light she was dancing. She couldn't have been afraid of falling over the edge of the stage because she was close to it. Too close. At the time he thought perhaps she was used to dancing on the edge; she had to have known what she was doing. Now he realized that it might have been because if she fell, Naomi would land on her toes and keep dancing. But he should have known better than to leave home for so long, especially at this time of night.

Once he arrived at his house, Saint quickly checked the time on his phone and unlocked the front door with his key. He had been gone for almost two hours. He flipped on the lights and had just locked the door behind him when he heard footsteps running his way. He spun, and a body dashed into him.

"Saint!" They both rocked back.

He reached down and hugged his younger brother. "Sully, what are you doing awake, man?"

The little boy separated from him and his nostrils flared. "I know I should be sleeping but I heard him coughing and so I went to check on him, and he asked for you and"—Sully paused—"I didn't know what to do."

Saint sidestepped his brother and gave him a pat on the

back. "Don't worry about it. Let me have a look and see what that old man is complaining about."

Those types of jokes, that minimized what was happening to their father, were beginning to work less and less on the little boy, and Saint knew that. Sully was getting older and wiser. But the ruse had been going on for so long by this point that without it, what else was there? The truth?

Saint left Sully in the living room and inhaled just enough for his back to straighten and his chest to make him as big as he needed to be in order to open the first door on the left in the corridor. Twisting the knob slowly, he pushed in and left it ajar behind him, allowing light, air, and other things needed for survival to step in next. Saint stopped at the foot of the bed.

"Where were you?"

"I went for a walk," Saint answered. He took a singlet from the package of baby wipes on the dresser and walked to the bedside. "I'm here." Saint found the dried mucus crusted on the corner of Richard Owens's mouth, his hands, even on the sheets, but it would take more than wipes to get that out. Richard squirmed out of the cleaning. He warned, "Don't."

The boy repeated, "I'm here now."

"Saint, if you're going to leave, say something."

That was pointless. If he told his father that he had wanted to escape for a while, the man would find some string to pull him back and tie him to an unmovable part of their house. And what type of son would he be if his sick father asked him to stay and he ungratefully could not bear to honor his request? Saint discarded the used wipe in the overflowing trash can and opened the night table to sift through the pill bottles for the one that would specifically help with nighttime relief. He had their names, colors, scratches on the labels, all memorized. But he still read them out loud under his breath each time just to make sure he was grabbing the right one.

He uncapped the bottle and shook two capsules into his palm. His other hand he used to hold his father's weak arm. Two seconds for comfort, another two for preparation, and the final three to help him sit up. Shakily, his father took a single pill from his son's outstretched hand and put it to his dried lips. Saint picked up the plastic cup filled with water (all the glasses had long since shattered) and handed it to Richard. He drank it down. Then the second one after a short pause. This he could still do without too much help.

There was silence as the man groaned while finding a comfortable position.

"I don't want William to see me like this. Don't go out this late again," he said, referring to Sully by his real name and not the one they had given him long ago from the boy's favorite animated movie when he was a toddler. Then after a moment, "He gets antsy when you're not around."

In the moonlight, Saint could make out all the lines like scars that changed his father's face. He wanted to tell him that Sully was in the fourth grade now. He knew what was going on. He wasn't antsy because his older brother was out all night. He was antsy because his father, his only remaining parent, was dying, and he was expected to sit in the living room and watch TV. Surely at his age he knew what the word *orphan* meant. But as Saint traced the lines in his father's face, he decided to give him at least this. He said, "Okay. Try to get some sleep."

Richard Owens turned on his side in response, flipping his pillow in hopes of a colder side. Saint had always hated that about his father. Whenever he ended a conversation, he did so wordlessly and simply looked away. It was rude. Didn't he care enough to ask what his son would do next? How was his night out? It was always the same, a good-bye demonstrated by the display of his back after he'd received whatever it was that he had wanted.

Saint tightened his lips. Silence it was then.

Out in the living room, Saint met his brother's eyes. "How is he?" Sully asked immediately.

"Asleep. Ring any bells?"

Sully pulled his feet up on the seat. "But I'm not tired!"

Saint shrugged and switched off all the lights. "So you want to stay out here all alone? In the dark? Okay," he sang, walking away slowly.

"Wait!" Sully shouted. Then sheepishly, "Can I have a snack?"

Saint searched his last mental image of the pantry. Empty, he remembered. "How about hot chocolate instead?"

His brother's eyes lit up and Sully nodded. Clearly the boy didn't know it was only being offered because it was the cheapest option. The one his older brother would be able to replace the easiest.

Around the counter while the water was set to boil, Sully asked to see his big brother's newest drawing. It was their tradition. Saint would draw something and Sully would ask to see it. That was the way things were between Sully, Saint, and Saint's art. But recently Saint hadn't drawn anything new. The past few days had been short on inspiration, and he'd rather not draw at all than draw something that didn't feel like him. Saint told Sully he would start something tonight, however. In fact, he'd already seen the image in his mind. A moonlit lake with white swans drifting across its surface, and, in the center, a dark-skinned girl standing on the water.

CHAPTER SIX

At six in the evening, the dusty studio windows of the Riverside Performing Arts Theater saw the yellow rays of the setting sun. Sweat dripped from everyone in the academy; no one was special. Despite the building's air-conditioning, sweat still trickled down their bodies, tickling the most inconvenient places. Regardless, the dancers knew they could not swipe any of it away while the piano was playing. There was simply no moving unless the movement was a part of your variation. In other words, unless it was dancing, it wasn't allowed.

When Valentino called class to an end for the day he didn't leave as quickly as he normally would. Instead, he stood for a few moments and watched all the young dancers remember themselves. Moving in the absence of Tchaikovsky now, they all seemed a little more recognizable. More human. It was as if the more they cooled down, exhaled, and talked with one another, the more pieces of themselves began to slowly resurface. They reattached their smiles and exercised their voices;

now the dancers didn't have to chip away at themselves in order to better fit into their ballet's thin lines. They managed to fill up the entire room.

It reminded Valentino of himself—when he was younger and had to deconstruct and reconstruct himself too. After an entire childhood rehearsing instead of studying, and winning medals at dance competitions instead of looking up at the ceiling, Valentino realized too late that this was all he was good at. Ballet had made him lonelier. Which was ironic because it was also the source of all his preoccupation. It gave him a few friends, a lifestyle, work ethic, and everything else that makes a man.

Then it gave him a career, dancing for a company. And when his body could no longer bend in the ways it needed to, ballet gave him another job—training others in the same way. Now, watching his dancers reassemble, the man wondered if it was already too late for them. At this stage of a dancer's adolescence, he remembered, you feel as though you are nothing without the thing that keeps you up at night.

Valentino cleared his throat and everyone turned around.

"As you all know, the Riverside Performing Arts Theater is closed on weekends. In the past, this was because this is a pretty big theater and the janitors need those days to go over everything. You know how messy an audience can be, much less the performers."

Before any of them could take the hint, one of the dancers, Josiah, Naomi thought it was, repeated, "In the past?"

Valentino pressed his lips together. Nodding he said, "Recently, my personal set of keys to the theater have gone missing." Naomi froze. "Now, I'm not saying someone in the academy stole them, but if that was the case because a dancer felt as though they needed more time to rehearse, I wanted to grant everyone that opportunity. I spoke with the theater staff, and they've agreed to leave the theater open on weekends as long as you all keep the dressing rooms clean. They won't be cleaning up after you. With Grand Prix getting closer I can understand the stress that may make some of you feel the need to be here on weekends. I only request that next time, just come to me. There's no need to steal."

All of the dancers were grinning brightly. Jessica, however, was gritting her teeth. She turned to Naomi in disappointment. *We've just lost our edge.* Perhaps dancing seven days a week was not ideal for any single person, but it was ideal for a dancer like Naomi, who had to compete. But now that everyone in the academy could dance the same hours she had managed to steal away, she was right back to square one.

"I won't be here, though. The weekends are the only time I get to relax. Neither will Eli." Valentino pointed to his intern sitting at the piano. "But if you decide you want to come in and rehearse with a portable speaker or something, feel free. I won't stop you. Doors open at eight in the morning and you can leave anytime you want, but they lock from the outside at seven in the evenings. I encourage all of you to make use of this opportunity."

"When?" Naomi's voice was layered simultaneously by a more assertive one. She spun to look and found where the other voice had come from. Naomi and Aspen made eye contact across the studio.

Aspen cleared her throat. She finished her thought. "When can we start coming in?"

"Tomorrow, bright and early. Staff might be around somewhere in the building if you need anything. Otherwise, you have my number. Call me if there's an emergency. And please remember, this is a privilege. Don't embarrass me." Valentino grabbed his things and left. The door reopened suddenly and he stepped back inside. "Oh, and now that everyone has been given this chance, if someone has misplaced my keys, I expect them to turn up again. Slide them under my office door if you must." He left again.

Jessica pulled Naomi's attention to the side.

Did she understand what this meant? Rehearsing on weekends was now a must if it meant everyone else could do it too. If it meant others could potentially outperform her on the big day. Now she had to nail her variation. Otherwise, a scholarship to attend the School of American Ballet was at risk. Which meant her future acceptance into the New York City Ballet was at risk. Tomorrow, she needed to be here.

Naomi recited all of this back to Jessica. Then again. A few more times. Until Jessica was satisfied that she understood the stakes. Jessica looked directly into Naomi's eyes and confirmed that if Naomi was going to steal her role as the White Swan in *Swan Lake*, the least she could do was get into the New York City Ballet. Naomi thought briefly that maybe she wasn't meant for the role at all. That Odette, the beautiful white swan, should be played by someone who could do her justice. Not Naomi.

Naomi hadn't even realized that the studio and most of the theater was empty now. It was just her. She gathered herself and avoided looking at the mirrored walls as she walked out. In the dressing room, she didn't fully change or take off all the tape on her feet either. Instead, she threw on her denim jacket and half shoved her feet into her sneakers. More than anything else, she just wanted to get home. Somewhere she could rest her head.

Outside didn't feel any lighter, however. The sunset pulled the colors of the sky downward. Meanwhile, the sky itself looked as if it was about to follow suit. Tumble on top of her head and send pieces of her splattering everywhere.

When the blinding light peeked behind a smaller building, Naomi quickly bounded down the steps of the theater and Jessica came up next to her, reminding her to not take the steps so harshly. She had heard of a girl snapping her ankle on theater steps before.

But when the girls got to the foot of the steps, they heard something that was rare on this side of Riverside: shouting. They turned to see that just a few feet over, in the tiny theater parking lot, a man seemed to be reprimanding a girl. It took the girls a fraction of a second, because she was standing so sheepishly, to realize that the girl was Aspen. Her back was facing them but they could tell it was her. Her frame and blond hair were recognizable anywhere.

Naomi couldn't recall ever seeing the girl's father before, but the man was screaming down at her now. The words themselves were inaudible from this distance, but Naomi wasn't quite sure that mattered when she could still make out the terrible look on his face. Anger had burned away any softness his features might possess and replaced it with something much, much darker. Naomi settled back onto her heel.

Then the man abruptly stopped speaking. His last sentence was the loudest and his expectant expression told Naomi that whatever he had just said was a question. Interrogative and in need of an immediate answer. However, Naomi had to assume that Aspen had given the wrong one because, in a flash, the back of her father's hand went across her face. Riverside stilled. Aspen held her ground. It looked like she was willing her head to remain attached to her body. The parking lot fell silent.

Though Naomi was several feet removed from Aspen, and even farther removed from the impact, she still felt dizzy. She touched her own cheek. The man flung open the door to his car and stepped inside. As he sat there, the tinted windows hiding him, Aspen didn't move.

Jessica smirked.

Naomi wasn't aware of how long she had been at the steps of the theater watching the blond girl until their eyes clicked. Aspen had turned around and found her there. Naomi took a step back. Aspen's jaw tightened. The look on her face morphed into something uncontrollable, just like her father's. Something was burning up in her too. And her face, in the same fashion, was readying itself to shout something at Naomi, but none of it came through before her fire was extinguished by an outbreak of tears.

Looking at her now, Naomi realized Aspen's eyeliner wasn't drawn on and the conviction she'd always had seemed to be slipping like her smudged lipstick. She didn't know exactly what she felt toward Aspen Letterman at that moment, but it wasn't fear. Aspen's nose opened with an uneven exhale and she spun away before clumsily getting into the car. Seconds later, the father and daughter peeled away from the theater and out into the road.

"Less competition," Jessica commented.

Naomi looked over at her. Usually, Jessica would be concerned, empathetic, anything other than elated at the other girl's misfortune. And the more Naomi looked at whoever this stranger was, the more she came to understand why Aspen's pain felt so similar. She recognized what it felt like when the person you were supposed to be closest to was the one hurting you the most.

Naomi continued to think about all the things she wasn't supposed to. The things that Jessica never wanted her to think about, like what Valentino had said to her about grief, and what had happened to Aspen. The thoughts seemed pressing, but Jessica was a strong dam.

She reminded Naomi of what was really important: the New York City Ballet. To get there, the School of American Ballet. To get there, the Youth America Grand Prix. She repeated this mantra again and again. And Naomi knew that ultimately Jessica was right, but it didn't feel like it anymore.

There were other things, she was beginning to realize, that existed outside of this straight line.

Naomi told Jessica this much.

Jessica shook her head in frustration. "You get distracted too easily."

Naomi told her, "It's not a distraction." She watched her best friend take up a pair of dirty tights from her bedroom floor and put them into Naomi's bag. Go into her closet for pointe shoes and retrieve those too. "What are you doing?"

"Getting your things," Jessica said. "We're going to the theater."

Naomi cracked. Before she could hold it in, it slipped out. "I don't want to."

Jessica paused. Slowly, she looked at Naomi sitting on the bed and blinked. "Naomi, if you don't rehearse, you'll never get into NYCB. We'll never get there together. Do you understand that?"

Naomi whimpered.

"Is that what you want?"

Naomi shuddered. "No, but—"

"So, help me pack. Let's go!"

Naomi watched the girl retrieve more and more things. Extra tights. Athletic tape. Numbing gels. But Naomi felt something within her shift. "Jessica," she said, "I don't think we're going to go to NYCB together."

The walls revved to life.

Jessica dropped the latest item in her hand, pointe shoes. She wasn't looking at Naomi. "And why's that?"

No one moved, but in the silence, there was an answer.

Jessica narrowed her eyes. She seethed. Finally, she spun around. "Out of every other dancer in that studio, you need to be the one rehearsing the most. You think everyone doesn't see how ridiculous you look? How broad and ungraceful you are? The role is called *White Swan*, for god's sake. And you really think that's you?

"Everyone in that audience will be laughing when you go on that stage, Naomi. You will look so goddamn stupid in your dyed tights and custom costume. I pity you. I pity you so much. Do you know why? Because every time you lace up your little pointe shoes and flat-iron your hair so it can fit in a bun people will watch you dance and think to themselves, *Is she supposed to be there?*"

Naomi fell back onto the bed, as if all the air had been knocked out of her. But it didn't stop there. Jessica continued to spit insults at her—something about the judges from the School of American Ballet. Something about being the best. But they all passed through her now, like lies told to a ghost. She felt the dresser come closer on her right. She felt the bed frame graze her spine. Naomi put her hands out to stop the walls.

"Why are you saying these things?"

Jessica took hold of the nearby things in the bedroom and threw them at Naomi. She began with pillows. "This isn't anything new!" Then she picked up Naomi's lamp. "You know deep, deep down that I'm right!" The lamp hit the bed and rolled off the other side, smashing on the floor. Jessica grabbed a chair. "You know how I know? Because you're always think-ing it! I'm just saying it for you!"

Naomi tried to dodge them, but the heavier objects came quicker than she expected. Tears spilled down her face, and her throat was so dry she couldn't release the agonizing scream she felt boiling within her. She turned and made for the door. She grabbed it. Release. But not before Jessica pulled her back. "Leave me alone!" Naomi screamed.

Jessica didn't let go. Naomi grabbed her back, digging her nails into her skin. They tugged at each other, struggled back and forth, spinning in the doorway. And when Naomi finally got the girl off of her, she shoved her into the hallway and grabbed the door handle to push it shut—to lock herself inside and the monster out. But somehow Naomi's foot was still in the doorway. When she pushed it with all her strength, the wood crushed her foot. Naomi let out a bloodcurdling shriek.

She stumbled backward, falling to the floor in a fit of silent cries. The door slammed open. Her mother was standing there, looking down at her. "Naomi, what's going on? Are you okay?"

Then Aja saw her clutching her foot, tears coursing down her face. "Oh my god, Naomi! What happened?!" She was all the way in the room now, dropping to the floor next to her daughter and holding her. Aja gently pulled Naomi's hand back and noticed the bandage wrapped around the girl's palm. She froze. The past few days Naomi had kept that injury concealed from her parents; she'd tucked her hand into her pockets whenever she saw them and kept it casually in her lap while she ate. Aja stared at the poorly wrapped bandage for a moment but decided against commenting on it. She continued to pull Naomi's hands away.

Now revealed, they could see Naomi's foot didn't look discolored or broken. But nothing ever appeared that way at first. Aja got up and went into Naomi's bathroom, stepping over the discarded pillows, chair, and shattered lamp. She came back, hurrying to open the first aid kit and setting it beside them. Naomi sank her teeth into her lips to silence her cries.

Aja Morgan thoughtfully unrolled the gauze before looking up at Naomi. "How did this happen?"

"I slipped," she lied, "and my foot was still in the door."

Aja slowly began to apply Topricin cream, working her way from Naomi's ankle gently downward. "Then explain the cut on your hand. And the pillows. And the lamp. Naomi, I'm beginning to worry about you."

Naomi tightly caged the next scream she wanted to let out. "I—I'm sorry. I'll clean all this up."

"I'm not talking about the mess, Naomi." Nothing dawned on Naomi's face. Aja continued to rub the cream in.

"I love that you do ballet." Naomi didn't answer. "Watching you dance on that stage, it's one of the most fulfilling things I could ever see. It makes me so happy to see you pursue something you really love." She chuckled. "I almost feel like I'm living through you sometimes."

Naomi wiped away her tears. She opened her mouth to say something but Aja had begun speaking again. "But if it's causing all this. If it's making you hurt yourself . . ."

"Mom, I'm not—"

"What's changed?" she asked finally. She was looking up at Naomi now. Her eyes were burning, searing into her daughter's. Naomi could tell she had been waiting to ask that question for some time now. "Is this all to do with Jessica?"

"No. Nothing's changed. And Jessica—" Naomi gulped. The distorted version of her best friend was gone, so she should have felt safer continuing, but the truth was that it still felt as though Jessica was secretly listening somehow. Naomi slowly scanned the room in search of her.

Aja used the back of her hand to wipe Naomi's tears. "Look at me. Naomi, she's not coming back. You have to live for yourself now. That's what she'd want."

No, what she wants is to take the scissors I use to etch my pointe shoes and slit my throat with them. Trap my head in the briefly open space of a slamming door. Make me dance until I break. "It isn't. It isn't about her."

Aja searched her daughter's face. "Does it still hurt? Do you think you need to see a doctor?"

"No. It's going away," she lied.

Aja nodded. After finishing applying the pain relief cream to Naomi's foot, she wrapped it in gauze. "It might swell tonight but it should go down by tomorrow." Naomi dove into her mother for a hug and whispered a thank-you into her ear. Separating briefly, Aja looked into her eyes. Just like all those years ago, she asked Naomi again, "Do you still love ballet?" It was the type of question that could define everything from here on out, Naomi knew. Not just for herself, but for her mother, her father, even Jessica.

Her answer wasn't much of a choice because of that. She said, "With everything I have."

CHAPTER SEVEN

When Naomi woke up on Saturday morning, the pain in her left foot was almost unbearable. To make things worse, she was late for rehearsal. Jessica hadn't woken her up today, and Naomi glanced around the room only to realize that, in fact, her best friend was nowhere to be found. She was completely alone. But her bedroom had been set back into place. The shattered lamp was gone and the chair was where it was supposed to be again, sitting at her desk. Her mom must have come back in the middle of the night to set everything right.

Naomi tried not to think about what had happened last night as she sat up in her bed. Her ankle and all her other joints were still painful, and she knew that this time it was not because of her pointe shoes or her injuries. There was something deeply wrong with her.

When Naomi undid the gauze her mother had wrapped around her foot, she saw it was clearly swollen. It even looked purple closer to her heel. Naomi got up anyway. As she stood and got ready, she realized her ability to walk was starting to feel like permanent stumbling.

She took extra care descending the stairs so as to not wake her parents. Neither of them had work today, but any slight noise in the house might bring them downstairs. This meant Naomi could only use the bathroom that connected to her bedroom and had to take each step on the staircase one at a time. She didn't eat breakfast either. She had to avoid the kitchen altogether because it was much too close to her parents' room. But, before she walked out the door, Naomi made sure to lather her feet in a heavy coating of numbing gel and swivel a roll of tape around her toes to reduce the pain. She shoved her feet into a pair of Converse and threw the tape into her backpack. She set off.

The heat outside was just as unforgiving as the pain in her foot. Its light was blinding and its heat sizzled on her skin. For a moment, Naomi considered turning around and just going back home. She had missed the bus and so she was forced to walk the entire way, limping and wincing as she went. It felt like the theater was miles out of reach. Perhaps it really would have been better to have practiced at home and nursed her injuries. But even that idea seemed hopeless. Without a proper studio, her dancing would surely deteriorate. And if she stayed home and nursed her toes, that would be worse. The other girls, she was sure, were not taking any days off.

After a series of agonizing hops and sharp inhales, the theater finally came into view. Relief washed over her. Briskly scampering down the sidewalk, Naomi glanced both ways before crossing the street and heading toward it. She slumped against the building for support. The cracks in the theater's redbrick walls were that much more apparent this close. The lights that were embedded within its sign had blown out long ago and now dust coated the outside and cobwebs joined the letters. It was no wonder the building always felt so lifeless.

Quickly, Naomi launched through the double doors and headed straight for the girls' dressing room where she dropped everything, including herself, to the ground. She reveled in the relief of that dirty tiled floor for a moment, and let her breath even out. Then, gently, she removed her left shoe. Nothing eased up; if anything, Naomi's heart sank. Sucking in her bottom lip, she slipped the sock off next. Her whole foot was tinted blue.

"This cannot be happening," she said aloud to herself.

Naomi dove into her bag and grabbed the supplies she needed to paint her feet back to normalcy. She scooped out more Tiger Balm to make them new and shiny again, doubled up on tape to prevent more pain, then covered them with her pointe shoes to at least not have to look at them anymore.

Ten minutes later, in leotard and tights, Naomi Morgan entered the dance studio. She held her head high and tried to make her walk seem as natural as possible. But when she looked around, there was no one else here. Briefly, she even thought she was alone until, in the corner of her vision, she caught Aspen balancing through a barre routine. She didn't turn around. Having the theater open on a weekend was a massive privilege, and after Valentino had told them about it, Naomi assumed that everyone would be here. She expected dancers to be rehearsing, probably fighting for mirror space the moment the doors had clicked open. And yet the studio door echoed shut behind her, and she was one of only two who had made the effort to come.

Naomi took her place at the barre a small distance away from Aspen and began stretching. The girls didn't acknowledge each other's presence at first. It felt as though, after what Naomi had seen Aspen's father do to her yesterday, they couldn't. Naomi assumed the other girl must feel embarrassed to death. She couldn't even maintain eye contact when it had happened. But Naomi didn't want her to feel embarrassed; in fact, she wanted to tell Aspen that she understood what that was like. For the worst pain to come from the ones you love, and to still love them in return.

Then, in a few moments' time, it began to feel inevitable, as though that was exactly the reason they needed to be here together. On Naomi's temple, right above her right ear, she felt the holes being burned into her skull. She spun.

Aspen didn't look away. She said, "Looks like we're the only people with the right idea." There was a pause. "Or the wrong one."

Naomi couldn't help but notice that Aspen didn't look embarrassed at all. She was here today with a tight bun and her pink water bottle as if nothing had happened.

Aspen watched her for a moment, and Naomi was grateful when she broke the stiff silence. "Look, about what happened yesterday in the parking lot, that doesn't happen often, okay?"

Naomi smiled weakly. "You don't have to explain yourself." *Even if it is a lie.*

Aspen straightened her back. "Good. I just don't want you calling child protection services or something over a onetime thing." She turned to stretch again. Exhaled. "I'm assuming you had a better evening than I did, then."

It was a good thing Naomi had not let her smile fall completely. She used that strung-up thing now. "Something like that."

Aspen put her hands on her waist and nodded. Now Naomi wasn't sure if any of them in the Riverside Dance Academy went home to something pleasant when all the costumes came off. She supposed they had to be a little too familiar with suffering if after all these years they still danced here. Pointing to the Bluetooth speaker on the floor, she asked Aspen, "Hey, do you mind if I play my composition when you're done?"

Aspen nodded. Then, wordlessly, she set the track on her phone and took her position. The music began.

Aspen was talented—everyone knew that. Her thinness normally made her seem surreal whenever she danced. But today it only made her appear fragile or, perhaps somewhere concealed, already broken. When her leg rose, it didn't go all the way. It barely went halfway. Even her pointe seemed wobbly, and her chin was low. Naomi suspected it had something to do with the gray-looking spot under her left eye. It only appeared that color because of all the layers of concealer on top of it. Naomi knew that underneath the spot was really a bluish-black color instead. She couldn't help but think back to what Jessica said last night about the White Swan.

Aspen stopped herself. She began to defend her dancing, gave a few excuses, it seemed, but Naomi couldn't really hear over the pain in her own toes. Then suddenly, Aspen was looking at her. Expectantly.

"Sorry, what?"

"I said, why don't you go first. I think I need to stretch out my hamstring a little more."

Naomi cleared her throat. She nodded. "Of course." By now,

she knew how to walk well with her weight distributed on the calloused part of her feet, so making it to the Bluetooth speaker was easy. She asked Aspen if she could borrow her phone to play the music, and when she agreed, Naomi searched for the song and hit Play.

Dancing was not like walking, but she had spent more time doing the former. It should have come easily. She took to the center of the room, inhaled, and began the variation.

Two long arms transformed into giant broken wings, twisting and bending downward as she lowered her body to deadened feet. Then to her sides, they flapped and her sharp pirouettes lifted her up and up. Sky-bound, Naomi felt the clouds surround her. The layers of numbing gel had finally silenced everything below the ankle, and her glances in the mirrored wall assured her that she was beautiful.

She could taste the lights now.

But soon, each time the box of her pointe shoes struck the Marley floor, a sharp pain sparked. It felt like rocks trying to make life. Then with every turn she instinctively swayed in the direction of least pain. Not that she should have been swaying at all. The athletic tape rapidly became useless and the numbing gel could not put out what was already smoking. Naomi attempted gliding across the studio floor, but there was something crackling loud and hot.

It quickly began to spread up her legs and, like a midflight bird set on fire, Naomi fell. She landed on her hands and knees, heart stopping. Her ears tuned everything else out.

This cannot be happening.

The music had stopped now; the only sound was her breathing.

Aspen came over. "Hey, are you okay?" Naomi kept her eyes on the floor. "Look, Valentino isn't here. You can take a break if you need it."

Naomi shook her head. "I just need some air."

Aspen offered to follow her, but Naomi refused and left through the double studio doors. She stumbled down the narrow corridor, using the walls to help her along. Then she resorted to hopping, then limping. It was a lifetime before Naomi found the dressing room door and all but fell through it.

She sat in a corner on the floor. Inhale. Exhale. Then she gritted her teeth and discarded her pointe shoe before slowly unraveling the rolls of tape. She winced just looking at her foot. Now her toes were swollen beyond recognition and the bruise had fused blues and purples on her dark skin. The thing looked like it was about to burst.

Naomi whimpered and threw her head back at the wall, staring teary-eyed at the dusty ceiling. For a second she was glad Jessica wasn't here to tease her. Then she was disappointed that she wasn't here to tell her what to do. Naomi wiped her tears and balled the old tape in her fist. She threw it into the faraway bin. It didn't make a sound. Glancing helplessly at the clock hanging on the wall, Naomi saw she had only been in the theater for thirty minutes. Her bottom lip quivered.

Then, as quickly as she could, she rolled on three times the amount of tape as last time and put on her sneakers. She grabbed her bag and headed out the dressing room door. She knew exactly what she had to do. It was something she had only heard of other girls doing, and occasionally seen the aftereffects of, but had never done herself.

In a rush, Naomi half ran, half hopped out of the back door of the theater. She took the shortcut alley behind the building and came out on the other side of Downtown Riverside. She stumbled down the sidewalk. Her feet felt like they didn't belong to her, like they weren't a part of her. And when the other girls whispered about these exact feelings in the dressing room, they attributed their only relief to ibuprofen and other drugs.

Naomi knew this was bound to have long-term health complications and that a particular analgesic could work differently for each person. But she wouldn't be dancing for the rest of her life anyway, and if this one didn't work, she would keep switching brands until something stuck. Until something put all this to rest.

When she made it to the pharmacy, she retrieved as many bottles with names that she could remember. That way, no matter what, the pain would go away. At least that was what she told herself as she paid for it all. Jessica wasn't here; who would stop her? Every dancer did it anyway.

She imagined it was the norm at the New York City Ballet.

Back outside, Naomi knew Jessica would find the irony in this moment. She never thought she would be here. Standing outside a seedy pharmacy, doing the same thing as the other girls. But the bottles were in her hand, and she had no other choice. Naomi realized that this would not be the first time she came to buy relief for all the pain ballet caused her.

She gathered herself and started down the street, but just ahead of her, she saw something that made her stop. A few blocks away, glistening in the sun, was her father's car. Naomi stopped moving. At least, she thought it was her father's car.

Wasn't it? But her father didn't work on Saturdays and rarely come to this side of town anyway, so she shook off the idea and continued limping down the sidewalk. She glanced at the car one more time for good measure.

Sure enough, the owner, a young woman complete with sunglasses and a messy bun, walked up to the car. Naomi let out a breath. The pain in her toes was clearly more than physical. She continued down the sidewalk. But then, without even thinking about it, she shot one last quick glance over her shoulder just in time to catch the driver's door opening and her father stepping out. Naomi froze.

He walked around and gathered the woman in a passionate kiss. Naomi felt as if the Riverside sun was melting some necessary organ inside her because she swore she was about to die right there. With his hand on the base of the woman's spine, Ethan led her to the passenger side and opened the door for her before walking around the car and getting in as well. In a flash, they had driven off.

By the time Naomi got back to the studio she could hardly see straight. The only thing that came into focus was her own reflection looking back at her in the mirrored wall.

"Naomi," Aspen called. The steps Aspen took forward were tentative but firm. "Is everything okay?"

She didn't turn. Aspen shouldn't have been asking her that anyway. As Naomi's competition, what would come out of her mouth next could determine the difference between first and second position at Prix. "Yes," Naomi told her, and in a way, she really meant it. In fact, when she returned to the theater she had beelined for the girls' dressing room and popped three pills into her mouth. Swallowing them, she then lathered her toes in large globs of Tiger Balm and wrapped them in athletic tape, all the while silently praying it would now numb something much, much worse.

Wordlessly, Aspen came up behind her, watching Naomi's reflection. Naomi swore not to glance back, though. If she did, the other girl might realize that something was wrong, or worse, Naomi might start crying. Naomi cracking was all a dancer like Aspen needed to have an edge over her in the academy.

Naomi walked back to where she had set the phone and speaker on the floor. She restarted the track. And when the cue came, she danced. It was that simple, really. She told herself that her father existed outside of this studio, and that she was inside. Logically, he had to wait. Stand out patiently in the hot sun by the door until she felt ready to let him in. Long enough, at least, for her to dance.

Again, two long arms transformed into two giant useless wings, twisting and folding downward as she bent her torso to her feet and lowered her body like a casket into a grave. With the walls this close to her, the barres had begun to feel like the rods of a lowering device too.

Aspen Letterman danced alongside her, silently watching the other girl turn her two-minute variation into an hour-long marathon. Perhaps rightfully so. They had come here to dance, after all. *But what good is dancing if your heart isn't in it?*

Sometimes they danced even if their hearts weren't in it.

Admittedly, it happened on a very few occasions, but there was nothing at all, not heart or anything else, in Naomi's dancing now. Not even her. Aspen watched her spin and spin.

When the girls had alternated the speaker enough times for their compositions to sound completely played out, they returned to the dressing room. It felt a little strange to leave while the sun was still high, but it was a Saturday and they told themselves that Valentino was not here to read off all the movements they got wrong. It made sense to leave before the Riverside traffic began piling up.

Aspen silently followed the other girl. Naomi was limping and overcompensating with an extra bounce in the opposite leg. As they moved down the deserted concrete tunnel, Naomi began to wonder if she could ever have a rest day, like the other dancers. In truth, she wouldn't allow herself one. As for bad luck and mishaps, these were things she was always prepared for, carrying all sorts of equipment and bandages and spare fabrics in her bag. But this, whatever it was, it was not something that she had prepared for.

The dressing room door opened with a slight push powered by Naomi's walking momentum more than the strength in her arms; Aspen caught it afterward. As empty as the room was without the other bodies usually moving about, it still felt crowded, and the feeling of a crowd even though there was none was enough to push Naomi to her usual bench in the corner of the dressing room, away from all the vanities and scales. It was where she felt most comfortable. She looked up and, of course, Aspen was gathering her things. Quickly, she looked away.

Naomi found that she was beginning to feel the growing

desire to simply stay here. She thought if she spent the night at the theater she could work on her routine and have the free-dom of avoiding her father. It was a win-win. She could keep him waiting outside forever. If she wanted to. Yes, she should. Keep him out there until the sun dried him to a crisp or his heart gave out from the waiting. She lowered her forehead onto her knees.

Aspen cleared her throat.

She was holding the dressing room door wide enough for the both of them when Naomi looked up. "Let's go," she said.

Naomi stared after her. "What?"

"Get up," Aspen said, like it was obvious. "I can't just leave you here. I'll give you a ride home." Naomi waited to see if she was serious. Aspen broke the silence. "Please don't make me ask twice."

Naomi let her arms fall to her sides and wiped at her eyes despite nothing having fallen yet. She said, "It's fine, I think I should just take the bus."

"Naomi," Aspen began. When their eyes connected this time, Naomi knew it was useless. Aspen was seeing through her now. There was no smiling away the trouble settling deep inside of Naomi. "We're both having a shitty day," Aspen said to her.

Naomi didn't want everything to slip out. Carefully she told her, "You have no idea."

"No," she agreed, "I don't. But it's not a good idea for any-one to be here alone dancing the night away. Even principal dancers have a life outside of all this."

Naomi swallowed her response. She didn't think that was true. A principal dancer's life was all this; that was the meaning of *principal*. Wasn't it? Exhaling, Naomi stood and muttered a thank-you. She turned to change into her sneakers, not wanting Aspen to see just how damaged her feet really were. She threw her pointe shoes into her bag and exited the dressing room through the door Aspen still held open for her. Before they walked off, Naomi wondered if Aspen thought she was slacking or giving up. If she thought this would be her opening to outshine her at Grand Prix. "I just might come back next weekend to practice too. I don't think this will happen again." Naomi wanted to make that clear.

Aspen closed the door behind her and adjusted the strap of her bag on her shoulder. "Me too," was all she said.

When the girls made it to the parking lot, Aspen clicked her silver Prius to life with her key fob. It was a considerable distance from where her father had picked her up just yesterday. Naomi looked over to that spot now, but, apart from an oil stain pooling on the asphalt, it was empty. Aspen tried not to notice her watching. She opened the back door and put her bags in. "Do you have your license yet?"

"Yeah, but I prefer to walk." Naomi got in the car. "I read somewhere it makes your legs stronger. You know, for dancing."

Aspen nodded. She put the key in the ignition and shifted out of Park. "And how's that going for you? That extra walking." Naomi opened her mouth to respond but Aspen was quicker. "And don't lie. I saw you limping today."

Naomi looked out her window and slumped into the leather of the seat as the car reversed out of the parking spot.

"Naomi, if you're injured you have to tell Valentino."

"I don't want to talk about it," she said.

"He's going to notice."

"It won't matter. I'll nail the variation anyway."

"With that foot?"

Naomi turned to her. "And you're what now? Perfect? Have everything figured out now?"

Aspen smiled weakly and put the car into Drive. "Now, we know that's not true." Images of a younger, rounder Aspen flashed into Naomi's memory. The girl who frequented the back of the line on the barre and rarely got any leading roles. Looking at the girl beside her now, flushed with makeup and with bony hands on the steering wheel, it was hard to reconcile those two people. In many ways, they were unrecognizable as the same person; only the ghost of a smile on Aspen's face reminded her of that other girl. "None of us in the academy have it all figured out. No matter how much we pretend like we do."

"Is that what you think? They're *all* just pretending?"

"Oh, Naomi." Aspen sighed. "We're all just pretending."

The rest of the car ride was fifteen minutes of silence but Naomi was just glad there was someone alive next to her. Someone she could talk to who didn't want anything from her. For those fifteen minutes, it didn't feel like she was struggling to keep her head above water.

CHAPTER EIGHT

Saint held his sketch pad up to the light pouring in through his bedroom window. Raw sunlight, he found, gave a certain life to his pencil strokes in ways his desk lamp simply could not. Not that this specific drawing needed much more life added to it. There was enough to birth a whole universe—sun, stars, planets, and all—within the image itself. He'd made it even better than he first imagined, a girl in pointe shoes dancing across a moonlit lake among swans. It felt so real when he looked at it that ultimately, Saint convinced himself that somewhere, it was real. Somewhere, that universe was spinning.

The other thing Saint told himself as he examined his work was that the drawing was not really of Naomi. The drawing was his interpretation of ballet from what she had shown him that night in the theater. How natural and calming the dance had looked, like real swans on a real lake, and he found that comforting. So he drew it. It had nothing to do with the girl herself. Or the way she carried herself outside of dancing. As he said, it was a separate universe altogether, real and removed.

Sully trudged in through the already ajar bedroom door. He was holding the television remote in one hand and the other was in the pocket of his shorts. Noticing his older brother inspecting the artwork on his sketch pad, the boy's eyes lit up. "Is it done? Can I see it now?"

Saint exhaled and turned around. He realized there were no sounds coming from the living room anymore. Their three-bedroom home was completely quiet. Sully must have gotten bored of whatever cartoon was airing and had come here to find something else to occupy his attention. Saint realized the boy must have been watching TV all day by now. "Yeah, it's finished. You wanna see?"

Time stopped for the nine-year-old. Sully had been waiting for this moment. For the past few days Saint constantly went back to this drawing in between doing chores. He worked on it while he made them breakfast in the mornings, allowing the stove to finish frying the eggs as he got in a few more pencil strokes. He worked on it before and after he helped their father clean himself up. He worked on it out in the living room long after he had put Sully to bed.

Sully had asked to see the drawing before, but in those early days Saint was territorial, saying it wasn't ready or that it needed to be perfect. Even now, Saint was telling him, "It could still use some work," before he showed it to him.

The words went right through the younger boy. Saint could tell Sully just wanted to see what all the excitement was about. There was a part of him that clenched. Usually when he showed his little brother one of his drawings, if it was good enough, you could see something in the boy's eyes grow hungry, as if he was trying to devour the image just by looking at it, but wasn't sure where to start. But these days, it was getting harder to make art that shocked or surprised Sully. He'd seen so many drafts over the years that now he was disillusioned about what good art looked like. Either that or he was just getting older.

Saint flipped the sketch pad around.

"Saint, that's incredible! The water looks so real. How did you do that?" Sully reached up to hold it but Saint snatched it back.

"Look, don't touch. I don't want you smearing it."

Sully let out a string of okays. He pointed. "Who's that?"

Saint was glad he had settled on his own answer earlier. He didn't even have to look at the drawing to tell him, "It's no one. It's just a dancer. A dancer who coexists with nature."

"She looks like a swan princess. She's pretty," Sully let out.

This time, Saint didn't look back at the drawing because he knew exactly what the boy was talking about. He had seen it too in the light.

Sully looked at his older brother to see if he'd agree, but he was already flipping the book shut. "Wait, will you paint it? You're going to paint it, right?"

"Sully, I can't paint on this type of paper. It's only for pencil."

"Color it then. Use your crayons. Or you can borrow mine. These ones are better now, not wax, remember?"

He chuckled. "Okay, maybe. In the meantime, why don't you go read something?"

Saint stood up and his little brother followed, waddling out of the room after him. "Can you read me something? One of the books you read. No more of those baby books."

Sully loved stories in the same way Saint loved art. They were alike in that sense, but while Saint's hobby was more expensive, Sully could get away with just going to the library with his big brother. If he'd let him, Saint was certain Sully would stay there for hours. Even now, he was positive the boy had books piling up in his bedroom.

He went into the kitchen and opened the pantry, taking out the cookies they had baked a few days ago. "Don't you already have a bunch of books? Just grab one of those. You won't—"

Sully gasped. "Can I have one?"

"After dinner." Saint continued, "—you won't understand mine." He took a bite of the chocolate chip cookie and put the jar back in the pantry.

"Yes, I will!" Sully said, offended. "I can understand them. I'm smart. My teacher says I read above my grade!"

Saint leaned against the counter and took another bite. He didn't doubt that. But it was hard for him to articulate to his brother the extent of the comprehension gap between twelfth and fourth grade literature. Perhaps it would be better to just demonstrate it instead. "Fine, let's see how smart you really are." Sully jumped excitedly, puffing out his chest. He was repeatedly telling himself how smart he was when Saint cut him off with, "Go grab a book off my desk. Any one you want, and we can read that."

Sully broke out a number of celebratory fist pumps. Then he dashed off, continuing to recite all the praise his teacher had given him for his reading level, his voice going nonstop, trailing all the way into Saint's bedroom. The older boy waited until he was out of sight, and finished the cookie.

Like Sully, he too wanted to experience something new. The last time he traveled deeper into Riverside, he had met Naomi. The inspiration followed seamlessly thereafter. Tonight, he was determined to go even farther into the city to see what, or who, else he could find that would be able to light a fire under him. Only, if he was to do that, he couldn't walk. And the bus would be too unpredictable if there was an emergency and he needed to come back home. Saint needed the keys to his father's truck.

He leaned off the counter, brushed the crumbs off his shirt, and walked around to his father's bedroom. He pressed his ear against the door and when the same silence persisted for a few seconds, he gently twisted the door handle and let himself peek inside. It was still dark. The curtains were fully drawn and his father was a silhouette resting on the bed. Saint didn't often have a need to sneak in here other than to retrieve the official documents that his father insisted be kept in the room, but he knew by now that the slower, the better. The quieter, the better. When the door was open just far enough, he slipped inside fully. From what Saint could tell, the rhythm of his father's breathing was consistent and slow.

Saint continued over to the dresser on the other side of the room and took the keys from among the old prescriptions and empty pill bottles. Then he turned to leave. Saint closed the door and went out into the corridor at the same time he heard his little brother's footsteps running down to meet him.

Sully shoved a book into his chest and said, "That! I want to read that one."

Saint pulled it back. *Macbeth*. The boy was probably drawn to it because of the bloody knife that adorned the cover. He might have thought it would be action filled and riveting. Saint supposed it was, just not in the way Sully's young, excited brain probably expected. It was a different story, not really about killing or wealth or death, but about what comes afterward. "A deal's a deal," Saint said. "Let's get reading."

Sully chirped up and followed his brother into the living room where they both slumped onto the couch. Saint flipped open the first page. "So, this is a play, meaning it's a little bit different from a normal story."

"How?"

"Well, first, you have to use your imagination . . ."

In the evening, Richard Owens coughed so much that he spat green into his crumpled tissue. Saint did not know exactly what green mucus meant, and they couldn't afford another medical bill in order to get a diagnosis, but he was sure it couldn't mean anything good. About six months ago it had looked a little more yellow, golden enough that Saint could convince himself and his brother that their father only had a simple cold gone bad. The green did not grant them those niceties. The tissue drooped in mockery, as if to say *This will be your father soon, too, discolored and limp. You will be disgusted looking at him the same way.*

Saint took the tissue from his father and folded it closed. Along with the rest of the discarded litter on the bed, Saint threw it into the bin. He thought he should be grateful the mucus wasn't red at least. Red meant another thing completely, something that Saint was sure it wouldn't take a medical practitioner to confirm. He wanted to hope that day would never come.

Richard Owens lay back down. "Don't look at me like that."

Saint hadn't realized he was looking at him at all. "Like what?"

"Like I'll be dead tomorrow." The man shifted to retrieve his pack of cigarettes off his nightstand.

Saint wanted desperately to take that box and break each stick of nicotine into something that could not hurt his father anymore. "Don't talk like that."

Seconds too late after the words left his mouth Saint realized they were doing it again. Ordering each other around. Wielding their dominance like a weapon.

Without looking at him, "Pass me my lighter," was all Richard replied in his deep, croaky voice. And Saint was reminded of the problem that always incited their fights. Richard Owens didn't care about what the cigarettes were doing to his lungs, and he didn't care what color they made his mucus, and he didn't care that they were the reason he hadn't been outside in almost two weeks. He still kept them by his nightstand, as if they ought to be the first thing he woke up to and the last thing he saw when he fell asleep. Which, these days, happened only hours apart.

"Saint," his father demanded with the cigarette between his teeth, "the lighter."

Saint stood up and took it off the dresser where he'd set it last night in hopes it would dissuade his father from deciding to smoke again. He walked back to the side of the bed and stretched out his hand, realizing now how his plan had backfired. He was aiding him. He was killing him. Saint hoped, at least, that as he was handing his father the lighter the man would read his face and see how obviously it devastated him. How aware his son was that he was handing his father the very thing that would eventually take his life and how it was his father, *him*, that was making Saint do it.

Richard Owens hardly batted an eye. He took the lighter. He lit the cigarette. For a split second Saint wished it would just burn his lips.

Saint waited three hours after putting Sully to bed before he changed his clothes and retrieved his father's car keys from the drawer in his desk. Out in the living room, the boy silently double-checked the door of his little brother's bedroom to make sure there was no light or sound coming from it. Asleep, he hoped. Then Saint did the same to his father's door, only this time he waited longer. He held his breath. Sometimes you could tell the man was awake at night by his groans or if he occasionally decided to turn on the television in his room to keep himself occupied. It was his personal routine, and he didn't do much outside of that. Tonight, though, his room was dead quiet.

Saint slipped out of the pitch-black house and into the streets he knew well. His father's truck was sitting by itself on the curb across the street, a single streetlight illuminating it. It only ever got driven when Saint went to get groceries. Outside of that, his dad hadn't driven it in a year, and Sully never wanted to go anywhere too far, so the 2002 Chevrolet

Silverado stayed put. Hopping into the driver's seat, Saint reminded himself again that he really needed to google where to get maintenance for the truck. It wasn't a conversation he was keen on having with his father. That man would go in circles with him, first asking why he felt he had to know these things, then if Saint felt as though he was more grown-up than his own father. Saint would want to say yes but he wouldn't, and then after juggling a few lies back and forth his father might finally give Saint the closest thing to a straight answer that he could: directions to a friend he used to know who might be better able to help.

Saint revved the car. The pair of red fuzzy dice hanging from the rearview mirror bounced each other awake. It hadn't always been like this. Richard had been a distant father, sure, but in the same way most fathers were, and Saint and all his friends from school could attest to that. But after Saint's mother died, something shifted in that little house. Suddenly, his dad was smoking a cigarette no matter where he was or the time of day, and he was out drinking nightly. He lost his job in two short years and must have made up his mind to never work another day in his life because he seemed comfortable, even happy, being unemployed. The memory of his father picking him up from school the day he found out Richard was jobless was still vivid.

Saint had gotten into the front seat and thrown his back-pack in the back. It was raining, so he was soaked. And he was thrice mad. First, because his father was picking him up because he had punched another boy in the face and the principal had called Richard to collect him. Second, because he knew his father would be mad at him for fighting in school and forcing him to leave his job. And three, because he knew his father would be mad at him for fighting in school and forcing him to leave his job *and* getting the car wet with his drenched clothes and dripping backpack.

"Watch your attitude," Richard had said, peeling out of the high school lot. "You fight now?" He sounded more amused than angry.

"I don't want to talk about it." And it was that easy. Richard didn't ask again. He put another cigarette into his mouth and kept quiet. Probably reserving the cussing for home, Saint thought. But when he realized they were driving straight home instead of back to his father's office he asked, "You're not going to work?"

The man was almost smiling. "Got fired today, my boy."

"What? Why?"

The bitterness came almost immediately, as if it was the easier emotion for him and all the smiling was straining his muscles. "They tripping. They know what I'm going through, and they still did this to me."

The way he had said it, so matter-of-factly, it was as if he didn't actually feel any of it. He was saying what was true, and he looked angry, but not sad. Looking back now, Saint had felt it in his gut that things would forever change again in their family. This time, however, it was his father changing and not his mother.

When Saint's knuckles began to hurt from clenching the steering wheel and he felt his throat tightening, he pulled over. All he could see now was his father on the day of the funeral. Sully's face as Saint tried to explain to him the reason their mother was never going to come back. His breathing was coming out ragged. Air. He needed air. Saint took the keys out of the ignition and stumbled out of the Silverado, running around the truck and meeting the concrete sidewalk just inches from his face. All fours. He tried to focus on feeling the scrapes and cracks in the concrete. If only his mother were here. She would know what to do. She should know what to do. How could she have left him here to take care of everyone? Maybe she hadn't known how badly Richard would take it, but she had to have known his smoking would get worse. When she was alive he only smoked casually, and even then, she couldn't get him to stop. And she had to have known a family never recovers from a death. She had to have known she was the only thing that was weaving their lives together into one; that without her their lives would be cut short, split, and overburdened.

Saint felt his breathing uptick. She wasn't here, and she wasn't coming to save him. He flipped his hand over and pressed it deep into the concrete. He rubbed it in. Saint shut his eyes. He rubbed harder. Soon he was holding his breath against the pain. And only when he felt like he didn't have to think about his breathing anymore did Saint open his eyes. The sidewalk was decorated red. When he turned his hand over, it was dripping.

His body had never failed him like that before, especially not while driving. It had only ever happened in his room where he could pinch himself back to reality or pick apart the things that he loved the most about his recent drawing. This time pinching was not enough and seeing was too much.

As he stood up, Saint's back brushed against the metal body of the Silverado. He hadn't fully come off the road like he thought he had either. Luckily, the few cars that were driving by had enough space to swerve around him. Saint grabbed hold of the cargo bed. Things could have been a lot worse. The realization, it felt like, dropped on top of him. Perhaps this was exactly the inspiration he'd been searching for. This: driving, his mother, what felt like almost never being able to breathe ever again, rubbing his hand into the sidewalk, relief. Relief. But he'd left all his art supplies at home.

The boy searched the Silverado for a pencil, paper, anything, but came up empty. Down the street was home, maybe twenty minutes away. Up the street was more road. But Saint wanted to remain here, with his blood. As he glanced back at the spot he'd made, Saint noticed a home improvement store across the street. His mind raced. *Close enough.* He gathered himself and jogged across the street, looking left and right when he was already midlane.

There were only a few people inside at this hour so he didn't have to look over too many heads to find what he needed. And there it was, in the back of the store, waiting for him—paint. Saint almost dashed in that direction. He bumped past workers and circumvented buyers until he finally was standing in front of a wall filled to the ceiling with paint, paint rollers, and smaller tubs of color samples. His immediate reaction was to get a bucket, but that much paint was hard to control and if he got that he'd need a brush, too, which was more money that he didn't have. He needed something else. His second idea bumped the elbow of his arm when he placed a thoughtful hand on his hip. A display of stacked spray paints.

Saint felt the inspiration burn brighter inside him. He rang up a single can at the cashier and sprinted back to the sidewalk. Out there he took off the safety seal and shook the can vigorously. Saint Owens began to paint the first thing he felt like he needed on the sidewalk. Two minutes in he realized he'd need a stencil perhaps, or maybe a different nozzle. But the slower he went, the more control he had and the better the portrait began to look. He also used his free hand, the undamaged one, to help stencil the few shapes he required. Half an hour later, he realized he had taken up more sidewalk than he initially intended to.

Finished, Saint pulled away. His mother, Miranda Owens, smiled up at him from the sidewalk, exactly how he remembered her, his own dried blood staining her face.

CHAPTER NINE

The dining table was already set when Naomi got inside. Aja was done cooking and all the plates were placed perfectly on their mats. Naomi decided against changing her clothes for something more comfortable to wear. It felt a little pointless, given everything.

Aja commented on how early her daughter was home today compared to weekdays, and Naomi's only reply was that things were ending earlier now. Ballet was being cut short by other things. Normally, Aja would press her daughter to explain exactly what she had meant by that, but after last night she accepted the answer as it was and gave Naomi space. In that time, Ethan descended the stairs and came into the dining room. The walls began moving.

He uttered some greeting, which fell on deaf ears, and moved into the kitchen to greet his wife. Naomi didn't expect the sudden taste of spoiled fruit in her mouth at the sight of him. She attempted to avoid looking at him altogether. This, of course, became harder when the couple entered the dining room, hand in hand, and took seats alongside Naomi. At the table, Ethan sat at the head. Aja was at the other end of the table, and Naomi was off to their sides. Jessica would usually sit across from her, but even she did not want to endure what would happen next. No one said anything.

Naomi knew that her mother deserved to know, but she couldn't find the words to tell her something like this. She could hardly tell herself. Would her mom be upset? Disappointed? What would happen to all of them after something like this was brought out into the light? Her mother only worked part-time as a paralegal—how would they pay for Naomi's career? It was easier to just keep her eyes down. Head down too. And sink everything she was feeling even further and further down, where she didn't have to feel it anymore.

Naomi felt the walls continue to close in on her. The dining room was becoming exponentially smaller the longer she refused to look at her father. She kept her gaze on her plate and allowed the world to close in. She waited to be crushed.

On Sundays, Naomi usually woke up early to stretch in her standing mirror while Jessica kept count, but Jessica had abandoned her days ago, and Naomi could hardly stand when her thoughts were this heavy. It felt as though the walls had not expanded at all since the previous night, and so all the things she was holding in were beginning to swell, like freezing water in a glass.

Naomi didn't leave her bed the entire day. She stayed

planted on her mattress because she knew a trip to the kitchen or the bathroom would mean she would have to carry this weight and size with her. She was no longer certain that she could manage to walk with it all. Between herself and the too-near walls, something would have had to give.

Rain had arrived in Riverside during the time it took her to eat nothing. Hours into the storm, lightning had joined too. Naomi was only grateful there was some sound. Noise to break the silence. Oftentimes, she imagined a thunderstorm, much like this one, coming toward her with a vengeance. It would lift the roof off their house and shift its foundation. Everything here would collapse in on itself, and she, along with her parents, would go down with it. But no one would hear a thing. Naomi pictured the Morgan house falling silently while the rest of Riverside kept going.

In the rainy darkness, Naomi reached out to her side and clutched a fistful of her sheets. At least she was putting up a fight. All day she had been forcing everything down. Her best friend, who was a master of cutting her down, from her food to her nails, to her life. Valentino's words on her grief. Her father's infidelity. All down. Away. And when they were far enough out of reach, finally, she exhaled. Thinking about other people and their choices would leave no room for herself, she decided. She still had to think about her career, Grand Prix, the School of American Ballet, the New York City Ballet. She recited that over and over again. Above all else, Naomi wanted to dance. And she told herself that was exactly what she was going to do.

So the young dancer sat awake all through the night and waited for the sky to change color. Time passed, and her spirit readied, and finally, when sunlight peeked in, Naomi lurched forward. Tiger Balm. Three capsules of ibuprofen. A change of clothes. The art of escapism. The Riverside Performing Arts Theater saw Naomi on Monday before anyone else did. She told herself that today belonged to her, not Jessica or her family or anyone else. She repeated it over and over again until every syllable had seeped into the very marrow of her bones. Then, when she entered the dance studio all alone, she sat in the center of the floor. She strengthened her mind with images of the elegant White Swan performance she'd spent countless nights analyzing. She imagined herself doing it as part of the New York City Ballet. Her toes twitched hungrily.

Naomi began her stretches thereafter by mercilessly bending her pointe into submission before the rest of her body underwent the same treatment. She largely tried to ignore any pain her injured foot exercised on her. For warm-ups she held the barre and threw her body forward then back again. Her back cried as she forced it past what it was used to and her knees buckled from exhaustion a few times, but her toes were muted. She could still go on. She even rehearsed her smile. All lips, no emotion. A dancer's bread and butter.

Just when the vigorous bending and twisting had ended, the studio doors opened, and the other dancers began to flood in. Pairs of eyes landed on Naomi, and immediately the girl came off pointe. Sweat drenched her tights and she knew they could tell that she had been up for what seemed like hours already. Whispers circulated. Naomi quickly spun around to avoid them, but it was useless. She was met with the mirrored wall, and it reflected all their penetrating stares right back at her. The face of the one person contorted.

Naomi looked at the floor. She remembered her decision and told herself it was her time to dance no matter what. She could still do this. She shamelessly resumed her own rehearsal, and every time she overheard a whisper or glanced at an unimpressed look, she danced even harder. She used it to fuel herself. That must be what the New York City Ballet and every other talented dancer did. How else did they make *this* a practice they did every day, for years, forty hours a week?

The studio doors slammed open in the middle of Naomi's turn. Her body rocked back onto her ankle. She recovered quickly, regaining her balance on the soles of her feet. Naomi took a fraction of a second to inspect her foot and under the satin of her pointe shoes, she couldn't make out much of the swelling or the bruises, and she hardly felt anything thanks to the ibuprofen. Valentino stormed inside, and the class fell silent. He discarded his sunglasses and trained his eyes on each of his dancers.

They needed no instruction. They all drifted to the barre, Naomi breathlessly two paces behind. She gripped the horizontal, waist-high metallic barre drilled into the left wall of the studio and squeezed. Her heart was picking up. But she kept her face hard like every other dancer did in here and tried to remind herself of the importance of this day. But she was tired. She had been here for an hour already on no sleep, and no food to give her energy. She felt her heartbeat speed up even more.

The intern, Eli, set his fingers on the keys of the piano and the music began. She wasn't sure when Valentino had told them which barre routine they were doing or how he explained it to them, but Naomi saw all the bodies in the Riverside Dance Academy begin to move. She gritted her teeth and quickly fell in line. Whatever they did, she just copied, and it managed to keep her two beats behind for most of the routine.

In between switching arms on the barre Naomi glanced at herself in the mirror. Bagged eyes and messy hair but nothing, she thought, that couldn't be fixed with makeup and a hair straightener.

In her peripheral vision, she caught a flicker of movement. Aspen was looking back at her in the mirror. Her blond hair was precise but her face wore a worried look. She mouthed, *Are you okay?*

Naomi tried not to think about how bad things must look for Aspen to feel the need to ask her that from across the room. She steadied her breathing and gently turned her gaze away. For the remainder of the routine she kept her chin high, squeezing the barre so tightly the palm of her hands scared the blood off. By the end of the warm-up, it became another numbed thing.

Valentino told the class, "I haven't received any email complaints from the staff yet, so I have to assume that means you were all on your best behavior this weekend. Although I still haven't gotten my keys back. I need those, by the way." No one said anything. "Who came in this weekend to rehearse?"

Naomi wanted badly to say that she had. She wanted to raise her hand and distinguish herself from the other girls here. Valentino would have liked that, she was sure. But there was nothing about coming last Saturday that she was proud of. She tasted a reflux of acidic vomit at the remembrance of her father kissing that woman.

"I did." The room turned to look at Aspen Letterman. "And so did Naomi."

Valentino nodded. "And the rest of you?"

Many of the boys blurted their excuses first. Trips into the countryside. College viewings. A lapse in memory. The girls said less. They knew their excuses didn't matter in the same way that the boys' did. While princes and heartthrobs didn't have much competition in the world of ballet so long as they were good enough, there was competition for princesses. Almost too much. All the girls knew they had to be perfect if they wanted to stand a shred of a chance. Girls in ballet were not the type to take vacations to their family cottages almost three months out from the Youth America Grand Prix.

Valentino tutted his teeth nonetheless. The boys, he said, since they were so eager to prove themselves, should go first today. He asked the dancers to move to the back of the room so the floor could be open for solos. A few people whispered to each other but mostly it was a quiet transition. They all stood against the wall and Valentino called up each boy individually to perform his variation.

Naomi examined each of them. Despite the fact that the boys did not go on pointe, and their variations were so different from hers, she still tried to pick apart their movements just as she knew the judges at Grand Prix would. Meticulously, she watched them. The skin beneath their tights and the way their heads followed their dominant hand. Only, by the third boy, Naomi began to realize she was not retaining anything she was looking at. The places she would have otherwise used to store studied techniques were at maximum capacity now. Occupied, unwillingly, by things that had nothing to do with techniques and movements.

The girls, in many ways, were worse. They were fluid and

quick, more than what Naomi was capable of copying. They were doing better than her, she realized. All of them. Even the ones who often received harsh feedback seemed more awake today.

Then Valentino called her name. Naomi bit into her bottom lip so hard she knew there was blood. She stepped forward, took her position, and exhaled. Promises had been made, she told herself. For the next three minutes she only had to keep everything submerged. Just a little longer. Just a little longer. Just a little.

When the music began, she was ready for it. Two long arms transformed into giant wings, twisting and folding downward as she lowered her body to the floor. Then she came up. And Jessica was standing in front of her. Her hair was haphazardly down and she was not wearing compression tights or anything else but a sundress covered in dirt, as if she had crawled out of a grave to collect something that was supposed to be buried with her in the first place. Naomi gritted her teeth.

Like her routine instructed her to, she flew up on pointe and began her raised pirouettes. The moment she did this, the pain in her foot struck again. The dead girl didn't move. Then as she executed her spinning fouettés, Naomi saw the worried look on Aspen's face. Naomi shut her eyes.

This way each turn landed her somewhere she should not have been and every jump she tried was flightless. But her eyes would not open. She refused to let the light in. And, finally, there was a sharp crack from Naomi's ankle. Everything set loose. Her scream shattered the music as her body bent unnaturally. She folded twice over when the pain came from her foot first, then from everything else.

The rest of the Riverside Dance Academy held still as Naomi Morgan took to the floor in an agonizing scream cut short by the impact of her head on the Marley flooring.

CHAPTER TEN

"Naomi, relax. It's not that serious, I promise." Jessica was shifting through the crowded Riverside sidewalk, skipping down the concrete like a smooth stone on water as Naomi lagged behind, trapped behind the bristling shoulders of strangers.

"Easy for you to say, you're dancing Odette. The lead."

"The key to getting the lead, honey, is not caring about the lead."

"That doesn't make any sense."

"Law of attraction, or something," Jessica responded with a shrug.

Naomi crinkled her brows and followed her best friend down the busy streets of Downtown Riverside. She observed the way Jessica glided through the mass of bodies and wondered what it took to appear that effortless. Practice? Good karma? And she wanted to just open her mouth and ask her right then and there, but she couldn't find the words.

How could she possibly ask without sounding utterly pathetic?

Maybe the fact that she wanted to ask in the first place had already made her that way, and now she was simply denying what had been true for a very, very long time.

There were, actually, a few pathetic things that Naomi spent hours wondering about her best friend. Like how her hair could fall down to her neck without being flat-ironed. Why she didn't seem to like dancing that much but was so good at it anyway. The fact that whenever they spoke in pairs, people kept their eyes on Jessica always.

And probably worst of all, Naomi was confused that Jessica was oblivious to it all. Even now as she shifted through the crowd with a nonchalant air and an easy smile, Naomi didn't think she'd seen anything else so designed. And somehow Jessica Kingsley was still a stranger to her own perfection.

"That's not true, you know."

Naomi blinked up at her.

She shook her head, as if she had seen a child attempt a task that everyone else had known was impossible for them to successfully do on their own. "I'm not perfect. Naomi, no one is." The sun was still high but Naomi did not feel hot at all. Jessica's smile faltered briefly. "But you knew that already, didn't you?"

"I don't know anything. Not anymore."

Jessica turned around fully, her back to the incoming crowd, but everyone simply walked around her. "Why don't you just say what you've really been meaning to say all this time? It's not really about being perfect or talented or beautiful, is it? It never was. So why don't you just say it and get it over with." No one in the crowd was looking at them despite the fact that the two girls were the loudest voices here. Everyone was silent and headed in the same direction, off to do whatever filled their days.

Naomi opened her mouth and shut it again. Within their tight little bubble on the sidewalk, she felt everything inside her shake. She looked up at her best friend, real as rusted steel, and said finally, "How could you leave me?"

Jessica stopped walking when she realized Naomi was no longer following her.

"I was alone and I needed you. You were all I've ever had. The only person I felt like I could talk to who actually understood me. Do you know what that means? What that feels like—talking to people and physically feeling it go nowhere? But with you, I never felt that. Not once. And we were supposed to go to New York City together. Start new lives. You and me. Maybe we could have made new friends who were more like us. Maybe, outside of this stupid town, we could have, I don't know, figured out who we are. Or who we're supposed to be. Or who we wanted to be.

"But you left. You left me here. And now, I have absolutely no one. I'm all alone and it's so suffocating."

Jessica took Naomi's hands in hers and squeezed them. If Riverside ever had birds, they would be singing sad songs right then. It started as a thought but Naomi's mouth opened again on its own. "But what did you expect? What else could you have expected, Jessica? If we make all these promises, and you're the only person who sees me, what else did you expect?" Her voice cracked on each syllable and her throat burned. She tried not to think about the tears at all. "All I ever wanted was for you to keep seeing me."

Jessica's grip on her hands was constricting now. Naomi searched the other girl's eyes and lips for an answer. But there was nothing within Jessica looking back at her. Her eyes were just dreadful and glistening. Jessica guided her forward with the grip she still had on Naomi. She walked them down the pavement, where the faceless crowd divided much more quickly to accommodate their increasingly rapid steps. Mustering just enough strength to tear her eyes away from the back of Jessica's head, Naomi looked up and noticed they were close to the Riverside Performing Arts Theater now. Really, they were only a few seconds out, and Naomi wanted to tell her best friend to stop tugging at her—stop stringing her along by what felt like too many threaded needles pinned and hooked beneath the surface of her skin. She did not want to go to the theater. She didn't even want to keep walking. But her mouth was still a little dry from her previous words, and she had no idea how she should curl her tongue to form those kinds of words.

When they turned the last corner Jessica said to her, "Naomi, open your eyes." She must have closed them somewhere back on the sidewalk as she was wincing and crouching her neck deep into her collarbone. Again, Jessica said, "Naomi, please. Open your eyes."

One eye at a time, Naomi peeked. The building, she was afraid, was awake, and Valentino was in it waiting for her to dance until her toes bled. But in front of her as she saw it fully under the baby-blue Riverside sky, the Riverside Performing Arts Theater was not a large building but rather a small structure barely standing on the urban confines of Downton Riverside. It didn't look like it could be much larger than a broom closet.

The door opened from the inside and Valentino stepped out. When he saw her, he seemed surprised. "Naomi? I didn't think you were coming today." He looked at the other girl. "Hello, Jessica, how are you doing?"

Before Jessica could reply, Naomi said, "Sorry I'm late, Valentino."

The man chuckled. "Late?" He dug into his pockets and pulled out his keys. He turned around, slipped one into the small keyhole, and locked it. Naomi's jaw slackened. "Naomi, we're closed."

"Closed?" She looked down at herself, then at Jessica, then back to Valentino. "Aren't we rehearsing?"

Valentino said, "Why would we be rehearsing? Don't you know what day today is?"

She didn't dare say no.

Understanding her nonresponse, Valentino smiled to himself. The man put his keys into his pocket and walked off, joining the crowd of people on the sidewalk. Naomi watched him leave like a raindrop into a river. The single theater door was a scratched and cracked thing. It had been painted a rich burgundy color once; that much was recognizable from the mangled thing now. Naomi reached for the handle.

"Don't bother," Jessica said. "It's locked."

She asked, "Why?"

When Jessica's mouth opened, the tone was not her own. "Do you really want to go to New York City?"

Naomi cocked an eyebrow at the seriousness in her friend's face. "Of course."

Jessica shook her head, gesturing with her small hands as she went. "I mean, yes, you want to go to New York City, but I mean you could just go to the city and not go to the ballet company." Naomi didn't say anything. "You could just get away. Get out of Riverside, you know?" She wasn't saying "we" anymore.

An infinity went by in their little bubble. Naomi opened her mouth slowly. "I don't—"

"Yeah, you're right. It's stupid." Jessica smiled like nothing had even mattered in the first place. "I guess some of us are meant for ballet. Born for the life of dancing across stages, standing on pointe for an unimpressed crowd." She laughed to herself but it looked like she was laughing at the world. "I guess it doesn't sound so bad."

Jessica slumped down to sit in front of the simple theater door. Naomi joined her. They watched everyone in Riverside pass by them out on the sidewalk, their heads pointed toward their own different destinies. Naomi wondered where they were all going. Part of her hoped that Valentino would not return so she could follow them and find out. But also, secretly, she wanted to follow them wherever they went because Jessica was wrong: it did sound that bad.

CHAPTER ELEVEN

The sun fell from the sky. It sank halfway into the bed of the horizon. Like the selfish ball of light, Naomi had left nothing shining behind. The dusk of her hospital room contained only crumpled pillows stained with her bleeding dreams and a soaked floor where all her mourning had spilled from her eyes and onto the crisp white tiles. It was fair to say that as she was now, folded into a creaking wheelchair with her head unbearably low and a brace wrapped around her ankle, Naomi Morgan had nothing left; whether in her or of her.

She sat silently in the lobby area. Her parents were bickering with her doctor, probably in an attempt to find out the cost of the quickest fix. But the conversation was long and unresolved. From where she was sitting, she could hear that much. She wondered if her parents were even aware that she could hear them. That even though she wasn't standing on her own two feet, and she wasn't moving, and her head was low, she was still *here*.

Aja and Ethan didn't say much as they returned to her. She hadn't expected them to either. She had known the truth already. Her dad's mouth adjusted itself as he took the handles of the chair and pushed her toward the exit. Naomi wanted to tell her father to leave her alone, that he had no right to touch any part of her after she had seen him betray everything their small family held dear. He was selfish for what he had done. Whether or not her mom knew, he had still disregarded his family and their feelings. He had lied, manipulated, and—then she realized how quickly she had given herself ownership of this contraption she was sitting in. She thought of it as a part of her even now, and the suggestion of what that meant for her career locked her jaw shut. Her spine stiffened.

So it was that nothing had changed for the Morgan family as they quietly left the hospital building and entered the parking lot. No one spoke or uttered condolences. Instead, Naomi watched the bustling Riverside traffic fake progress just beyond the parking lot where cars stayed still and streetlights flickered on. Ethan picked Naomi up in his arms (she bit her tongue) and placed her in the car. Then he folded her wheelchair and went to place it in the trunk of their Audi Q7. Aja got in the front passenger seat and looked back at Naomi.

"This isn't the end," she said. "Valentino understands your condition, and I'm sure in his next ballet he'll give you the lead. No questions asked." Naomi decided against telling her mother that was not how ballet, or Valentino, worked. She looked at the traffic outside. "The doctors were telling us about how we can get you back on your feet too. They say seeing a physiotherapist will be good. You'll be able to walk in no time, too, since your ankle is only sprained. But they suggested a lot of sleep for strength. Maybe some vitamins and antibiotics," she added.

"Honey," Ethan said when he got in the driver's seat, his voice strained like the vocal cords would tear any second, "ease up. She needs time."

"I know that," Aja snapped. "But we need a plan. This is something—"

Naomi watched the two of them in the front seats go at it again, waiting for either of them to include her, maybe ask her what she thought was too soon or too late, but they never did. Maybe it was best that way. At least now she could watch the sun carry all the color out of the sky. She wanted to be one of those shades. Swirling hues of color bowing and leaping over soft clouds. They were mocking her. Those movements looked too familiar to not be the variation of a final act—where the girl dies and the audience is forced to watch. Naomi couldn't find it in herself to look away. Unable to feel her feet, or any other part of her for that matter, this ounce of ballet in the sky that she was witnessing felt like a stolen gift. The whole way home, her temple attached itself to the car window and she watched.

The car finally came to a stop outside their house. Her parents got out first and walked around to the trunk. Even from within the metallic death machine, she caught bits of their newest argument. Aja was urging Ethan to install ramps around the house as soon as possible. Ethan was insisting that ramps were unnecessary because Naomi only had the wheelchair for today and she would be using crutches afterward. They would be easy to remove, Aja replied. She wouldn't be the one removing them, Ethan threw back.

Naomi didn't think much about either option. She already knew she would not be leaving her room for a very, very long time. The car door opened next to her and the wheelchair rolled up. Her mom appeared and helped her into it, wheeling her around to the front of the house before stopping abruptly at the driveway. Whispers followed. In the end, the pause lasted only a few seconds and then Naomi's wheelchair was moving forward again. This time, she could tell her father was the one pushing her. The pacing was different.

They stopped briefly at the front steps, where he came to Naomi's side and lifted the wheelchair, carrying her up to the wooden porch. When inside, he paused. "Do you want to go to your room?"

She nodded.

Only a second later, her father was lifting her out of the chair and into his arms, carrying her up the staircase. The sensation dropped Naomi's mind back a few years to times when she would fall asleep in the living room and her father would pick her up just like this and take her to bed. Sometimes she'd pretended to be asleep just for that moment. Those days he carried her everywhere, either on his capable shoulders or in his guarding arms, and back then, he really seemed invincible to her. She supposed he still was.

Ethan slid his daughter out of his arms and onto her bed. She saw him bunch the comforter up in his fists and put it over her. When their eyes met, she turned her head away from him. Ethan stood over her, waiting, looking at her wrapped in fabrics that made her seem bigger than she was. Naomi wasn't sure what he was waiting for. Maybe he felt as though it was the right thing to do. Maybe a little more time standing there would give him something he had not waited long enough for in the past. Something he should have stuck around for?

But her body was immobile, and her eyes were glued to the empty corner of her room, in the direction opposite him. When neither of them spoke, she heard Ethan's footsteps recede, making their way back to the door. She heard him say, "I know this is a lot for you. But you should know the doctors at the hospital recommended a lot of rest. Your mother heard what she wanted to hear but . . ."

There was a tsunami Naomi was holding back with drywall.

He continued, "Whatever happens, you can overcome it. Your talent is legendary, Naomi, and an injury like this can't stop you." Naomi thought the worst part of this had to be that he thought the injury was the only reason she didn't want to be around him. "You're still my baby girl. If there's anything that you need, I'm here, okay?"

For a second he didn't move, and Naomi thought the world had finally stopped spinning. "You'll get through this." A tear, something she thought she'd run out of by now, slipped down her cheek. Then he left, shutting the door behind him.

When Naomi was thirteen, her heart broke. The Riverside Dance Academy was performing *The Nutcracker*, her first-ever ballet, for the entire town. It was her first opportunity to be something great. But Jessica got the lead instead of her, and Naomi always paled in comparison whenever they hit the stage together, so it was pointless from there. In that same week her first crush, Daniel, left the academy and moved away before she ever got the chance to tell him how she felt. Back then, Naomi was convinced her world was falling apart bit by bit and just breathing made her miserable. The same feeling had taken her under when she'd found herself in the hospital the previous day, hollowed and meaningless. And it hadn't gone away since.

Naomi slept until noon. Her eyes struggled open against the harsh sunlight. As she looked next to her, the heavy reality crept in. That the bed beside her held nothing where Jessica used to be, and that the cold air that once accompanied her was gone; Riverside's scorching heat was its painful substitute. Naomi inhaled deeply and turned on her side, her gulps of air prickly as thorns.

By evening, it took her a few futile attempts to realize that she still couldn't move. The hospital had said that her wheelchair was only a one-day privilege; there was technically nothing preventing her from actually standing on at least one foot. But Naomi refused to believe that was true as she struggled to feel any bone or muscle or anything else inside of her.

She was crippled, whether the doctor or her parents or anyone else saw it. Something was broken.

That fact seemed natural. And because of it, there was nothing left for Naomi. There was nothing to do, nowhere to go, no one to speak to. Naomi was more alone than she ever thought she could be, and she had only her empty bedroom to entertain what was left of her. She stared at the squared outline on the wall where her television used to be. She had removed it because Jessica thought it was a distraction. Her dresser was empty, too, as was her nightstand, which didn't even have her lamp anymore. In one corner, atop a lonely desk, was a laptop she hardly ever used. Even her floor was bare because Jessica said she would need the space to practice, and carpets and other miscellaneous things were all hindrances.

Looking around, Naomi tried to find something in her room that reminded her of herself. That was when she noticed something out of place: her closet door was ajar. She quickly blinked away the tears that had formed and realized that the door was wedged open by a pair of her pointe shoes. Helplessly, she stared. Permanent dirt had curved around the box and scratches were sliced into the soles. They had served her longer than she expected when she thought about all the things she went through. Pointe shoes usually withstood torture for about two weeks, but this pair had defied those odds.

Despite her sloppy technique throughout the summer and Jessica's berating, the pointe shoes stayed with her. Then all throughout her late-night relentless rehearsing in front of her bedroom mirror to materialize a future she was tired of dreaming about with Jessica, a girl she never grew tired of seeing. The pointe shoes' survival even lasted until she got the role of the White Swan, just when things had begun to fall apart. And even after that, when she was struggling to fit them on her feet after seeing her father love a stranger.

She turned onto her other side. A shiver crawled up her spine as the sheets shifted with her. But now she was looking at her dresser again and atop it, the keys to the Riverside Performing Arts Theater that Jessica had stolen. Or that she had stolen. Regardless, they did not belong to her, and she knew it but had kept them anyway. And it was ironic because the set of keys was with her here yet she knew that the theater was locked away from her in a way that it didn't even matter. She couldn't pull that door open again. What purpose, in the end, did the keys serve?

Naomi flipped onto her back this time. She tasted salt tickling her lips. She sniffled, her thoughts retreating to the overcrowded dark of her mind as she felt terrible tears stream down her face. She remained like that for another hour until she eventually drifted off to sleep.

A knock came at the bedroom door. Naomi said nothing, but it creaked open anyway and weighted footsteps came inside. Aja stood by the foot of the bed and cleared her throat. "Naomi?"

The girl didn't move. The quiet came for them again, like tides do for dead bodies. There was a long pause.

Aja tried speaking again, her words fumbling over themselves. "Naomi?"

The girl eventually stretched herself just far enough to spare her mother a glance from the corner of her eye.

Her mother exhaled with relief. Naomi returned her gaze to the closet door and wondered what exactly was her mother relieved about? She was here after all, was she not? In her bedroom, where she spent the majority of her time that wasn't already spent at the theater. Perhaps it was because she wasn't dancing in her mirror anymore and so there was no knock of pointe shoes against the wooden floor. Instead, she was lying here, motionless. Naomi wondered if the relief was because her mother had assumed that she was dead up here this whole time.

Aja sank into the mattress, sitting on its edge. She began

speaking, mostly hopeful stories about recovery that she had read online, and how Naomi could mimic that kind of success. When Naomi didn't respond, Aja held her breath again.

She said, "You didn't come down for dinner yesterday. You know you can't get better if you don't eat." After a few moments of silence she continued, "Last night, your father and I were talking, and I understand that you might not want to walk right now. Going downstairs might be hard, I get that." She paused, testing her words. "But food helps, Naomi. I don't mind bringing your meals up here. Just for the first few days. How does that sound?"

Naomi glanced at her mother again. She must have interpreted the look in Naomi's eyes well enough, because she smiled down at her then briefly left the room to retrieve a tray full of food from the kitchen. She rested the waffles, berries, toast, and eggs on the night table and helped Naomi sit up, hoisting her up by her underarms and helping her back against the wall. When Naomi finally raised her head, Aja saw her face. Her eyes were sunken in, lips chapped, hair undone. Aja handed her a glass of orange juice then sat on the bed's edge again. "Drink up."

Feeling its coolness in her palm, Naomi wondered what would happen if she simply decided to not drink it. What if she just sat there and did nothing? Or she squeezed the glass as tightly as she could before throwing it straight into one of her walls. Then, with broken glass scattered on the floor and the orange juice running down the walls of her bedroom, what would her mother do?

Naomi took a sip. Aja told her that they had their first session with a physiotherapist next week. "She's worked with recovering dancers before, so she really knows what she's doing, Naomi." Reaching over to the nightstand, she drizzled syrup on some waffles for her daughter and continued, "Don't worry. You'll be fine."

Aja went to cut the breakfast meal but realized that she didn't have a knife. She laughed at herself and flew out of the room. When she came back with a butter knife, she then realized that she had forgotten napkins too. She left again. She returned, and this time took a seat. Besides telling her daughter about the importance of food in her journey to recovery, most of the meal was fed to Naomi wordlessly, in true Morgan fashion. Aja had just about finished feeding her the waffles when Naomi attempted to reach for a strawberry.

She did a deep, long inhale and forced her arm to budge. When Aja noticed, she angled her body outside of the arm's path, watching it shakily extend to the breakfast plate on Naomi's lap. Naomi picked up the strawberry and curved her arm back toward herself, touching the fruit with her lips. Aja smiled.

Naomi held the strawberry there. She wondered how she was supposed to exist now, without Jessica. She wanted desperately to just welcome her back into her bedroom, like she had been doing for the past few weeks. But her friend was dead, she knew that now, and whoever had been talking to her, criticizing her, and tormenting her was not her best friend. It wasn't Jessica. And no matter how upset she was at her for leaving, Jessica had still left and there was nothing Naomi could do about that. She had to find a new way to exist, not only as a dancer, but as a whole person altogether.

Limply, Naomi looked over at her mother. She cleared her throat. It took her a few attempts but each syllable came out stronger than the last. When she felt her voice was working, she attempted a full sentence. It came out cracked and hoarse, but it served its purpose, nonetheless. "I want to see her."

Aja continued cutting the toast into halves, then dividing the first half into two. "See who?"

"Jessica. I want to see her."

"Naomi, I don't think—"

"I want to see her."

Aja looked up from the plate. "Where's all this coming from?"

Naomi looked into her mother's eyes and frowned. Then, agonizingly, she slipped out, "Everywhere . . . it feels like everywhere."

"Naomi, she's gone. Jessica's gone, and I don't think going back there would be good for you."

"That's exactly why I have to see her." *There are some things I still haven't said. Things that, in my head, have expired like milk. Chunky, rancid.*

Aja Morgan's eyes fell to the porcelain plate and she was about to start cutting again when she noticed that she had already turned the bread into quarters. She stared at them quietly. "Okay, we'll go."

"When?" Naomi asked.

Her mother twirled the fork in her fingers. Thoughtfully, she said, "After your appointment. When you're ready." Then she stuck a fork into a sliced, squared piece of toast. "Open up."

ACT
TWO

CHAPTER TWELVE

Naomi stirred. At least today she could bear to move before the day slipped into the afternoon. Yesterday and the day before she had barely caught any sunlight at all. As she came to, the noise of knuckles rapping against her bedroom door jolted her awake. The door opened gently.

"You're up." What sounded like amusement laced her mom's words as she stepped inside the room holding a tray of freshly made breakfast. "I thought you'd still be sleeping," Aja said.

The aroma of pancake syrup and butter made Naomi's stomach grumble. She twisted and just barely managed to sit up on her own so that her mother could place the brimming tray on her lap. It was a heavy thing on top of her, and Naomi's hunger felt as if it had been building up for this exact moment. She resisted the urge to lick her lips.

Peering down at the tray sitting in her blanket-covered lap, Naomi saw there were steaming eggs and pancakes and cereal and fruit and toast, and she realized instantly that this was much more than her mother had given her yesterday. This was too much. It didn't matter how hungry she was, there were places inside of her food simply didn't touch. Even before Jessica had visited her and begun dividing her portions, Naomi always knew what was excessive and what was required, especially if she was to be dancing all day at the academy. This was excessive. She looked up at her mother and wondered if she really expected her to eat it all.

But then again, she wouldn't be dancing all day—not anymore. Under the soft bedsheet, Naomi could feel her damaged ankle wrapped in a brace, reminding her that she wouldn't be dancing today or the day after or for however long it took for her feet to feel like feet again. Naomi examined the tray sitting silently in her lap for longer. The food, no matter how many calories or how much fat it contained, didn't matter anymore. She could, in theory, eat everything here and more, and there would simply be no consequences waiting for her. The thought, instead of liberating her, made her sick.

Aja took a seat on Naomi's bed. "I'm glad I caught you while you were awake. How are you feeling? Better?" The past two days Aja had come in the mornings to give Naomi her breakfast, but the girl had been dead asleep each time. Aja had simply left it on the night table. By lunch when she'd return to replace it most of the food was finished, and Naomi was back asleep.

Naomi swallowed. She was looking directly through, not at, her mother. She refocused. Today was different, she remembered. Her mother had scheduled the physiotherapist to come today, and if she wanted to see Jessica, Naomi had to be present enough to appease her mother. This, she realized quickly, explained the excessive food. Naomi tasted the roof of her mouth for a moment and decided on speaking whatever felt the most truthful. "Tired," she answered. "Hopeless."

Aja frowned. She took the utensils from the tray and began cutting Naomi's food for her. "Naomi, you're not hopeless. Dancers get injured all the time, or did you forget? Remember that time you pulled a muscle, or even when you had all those blisters on your feet and you couldn't go to the academy? You had to stay right here in bed, and I called in sick for you, and Valentino was fine with it. In a few days you were back on your feet. There hasn't been a serious dancer who didn't endure a career-changing injury. But they always bounce back."

Naomi thought she and her mother had completely different ideas of what injuries were considered career changing as opposed to career ending. She supposed her mom had gotten used to the tutus and the tights of ballet—their stitching and dyeing—even restocking Naomi's personal first aid kit in her bathroom and using gauze to cover persistently worsening flesh, but never this. Never a bedridden girl with an ankle brace where her pointe shoes should be, not even able to wake up before noon and eat three pancakes without feeling the need to throw them back up. These were not the signs of her career simply changing.

Naomi thought back to what her mother had said about living vicariously through her. This whole time, had her mom felt as hopeless as Naomi did right now? It might have been the reason she was trying her best to get Naomi to recover as quickly as possible; trying to convince her that she would get better. Because the truth was, Aja needed Naomi to recover so that she could too. She needed to convince her daughter because she was the one who needed convincing. Naomi watched her mother slice the pancakes thoughtfully and wondered how long it would be before either of them became accustomed to this. To the nothingness that filled the void where ballet used to be.

She, for one, had spent all of last night looking at her ceiling, crying. Ugly, at first. Snot everywhere with her chest pulsating as if the bone itself would snap away, just to feel a little release. Then melancholy followed, settling over her with the knowledge that everything she had been working toward for years had been for nothing more than to make this disaster hurt that much worse. Naomi became full on those thoughts again this morning, and only ended up eating about half of what was on the tray.

Finally, Aja said what Naomi had been waiting for all morning. "Did you remember Dr. Gonzales is coming to see you today?"

How could she forget? While many of the things Aja had said in the early days Naomi hadn't been able to hold in her head long enough to fully process, much less store, this she was clinging to for dear life. For this, she had been crossing off the days. Her mother had promised her that as soon as her appointment with this physiotherapist was through, she could visit Jessica's grave. Naomi still didn't know exactly what she would say to her best friend, but she told herself she would cross that bridge when she got there. For now, she only had to get through her appointment. That was all she had to worry about, and she already knew quite well what the doctor would say to her.

Naomi nodded her answer.

Aja said, "She'll be here in a few hours. This kind of thing is her specialty."

Hopeless dancers?

"Athletes with injuries," Aja continued.

After Aja had cleared away Naomi's plate, she reentered the bedroom and announced it was past time Naomi bathed. Aja didn't ask her daughter when the last time she had showered was. Perhaps she didn't want to know. Instead, she helped haul her out from under the sheets and into the connected bathroom.

It took the pair of them to get her clothes off. As the water ran, Aja helped ease Naomi into the bathtub. Everything seemed harder with the inflexible leg. Naomi felt like crying again as her mother's hand gently traced around the ankle brace with the washcloth. They clumsily stumbled out of the bath and water pooled on the tiles. The ankle brace and the bathtub and the tray of food delivered to her in the morning were all pulling Naomi under again, just as she was beginning to feel like she was breathing air again in her new, balletless life. But that was the problem. She couldn't get comfortable. Everything that was wrong would always be lapping at her neck from this day forward; the moment she relaxed too much, it would all simply drown her.

Later that afternoon, Aja entered the bedroom with another soft knock at the door. Behind her was a taller woman, dressed in scrubs and carrying a medical bag in her right hand. Aja introduced her and said, "Dr. Gonzales is going to help you get back on your feet."

Naomi tried to offer the woman her best smile while her mother stood in the doorway, anxiously holding her elbows.

"Hi, Naomi. I'm here to check up on that ankle of yours. See if we've made any progress. How does that sound?"

Progress? That wasn't the real reason she was here. The doctor was here to give Naomi a verdict. A death sentence. But in order to see Jessica, Naomi nodded.

Dr. Gonzales turned to Aja first, whispering something under her breath that Naomi was too exhausted to hear. She assumed the worst anyway. Naomi braced herself. What exactly would she do if she couldn't dance anymore? She had been homeschooled all her life and never took to any particular class. Would she just have to suffice with an office job? She had never planned on going to college; she always saw herself dancing for a company after she graduated high school and continuing to do that for the rest of her life. But was she destined for a cubicle instead, after all this time? All her life soaring, just to land in a spinning chair.

Dr. Gonzales stuck out her hands when she noticed Naomi's attempt to get up. "Oh no, stay where you are." She placed her medical bag at the foot of Naomi's bed. "No need for that. I can work right here." She took a seat on the bed. "Is that all right with you?"

Naomi nodded.

Dr. Gonzales gently opened her palm, gesturing a request to examine Naomi's foot. Naomi gave it to her.

Unstrapping the ankle brace, the doctor asked, "So, your mom tells me you're a dancer, is that so?"

Naomi nodded.

"What kind of dancing?"

Naomi was sure her mother had told the doctor all this already. Still, Naomi decided to humor her. "Ballet," she answered.

She said, "That's pretty cool. And how long have you been dancing?"

Naomi shrugged. She looked to her mother for an answer, but even she couldn't offer one. Naomi decided on, "For as long as I can remember. As long as it takes."

Gonzales nodded. After she said, "Let me know if it hurts when I do this," the doctor told Naomi, "That sounds pretty intense. I work with a lot of athletes just like you, Naomi, and so far, I've gotten them all back in the game. I plan to do the same for you." Naomi smiled and nodded, but perhaps the doctor had been too focused on her ankle to see any of it because she then said, "That is, if that's what you want."

After a moment's brief pause Aja chimed in. "What do you mean by that?"

The doctor looked up now, at Aja. "Just that it's not rare for athletes to take out their emotional and mental stress on their bodies. Doing what they do is hard." Then she turned to Naomi, and it was here Naomi realized how hazel her eyes were. "Isn't that right, Naomi? Not everyone gets quite just how tough it is. You know that better than most." Naomi didn't answer. "But the game, competition, championship, Prix, is never as important as your mental well-being. The body can't keep going if the mind's already checked out. Don't forget that."

Aja opened her mouth to respond but never did. Naomi remembered what she had told her mother this morning. *Tired. Hopeless.*

Dr. Gonzales gave Naomi a steady look. The girl just nodded although she wanted to do so much more. She wanted to say that she wished she had received that advice earlier. She wanted to confess that she had been checked out for months. Or maybe too checked in? Or just checked in to the wrong things altogether. But the truth had never exposed itself to her like this. Even thinking it sounded explicit, daring. Her throat dried up.

Seeming oblivious to the extent of the effect her words had on either woman in the room, Dr. Gonzales continued her inspection. She gently twisted Naomi's ankle to the right. "Well, your doctors at the hospital were right. It seems to be just a sprain."

Naomi's eyes flicked down at her foot. The metatarsal was still bruised and the toenails discolored. Her ankle had swollen into the largest single thing on her body, aside from her head.

Aja crossed her shaky arms. "What does that mean? Will she be able to dance again?"

"Eventually, yes. Though I can't tell you how soon that will be. Walking will come back fairly quickly, maybe in a few days, but ballet is an intensive activity. It might be weeks before you're able to safely go on pointe again."

Naomi asked this time, "What does that mean?"

Dr. Gonzales sat up straight and looked at the both of them. "It means I think we should play it by ear. Put you on crutches and do some daily light exercises and see where we are in a few weeks."

"A few weeks?" Naomi repeated. "What about Grand Prix? Will I be able to perform?" She already knew the answer. It did not have to be said but she found herself wanting to hear it. At least once. Just to be sure.

The doctor turned to Aja pointedly. "It's too early to tell. Let's try to not think about Grand Prix right now. Let's just focus on getting better." She patted the bed gently. "Why don't I grab the crutches I brought for you from my car? We can get started on those and then I can walk you through some exercises? Sound good?"

Naomi exhaled. She had always heard of the talent whose feet were never the same after an injury. She knew that would be her one day. All the best dancers had an injury that broke them. But Naomi hadn't thought she would break this early on. She would have sworn she was more malleable than this.

As Dr. Gonzales left the room, Naomi watched Aja silently stare at her feet. Then her eyes traveled up to Naomi's hand, still bandaged from the accident only a few weeks ago. She cleared her throat then asked her daughter, "Naomi, did you do this on purpose?"

"What?" Naomi's head flew up. "No, of course not."

Aja didn't answer. By the way her mother was looking at her Naomi felt as though Aja was replaying her answer over and over again in her head and examining Naomi's posture to try to decide if she was being lied to.

"Are you seriously asking me if I sprained my own ankle on purpose?" Aja crossed her arms and waited for Naomi's answer. "No, I would never."

As their gazes tested one another, Aja finally released a breath. "Okay, I just needed to ask." Her voice cracked on the final syllable. "I had to make sure after what the doctor said."

Naomi wanted to tell her she didn't even know what Dr. Gonzales was talking about. That the concept sounded alien to her, and she couldn't even begin to imagine hurting herself deliberately so she could stop dancing for a moment. But she hadn't lied at all today so far, and she wanted to keep it that way. Saying nothing was cowardly, but better.

When Dr. Gonzales reentered the room, she set the crutches against the wall next to Naomi's bed and began to walk Naomi through two basic range-of-motion exercises. They included tracing the alphabet with her toes and rotating her knee with the sole of her foot flat on the floor. Naomi was too afraid to ask how many of these she'd have to do for her ankle to heal well enough to start dancing again. A million? Two million?

"Don't start these until maybe next week, though," Dr. Gonzales said. Then, looking over at Aja, she continued, "This week, *rest* and lots of ice will do. Nothing more."

Naomi's eyes traveled to the crutches beside her head. "What about those?"

"Ah, these bad boys? They're a lot less intimidating than they look, I promise." She took them into her lap and demonstrated how to properly adjust the wing nuts and wiggle the bottom just right to make it slide out of its nestled home. The crutch came into itself with a pop, a sound that according to Dr. Gonzales meant that it was safe to use. Naomi looked over at Aja, who was intently paying attention. She caught her gaze. "Naomi, did you catch that?"

Naomi turned back to the doctor. Nodding, she told them she understood. Although the crutch was stubborn, for her purposes she should twist it and pull it until, unwillingly, it finally did what she needed it to.

"Exactly," Dr. Gonzales said. "You adjust it to the height that feels most comfortable to you. And don't feel shy about readjusting it either. Sometimes it may feel comfortable in the beginning but the more you use it, you realize it's set all wrong. Change it if you want at any time. It's yours."

Naomi felt her chest tighten.

After handing Aja an ice pack from her medical bag and instructing both Aja and Naomi on how to use it, Dr. Gonzales said a final good-bye. She reminded Naomi one last time to take it easy and told her to call if she forgot something or if anything came up. The rest of their conversation happened downstairs where Naomi couldn't hear it. They were probably discussing her future in more detail down there, or the lack thereof. But when Aja returned, Naomi couldn't learn anything from her mother's expression alone. Aja seemed, to Naomi, normal. Only a bit timid, as she had been these past days, but nothing out of the ordinary.

Aja spoke first. "See? Was that so bad?"

Naomi didn't answer her. She could tell Aja was saying it more to herself than to her. "Did she say anything else? About Prix?"

Aja shook her head. "But we can make it. If we stay focused, eat right, and exercise, I know you'll be back on track before the end of the summer."

Naomi did not want to think that far ahead yet. Doing that was part of what had landed her here in the first place. Instead, she wanted to think a little more shortsightedly. Starting with tomorrow. "Can I see Jessica now? Like you promised."

Her mom exhaled. "Is that still what you want?"

She was not doing this. Aja had promised her. She could not go back on her word now. Naomi's jaw set and her eyes iced over. Without speaking, her answer was stronger than a yes. It said *Yes, or else.*

Aja craned her neck to look over at Naomi's feet. "Sure," she said finally. "We'll go tomorrow."

CHAPTER THIRTEEN

The trees in Evergreen Memorial Park moved with the wind. Their leaves rustled in succession, like applause in a stadium, except there was nothing to cheer for here. In the clearing, just past the trees, there were rows and rows of graves and their accompanying headstones marked with a name and the other things that mattered most about someone after they died. Naomi wasn't sure why they called it a memorial park when this much death in one place would always feel like a graveyard, no matter how green they managed to color the grass. She should know. She too used to mask dead things so they appeared less so.

Using her new crutches, she passed the bodies buried deep in the earth. Many of them were left with a bouquet of fresh flowers set atop them. These were the graves that stood out from the rest. Passersby would know quite clearly that there was someone resting beneath that plot of earth and that they were missed; that it wasn't just another patch of grass they could step on thoughtlessly. Naomi finally found Jessica's grave deep inside the graveyard and saw that there were flowers here, too, probably left by Jessica's parents, whom Naomi still hadn't seen since the funeral. But the flowers were dried and untended. In need of replacing.

She neared it and eased up off of her crutches. Naomi haphazardly plopped herself onto the soft grass then set the crutches next to her and stretched out her legs. If Jessica were alive and Naomi wasn't injured, Naomi imagined, the girls would be sitting across from each other just like this on the dance studio floor, reading into the contours of each other's faces in the quiet. A part of her still wanted that. But, as Naomi looked at the headstone, she reminded herself that this was what had physically replaced her best friend, and they wouldn't be getting up off the floor together this time. She let out a sharp exhale.

"I imagined this part would come the easiest. I just pictured sitting here and looking at a stone that represents you now and just kind of talking, you know? I thought everything I wanted to say would kind of . . . come out? Like a long breath I had been holding in all this time. It's not quite that, is it?"

No response.

"Anyway, it's still easier than talking to you in person. I don't know if you knew this but you always had this sort of confidence about you, and it always made me feel a little stupid. I don't know. It's hard to explain. I guess I still feel a little stupid. Even though I'm just talking to a rock. Probably *because* I'm just talking to a rock.

"I know I haven't really been here to visit you since the funeral but I still think about you. Do you know that? These last few weeks I've been constantly remembering you because I just wasn't able to really forget you—which, actually, I'm beginning to learn are not the same thing. Remembering you and not being able to forget you. I know that's not really an excuse but I thought I'd say it anyway. I still think of you.

"I guess, Jessica, what I really came here to say is that you were a great friend to me. You were kind, caring, a little bossy sometimes, but we balanced each other out like that. Looking back, a lot of people didn't understand how we got along so well. To them, I think, you were just so extroverted and carefree, and I wasn't at all, so it was a little confusing. Little did they know you weren't always so outspoken, though. You had your shy moments. But then there were also people who thought we were sisters. Remember that guy from the bowling alley who thought we were sisters? Yeah, I think that was just because we're Black, though.

"And that's another thing. If I'm honest I just—I think we had a very different experience. Every ballet instructor I had before Valentino kept me at the back of the class because they were convinced that I would drop out, no matter how good I was. And my mom spent night after night dyeing my tights. My pointe shoes are like, double the price. And you get to be Black and not deal with any of that. To look the way you do, and dance the way you do, and not care the way you do? It was painful to watch.

"And the worst part is I'm mixed. My dad's white but somehow my complexion is still this dark. I guess, in a way, it feels like I was robbed. Like I was supposed to be you.

"That sounds so messed up. I love being Black. I love my skin—it's just that on a lot of days it's hard to live in it. And your Blackness just looked . . . easier? I don't think you ever knew what it was fully like. When people assume everything about you before they even meet you. To feel constantly out of place. To have to prove people wrong before you even meet them. With you, though, people thought, not the best things, but the somewhat better things. With me, people immediately think the worst. And even when I prove them wrong, I'm just an exception. I don't know how to make sense of that.

"But instead of talking to you about it, I let it eat me alive from the day I met you to the day you died. Even after. I saw you everywhere, and it was like you were haunting me and all these things I resented you for and all the things I hated about myself I projected onto you. And that made you, in my mind, the villain. Because that's who I wanted you to be in a really weird, unfair kind of way. Maybe it just made missing you easier.

"I almost forgot how kind you really were. Before we started using Tiger Balm you would always carry enough newspaper for both of us to stuff our pointe shoes, remember? You never let me leave the theater alone. You triple-checked if I had eaten that day. In a lot of different ways, you were what made my experience at the academy bearable. Maybe that's why it was so hard to keep going without you in the first place? Not that it matters now anyway.

"See my ankle? I won't be dancing again for a while. I've lost you and the academy, one after the other. Now I wake up and I have to keep going without either of you, and I have no idea what that even means for me. I wish you were still here. I wonder if, wherever you are now, you wish I was there too?"

Naomi would have liked to believe Jessica's answer was yes. And if it wasn't, she felt at peace with that too. She would, she told herself strictly, come back to visit her best friend in the future. Jessica's body was buried deep in the earth but Naomi didn't have to pretend as though she was gone, nor did Naomi need to bring her back to life either. Both would be a dishonor. Instead, Jessica resided in the middle. Here, because she had lived and loved, but at the same time away, because she was no longer continuing to do so. Here and away. And there was a calm in knowing that both of these things were true.

Footsteps sounded behind Naomi. She didn't think of turning around at first because she had asked her mother to wait in the car, and Aja had agreed. Anyway, this was a public space after all. But then a voice called out her name. When she turned there was a boy standing a few graves away, looking down at the ground where she was sitting. He grinned. "Why, hello there." Saint greeted her.

Naomi grabbed her crutches from her sides and used them to stand as quickly as she could. When she collected all her scrambling thoughts she fumbled out, "Hi. What are you doing here?"

"Visiting." Saint pointed to the grave that he was standing in front of. Then, despite the dirt and grass, he watched Naomi grab the handles of her crutches again and walk over to him.

He frowned. "Wait, what happened to your foot? Are you okay?"

Naomi looked down at it. "It's a long story," she told him. The story of how she rose, fell, and ended up here. Naomi supposed it wasn't that long of a story, really. Still, she wasn't sure if the boy would want to hear it. Long or short it was still the story of how a dancer was rendered flightless, and that premise alone was enough to dim the lights behind anyone's eyes.

It had already done so to her. Naomi got just close enough to Saint to notice the scarring on the back of his right hand.

She said, "Your hand."

"It's a long story." He mimicked her.

Naomi accepted defeat there. "Fair." Then she came close enough to read the headstone he was standing in front of. It said MIRANDA OWENS. She looked back at him, the question unvoiced but still asked.

"My mom," Saint said finally.

"I'm sorry." Naomi adjusted her weight. "That must have been hard."

Saint's smile didn't fall, but it changed. "It's fine. She died a long time ago."

Naomi watched him. The way he was looking at her told her that he had gotten very used to hiding things behind that smile. "Still, I can't imagine going through that."

Shrugging, the boy was already coming out from her shadow. "What about you? Who are you here visiting?"

"My best friend. She passed away not that long ago." Out loud for the first time, the sentence didn't scare her like she'd thought it would. High on bravery, Naomi continued, "Her name was Jessica. She meant a lot to me but for some reason, this is the first time I've actually been here to visit her." She searched his face next. "Do you visit your mom often?"

"I try to," he said as he analyzed Jessica's headstone. When he looked back up at her he continued, "Whenever I'm here I remember exactly what she was like when she was alive. Sometimes that's a good thing, other times not so much. It's like the very air here has her in it. Maybe in a few years you'll come to feel the same way about your friend."

Naomi said, "I think I know what you mean. For a long time it felt like Jessica was everywhere too. In my bedroom. At the theater. Just, everywhere."

"They always are at first." The sun went behind the trees now, casting shadows across their bodies. Saint asked, "And is she still? Still everywhere, I mean?"

Naomi thought about it. "In a different way, I think so. In the same way I'm sure you carry your mom with you everywhere." Saint's mouth opened, and, from the look in his eyes, Naomi could tell there were thoughts sputtering in his head. "Sorry," she apologized quickly, "I've just been in my head. You don't have to answer that or explain."

He smiled again, something more akin to the one he gave her when he had first arrived. Then he said to her, "Tell me what happened to your ankle."

She looked toward Jessica's grave, as if for advice, but of course, it never came. There was no one sitting there looking back at her. No one telling her what to answer or how to say it. There was only her left to decide. She looked back at the boy again. "It's a pretty depressing story."

"I'm sure," he said. Then he waited.

Watching him, Naomi said, "I'd been injured for a while. But I had to keep dancing so that I could compete in this competition and eventually join my dream company in New York." Impressed, the boy's eyes widened. "But the pain just kept getting worse. And I guess, the other day it got to a point where I couldn't keep dancing anymore. In rehearsal, I just kind of fell apart?"

The leaves gave another ovation. "Fell apart?"

"My ankle is sprained." She'd never said that aloud before either.

"Sprained," he repeated. Looking down at her ankle brace for what felt like the first true time, he asked her, "And is that why you're here? Because you can't dance, and so now you have the free time to visit your friend?"

Defensiveness came first, like the spark that starts a fire or the tremor that begins an earthquake, but the boy's face remained unchanged. Naomi thought for a moment. She tried to be honest. "In a way, yeah. I guess it is." A beat passed. "That sounds kind of bad, doesn't it?"

The boy laughed. "Yeah, a little bit. But there are worse things you could be doing in your free time. You could have not come at all. Stayed home and kept that leg elevated, as I'm sure the doctor recommended you should." Naomi sheepishly looked away. Walking closer to Jessica's grave, Saint continued, "There are also better things you could be doing." He turned to her. "She's not going anywhere. My mom hasn't."

Naomi pointed at her brace. "Like what?"

"Well, there are lots of living things out there to be seen. Alive and waiting." Naomi watched his mind work behind his eyes. "Like the city bridge."

"A bridge?" Saint nodded. Naomi smiled. "What's so special about a bridge? And bridges aren't living things."

There was a smile teasing the corners of his mouth. It was incredible how quickly he went from solemn to chirpy and back again. Naomi didn't even think twice about what that might mean. "Have you ever been under it?" When Naomi's silence gave him the answer he needed, Saint said, "Exactly. See, this is something you have to see. I can show you if you'd like."

Naomi paused. She thought of what Dr. Gonzales had said to her yesterday. *Let's try to not think about Grand Prix right now. Let's just focus on other things, like getting better.* Maybe this was part of that process. It could be. She made a conscious effort not to look back at Jessica's grave. She inhaled deeply, allowed the air to go right through her. Then she stood a little straighter. "Okay."

The boy grinned. "Okay."

She stuck out her wrapped foot at him. "But, I mean, it might be a little hard to get that far."

Saint looked like he did not even care. "I'll drive you there. Meet me here tomorrow at, say, noon?"

"Here?"

"Of course," he said, gesturing all around them. "Isn't it obvious? From the dead things, we move on to the living."

Naomi resisted commenting on how poetic that sounded, even if it would have been just to make fun of him. She suspected he heard those kinds of things a lot. She let his sentence linger for a little while longer. Then she said, "Sounds reasonable enough. I'll see you at noon."

"I'll see you at noon."

Deciding she'd said everything she needed to say to Jessica for today, Naomi waved a good-bye to Saint and walked back to the car. Stretching over the console, Aja opened the door for her. Watching her get in, Aja asked, "How was it?"

"Good," came first out of Naomi's mouth. But the boy's words were still playing in her head. *Isn't it obvious? From the dead things, we move on to the living.* Naomi added quickly, "But the flowers on her grave need replacing."

Aja smiled. She locked the car doors and started the engine. "We'll replace them, honey. We'll come back."

When Naomi and her mother returned home, Ethan's car was parked in the driveway. Naomi didn't ask herself what her father might have been out doing today. Instead, she turned to Aja and asked if she could help her up to her room. Aja, glad her daughter had even asked, obliged. She took the crutches out of the backseat and helped Naomi onto them, after which she patiently guided her up the driveway and held the front door open for her. She diligently stood behind her daughter to make sure she didn't fall going in and heading up the stairs. The chances of that happening were low, but her arms were outstretched anyway. If Naomi was to slip, there would be no question as to whether or not Aja would be there, ready to catch her.

When they finally stepped inside Naomi's bedroom, Aja asked her, "Do you need anything else?"

Naomi plopped herself flat on her bed. "No, thanks. Thank you for taking me today."

Aja let the crutches lean on the wall next to Naomi's bed. "Any time, baby." On their way home Naomi had devised a plan for how she might return to Evergreen Memorial Park tomorrow, but her mother had to be the one to take her there. If she didn't, there was no way Naomi could sneak out of the house unnoticed. And yet if she did, Aja would never allow Naomi to leave with Saint—a stranger she didn't know—when Naomi should be preparing to heal and dance again. She had to make this foolproof.

When Aja went to leave Naomi said, "Wait." The likelihood of this working would be immediately clear—based on what expression showed on Aja's face. And her mom was standing in the doorway looking at her daughter eagerly. Naomi knew she could get away with *something*.

"I've been thinking about what you said about this not being the end for me."

Aja nodded. "It isn't."

"And I know that," she agreed. "That's why I was thinking it might be a good idea to go back to the theater, you know? See how things are going, try to get my mind back into ballet."

Naomi watched her mother release a breath. Aja said, "Of course. When do you want to go?"

Naomi nodded, chewing, swallowing, and digesting the truth. Then when she was ready again, she asked, "How's tomorrow?"

Aja smiled at her daughter and said matter-of-factly, "Come, let me do your hair." In other words, *anything for you* in a Black mother's native tongue. A special kind of love language.

Naomi's hair had been frizzy for the past week since she had rolled and rolled around in bed, not straightening it for days, but Aja hadn't done Naomi's hair since she was a little girl—when they had both decided it was easier for Naomi to just straighten it if she was to keep doing ballet and required a classic bun. But the years didn't matter. Naomi knew to pull a chair to the bathroom sink so she could sit, and Aja's hands found the drawer of hair supplies on muscle memory alone. This was because it wasn't really about the hair at all. It was about them and the sweet-smelling bottles as reminders that this was home.

After a thorough wash and conditioning, Aja returned with the Jamaican castor oil, curl defining cream, leave-in conditioner, and a spray bottle filled with water, then helped her daughter out of the bathroom and onto the bedroom floor, where Naomi sat between her legs. Aja sectioned her daughter's hair with clips then uncapped the jars and lathered her hands, working the product through. She said, "Do you know why your father and I spend so much for you to do ballet?" Naomi didn't answer. "It takes strength and determination and practice. It forges people in a good way. When I was young, I was forged by unspeakable things. This isn't to say it was all bad. I had good times too in my community. But still, I always knew I wanted you to be strong, just without having to experience the things that I did."

Naomi thought her mother was about to stop there. It left her thinking about how Aja had uprooted her entire life in Jamaica so that she could have a better life here. So Naomi could one day do ballet. Aja had to work part-time and dye all Naomi's tights on discarded newspapers, and even after all that, this injury was the way Naomi was repaying her. Lying to her face right now was the way Naomi was repaying her. Keeping her father's infidelity a secret was the way Naomi was repaying her. She glanced away from her mother.

"And you are strong, even if you don't think that right now. And it's not just because of ballet, Naomi. It's because in spite of everything you are still here, and you are still making life happen for you." She exhaled. "When you said you wanted to visit Jessica, I was a little nervous at first because after her passing I could tell you weren't dealing with it well. But you know what? I'm glad you went back. She was your best friend, after all. We can't pretend she never existed."

Naomi didn't dare nod.

"I'm so proud of you, Naomi. I'll take you to the academy tomorrow. Maybe we can replace Jessica's flowers on the way."

Naomi's stomach twisted. All she trusted herself to say in response was, "Thank you." And already she was lying to her mother again. She had done the reconciling she believed was necessary to move on and yet she was still stuck. Something was still wrong if she needed to escape home and had to lie about it.

Later that night Saint returned to his father's bedroom for the keys. As always, he waited a few seconds, four, five, six, seven, before he opened the door and went inside. He'd had the same routine for over a week now. By this time he was sure the man was asleep. Glancing at him on the bed, Saint went to retrieve the keys and turned to leave.

"Going somewhere?"

He exhaled. "Tomorrow. Getting groceries." The lie came so easy.

The man coughed and it was louder than when he spoke. "We're out already? Why didn't you tell me?"

"I didn't want to wake you. It's not a big deal."

Richard thought for a moment. "Don't forget my cigarettes." *Of course that's why he was asking.* Saint's father turned on his side, his back now facing the way Saint had come in. "And don't be out too long. Your brother will get bored if you leave him here alone."

Saint watched his father. "Don't worry, I won't be out long."

His dad didn't answer him, and Saint knew that meant their conversation was over. This time as he left he didn't care about making noise. He walked out of there as he would any other place, silently hoping with each loud, prominent footstep toward the exit that his father might change his mind about the cigarettes. He never did.

CHAPTER FOURTEEN

The first thing Saint noticed about Naomi when she arrived the next day was that her hair was all out. She was standing in the exact spot where he had left her yesterday, and her coils were loud and unashamed, framing her face. "Why don't you always wear your hair like that?"

The sky was even brighter than when they had left yesterday. All the leaves' shadows were fluttering around them and the clouds had parted to give way to the big blue. Today was different, and neither of them would be able to describe exactly why other than the feeling of something fresh swimming deep within their rib cages. Naomi watched him close the distance between them.

"Really?" Adjusting herself on her crutches she continued, "I haven't had my hair like this in years, actually. I always straighten it for ballet."

Saint hummed thoughtfully. He wondered if she heard what exactly it was that she was telling him about ballet and the way it flat-ironed her. He didn't mention it. "Well, this suits you. More than straight hair, I think." Then after a moment's pause, he retraced his thoughts. "Not that you should do it how I like. If *you* like it is what matters, really. Do you like it?"

Naomi smiled at him. "Yes." She laughed. "I like it. My mom spent a good two hours on it, so I'd hope someone else would like it too." Naomi remembered instantly that she was lying to her mother even now.

This morning Aja had brought Naomi to Evergreen Memorial Park first. They had replaced the flowers on Jessica's grave with a new bouquet Aja had bought from a nearby florist, and then the pair of them stood for a moment of silence. Aja gave her daughter a hug and reminded her that Jessica would be proud of her, after which she dropped Naomi off at the theater. Naomi had only pretended to go inside to see the academy. In reality, she stood by the door and waited until her mother had driven off. Then she left the building and got on the next bus that would bring her straight back here. Back to Jessica's graveside, but also back to this newly familiar boy holding a bunch of car keys in one hand and a bulky backpack on his opposite shoulder.

She tried not to think about what a betrayal of trust this was. Perhaps if her mother was still living vicariously through her then all that mattered was getting out of the house and doing something that made her happy. Maybe Aja would feel that, and it would all be okay. "What's in the bag?" Naomi asked.

"You're no good with surprises, are you?" Saint motioned for her to follow him. "Come on."

Moving in pace with him, Naomi replied, "Hate them. I'd

rather just know than be surprised. I mean, what if I don't like the surprise? Then what?"

Saint smiled. "You'll like the surprise."

"What makes you so sure?"

"Because," Saint said simply, "we're going to leave our legacy on that bridge." Naomi looked at him in confusion, and his smile widened. "Who doesn't want a legacy?"

But through ballet Naomi knew a little too well that legacies weren't always what they were chalked up to be. You could end up with a legacy of lies, pain, and death. She wasn't sure how to tell him this.

When they got to the parking lot, Saint led her to an older-looking pickup truck. The Chevrolet didn't gleam or shine. There were various coats of dirt all over its metallic shell and the headlight lens seemed almost opaque, but Naomi thought the thing in its entirety had character to it. Things that did not last long, like her pointe shoes, were pretty and disposable, but something like this, with dirt and a lifespan, just seemed like it would have a history to tell. Something to show for its living and something to keep going for. Naomi asked Saint, "Have you named her?"

"Not mine to name, unfortunately. It's my dad's." He held open the passenger door for Naomi and helped her inside. "I'm pretty sure even he doesn't have a name for her, though."

"Why not?"

He shrugged. "Not his thing. He'd rather just drive it to where he needs to go then forget that it exists until he needs it again." It wasn't a complete lie. When his father had driven this car that was how he'd treated it, although that had been almost a year ago.

Naomi watched him hold on to her door. She said, "Sounds like a father to me."

Saint almost offered to take her crutches and put them in the back, but he had second thoughts and decided she might feel more comfortable if she had them next to her. He shut the door and went around to his side of the truck. It took Saint a few key turns to get the engine going, and, in between each failed attempt, he apologized and described again how old the truck was. When it finally came alive, he told her, "She's still got a few good years in her, though." They drove out of the parking spot in a cloud of dust.

Saint kept the windows down all the way, explaining that the air-conditioning had stopped working long ago. But she didn't mind. It meant that there was less standing between her and all the things that were happening outside, a stark change from her walled-in bedroom or the dance studio inside a concrete basement. The breeze took to her kindly, too, running across her face. Naomi assumed they were going in the complete opposite direction of everything she knew in Riverside because there was nothing out here that she recognized. There were plazas, not malls, and more people were on the sidewalks.

After a few minutes Saint asked, "So, which school do you go to?"

Naomi looked back inside the car. "I'm homeschooled, actually. Normal high school wouldn't have allowed me the time to dance as much at the academy."

Saint's eyebrows raised. "Ah, yes, the academy. Of course." Naomi nodded, oblivious to the way the boy was teasing her. "Tell me, what was that like? How did you meet literally anyone if your school was your house?"

"It was okay. Not as bad you might think. I had the same teacher for years, Mrs. Norris, so that was nice. She's kind of strict but I appreciated that some days." Riverside was passing beside her, and her eyes drifted back to all these things she'd never seen. "And I met people at the academy."

Saint corrected her. "Other dancers."

"Well, yeah, but they're still people. Actually, if I went to normal high school, I don't know that I would be better off, if I'm honest. Who would I relate to?"

Saint chuckled. He thought of all the times he thought he'd be better off if he didn't have to go to high school too. If he could just work full-time to better support his brother and his father. "Yeah, you probably dodged a bullet there."

She turned to face him again. "What about you? Do you have many friends?"

"I'm not sure how I'm supposed to answer that."

Naomi laughed. "What I'm trying to say is that you just seem like you'd make friends pretty easily."

"Jeez, well, say that next time." Here she had picked up that he was teasing her. "I mean, I have friends, but I'm not *popular*. I'm probably an extra in the main storyline of a lot of those people's lives. You wouldn't believe how they act."

Naomi narrowed her eyes at him. "Why do I find that hard to believe?"

Saint glanced at her briefly, grinning. "Oh yeah? Why's that?"

"Our meet-up spot was a graveyard. You talk like you're reading a poem almost all the time. Those are the things protagonists are made of."

Saint laughed. "Maybe." When his smile wore off a little,

Saint humored her. "Okay, here's something. What if we're all just the main characters of our own stories, but the side characters in everyone else's stories?" Naomi stared at him. He gave her a double take. "What, you don't think that's possible?"

She looked ahead of them, to the reaching road and all the sky it was holding up. "No, I think it's possible. It's just that I also think sometimes two people can share a story."

They got to a red light, and Saint used that time to look at her when he asked, "But wouldn't one person always outshine the other?"

"Maybe. But I don't think outshining matters in the first place, it's about how those two people affect each other. Like in *Giselle*, the ballet, I mean sure, to many people it's about Giselle, but I think without Albrecht there wouldn't be a story. So in a way it's about him too. His love for her and the extent he's willing to go to get her, and vice versa. The ballet is about them. They both make the story. So in a way, they're both the protagonist."

He turned a little more in his seat to face her. "So you think two people can share the spotlight?"

"I don't think it's about the spotlight at all." There was traffic picking up behind them. "There's a part of the story that the spotlight doesn't catch. Doesn't mean it's not still a part of the story." She turned to him. "What do you think?"

The light turned green and Saint shifted gears. "I think"—he paused—"I think you may just be onto something, Naomi—what's your last name?" She sat up and told him. He finished proudly, "You may just be onto something, Naomi Morgan."

The roads began to feel more congested as they went.

In the traffic, they met the deep afternoon and searing sun. Every now and again they would lurch forward just briefly, a reminder that they were supposed to be moving ahead of all this. After another few moments of silence, Saint cleared his throat and asked, "If you don't mind telling me, how did she die? Your friend, Jessica?"

She knew this question was coming eventually so she had her answer prepared. "There was an accident. She was walking and there was a car she didn't see. It was really horrible."

"I'm sorry." She wanted to ask him the same about his mother but she didn't know if it would seem fair. After all, a mother must be more painful than a best friend. Although, he hadn't seemed too upset yesterday, and even as he asked about Jessica's death just now the idea of dying didn't seem to upset him. Still, she decided it might be best to let the moment pass instead.

"Breast cancer took my mom." She turned around. "When we found out it was too late. But you want to know something?" She didn't realize he was waiting on actual affirmation until he glanced over to look at her after a few beats. Naomi nodded at him. He said, "I think she knew and kept it a secret. Maybe she knew it was cancer, maybe she thought it was something else, but I think she knew it was her time.

"Just days before we found out her cancer was stage four, she looked me in the eye and told me how she knew she could leave everything up to me. That there would come a time when I would have to take care of our house, and she knew I was ready. I think everyone knows they're about to die before they die."

"But wouldn't she have told you?"

"Not if she didn't want to believe it either. Who wants to believe they're dying?"

Naomi thought she would like to know when it was her time to go. And almost immediately she realized what a lie that was. For the past few weeks she'd felt as though she was dying, and she'd married the feeling sourly. Like an old, long-suffering couple that didn't say anything or mention each other. They turned their backs when they went to bed. Woke up together and politely asked for space to pass in smaller spaces, silent for as long as they could bear. She would hate to live with her death. When it was her time to go Naomi wanted the moment to peacefully surprise her. Like a delayed package lost in the mail that she couldn't track. She wanted it to arrive at her doorstep unopened.

"Do you think Jessica knew, even a little, that it might have been her time?" Saint asked.

Jessica definitely wouldn't have told her. "I don't know." Naomi glanced at him as he turned them off the main road. "Your hand," she said. "It's not healing."

"It will," Saint replied.

"You should get it checked out. Go to the doctor. It could get infected."

Saint didn't quite answer her, but the look on his face was telling her something. Kind of like he was saying thank you, he would go to the doctor, but in the way both of them knew he really wouldn't. Neither Naomi nor Saint spoke much after that, and the wind was the only sound in the truck.

The Riverside Bridge soon came out from behind a building when they made a left turn. Now it was straight ahead of them. It wasn't even a big thing, but to Naomi it felt grand. Large and mysterious. When they neared it, the car made a sharp turn before they could actually get onto it. Saint veered onto a dirt path that sloped to the waterfront. The old Chevrolet bumped all the way down to the part where the river came close to the town, and then Saint hit the brakes. He slipped the gear into Park and turned to her to sing, "We're here!"

In seconds, he was clambering out the car door and jogging toward the underbelly of the bridge. Naomi grabbed her crutches and followed him. The ground was rockier than she had expected, less sand and more pebbles, so it took her a while to reach the boy on this new type of terrain. Then when she finally got close enough, she followed his gaze up to the pillar holding up the bridge. They watched the concrete together. He said to her softly, "What do you think?"

He was pointing at a wall. The thing that held the bridge up and supported it over the river. Nothing but gray concrete. Naomi looked up at the tall thing and back at Saint. "This is it?"

He looked at it for a moment that felt too long before finally returning her gaze. "Tell me, what do you see?"

"Saint, it's a wall. I see a big, giant wall."

"Yes, it's a wall, but what about the wall?"

Naomi stared up at the thing again and her eyebrows furrowed. Blue grazed the clouds just beyond the zipping cars speeding to escape. This low, the sky and the road looked like sisters.

"Just try," Saint told her. "Say whatever comes to your mind first when you look at it."

Naomi inhaled. She scanned it. "Hard. Gray. Unmoving. Solid. High. Smooth. Bare."

"Exactly!" Saint almost jumped. He repeated, "Bare. There's nothing on it. It's empty. Blank. It can be absolutely anything you want it to be."

Naomi turned around and smiled at him. "I'm not sure that's how that works. It's still a wall, Saint."

"In a way it will always be a wall, sure, but we can make it other things too. It can say more than whatever walls say. It can go beyond a wall. And that's what we're gonna do." He saw Naomi's mouth moving to form a question but he stuck his index finger up before she could get it out. She asked it anyway.

"What? How?"

Simultaneously, Saint answered, "With these."

Saint jogged over to the pickup truck again and opened the back door to retrieve his backpack. The mystery bag, Naomi remembered. Only when he returned to her and the wall did he smile mischievously and unzip it. Reaching in, he pulled out a can and held it out to her. Naomi peered down at it.

"Take it."

She took the cylinder in her hand and immediately felt that it was metal. She turned it around in her hand and read the label. It was spray paint. "We're going to spray-paint it? The bridge?"

Excitedly, Saint nodded.

Nothing was funny but she felt like laughing so hard. "But—but it's broad daylight! This is public property. Won't someone see us? Isn't this vandalism?"

Saint took out a blue bottle for himself and shook it. "People usually look over bridges, Naomi, not under them. Plus, I've been doing this for a few days now. There are so many walls in this town that have me on them. No one ever notices."

He moved closer to the bridge, giving his bottle a hefty shake. "You can draw whatever you want or say whatever you want. It's a blank canvas. Bare, as you said yourself." He quoted her as if to say *A-ha, you've fallen into your own trap.*

The boy began on the wall. His arms moved in bigger and wider ranges than Naomi thought was necessary to spray-paint a wall. Even though, reasonably speaking, the thing was huge and there was a lot of surface area to cover. Anything that didn't match up to the bridge's size might have gone unnoticed, which was the opposite of the point, it seemed. In some parts of his painting, Saint jumped too. He'd never cover it all but he seemed intent on trying. Naomi looked over her shoulder, but there was no one watching.

When he stepped back, there was a dripping THIS TOWN SUCKS.

Naomi smiled. "Oh wow, don't know how I'll top that. I might as well just leave."

Saint gave a graceful bow. "Lucky for you, you don't have to. See?" He pointed at the concrete canvas behind him. "All blank. No expectations."

Naomi looked over her shoulder again, where the water was her only other witness. It was the baby-blue color of the sky, reflecting the bridge and the barely there bodies of the different cars driving over it. Everything that was above her. Naomi cleared her throat and walked up to the wall. She looked at it. "Write whatever you're feeling," Saint reminded her. Naomi held the metallic can in her fist and shook it. She pressed the nub and began. She wrote out, as a large as she could, I AM INJURED. Then, after adjusting herself to the right, she added, BUT RIGHT NOW I DON'T FEEL LIKE IT.

Her words were a lot smaller than his, but he was smiling at them as if they were the size of the bridge itself. Saint grabbed another can and added, WE ARE UNDER YOUR BRIDGE BUT WE ARE ALSO WHAT IS KEEPING IT SO HIGH. Then he looked at her, inviting.

So she wrote again.

And they went at it together, one after the other until they simultaneously began to decorate the entire wall with scribblings of their thoughts and occasional drawings. Now Naomi understood exactly what Saint had meant when he said they would be adding to the bridge. Because after today, the Riverside Bridge would forever be changed, even if no one saw the changes, like Saint said. The bridge would still be different, and no one would know how or why except them. It just would be from this day on.

That night, Naomi decided that when she got home she'd blow the dust off her phone and download some new music. Maybe something with a piano and cusswords if she could find anything like that. Something that, upon first notice, appeared as though it was meant to be innocuous and soft but once you got to know it, demonstrated a power that shocked you, one that you could only either admire or envy. Something a little like who she wanted to be from now on. Something like Saint Owens. Then she would save Saint's number and text him. Let him know that she was not as out of touch as he had said she was when she told him she didn't use her phone that often.

Homeschooled and *digitally illiterate. Wow, you're full of surprises, Naomi Morgan*, he had said to her.

After that, Naomi decided she would also unroll her fluffy rug from the corner of her closet and set it in the center of her room again. She'd open a window and light a scented candle in her bathroom. Then she'd push her desk under the rectangular shape on her wall, ignoring the noise it would inevitably make on her wooden floor. And finally, she would take out her television from under her bed and struggle with it all the way to the top of the desk, where she'd hang it back on the metal brackets left in the wall.

Naomi Morgan got close to all that tonight. She blew the dust off her phone like she said she would and turned it on. But before she could listen to any music or save Saint's number, which she had repeated to herself throughout the drive home, there was a knock and her bedroom door opened.

Her father turned the corner. "Hey there, kid." He gave a big smile. "How's it going?"

Naomi flinched. "Good, Dad. Everything's good."

His smile only got bigger. "That's good. I'm glad to hear it. Your mom told me when she picked you up at the theater this evening you seemed pretty excited. You think you can do this?"

She wanted to ask him what there was to do, exactly. Her ankle was sprained and she couldn't dance, and that was just that. The better question he should be asking was one directed to himself. *Do you think you can get away with this?* But all Naomi said was, "I think so."

Ethan Morgan stepped farther into her bedroom. Naomi's phone started to go off, all the unopened texts and notifications vibrating in her hand. "And the crutches are all right too?" She nodded. "You know, when I got stung by a stingray back in my day, I had to walk with one of those too. Yeah, it was an adjustment, but you know what? If you play your cards right people will give up their seats for you on the bus. Or cashiers will give you discounts." He wiggled his eyebrows.

The smile came before Naomi could think twice about it. Ethan laughed. "Don't tell your mother I said that." He winked at her. "But you know what to do."

The phone was still going, and Naomi's grin fell away as she looked down at it. Her father said, "Anyway, I'll leave you to it. Seems like you've got plenty of company right there." He came all the way in and took up one of the discarded plastic cups Naomi had left on her night table. "Just don't stay up too late. And keep that leg elevated, okay?" He walked back through the door and shut it on his way out.

Her father hadn't visited her often at the academy but he was visiting her here and now. Perhaps when it came to ballet he was only absent because he thought he had to be. Because Aja was the one who took her to performances and dyed the tights and helped her stretch. Ballet was a thing, maybe, he felt he didn't have permission to participate in. And since it was just the three of them in this house, he was inevitably left on the outside. Naomi couldn't help but imagine that being put out was almost the same as an invitation to wander.

Naomi looked back down at the phone going off in her hands. All the notifications coming in were the unread texts and emails from family members and friends she hadn't spoken to in weeks giving their condolences on Jessica's passing. There were also a few messages in the Riverside Dance

Academy group chat, some in her family group chat, and new app updates that were asking to be installed. Naomi swiped them all away. She sent a quick text to Saint, something smart and teasing, so she could have a conversation that would take her mind off every other pending thing.

As for the rest of her room, Naomi only managed to fulfill the part about her fluffy rug. She tried the desk, to be fair, but only got it about halfway before she realized she just wasn't as ready to change the room as she thought she was. She got into her bed instead, pulled the sheets up to her chin, and checked for any new messages from Saint Owens.

CHAPTER FIFTEEN

All the light from the sunrise washed Saint's bedroom yellow; he had forgotten to shut the blinds. Everything was calling him out of sleep: the children playing outside in the soft drizzle beating the sidewalk, his mirror magnifying the sunrays onto his eyelids, the smell of fried eggs filling up his small space. But he wasn't ready to wake just yet. He was attempting to pull back the very ending of last night's dream.

He was back under the bridge with Naomi, and this time she was the one handing him the spray paint. Her crutches were in the back of his father's truck and she was hovering inches above the ground, as if that was easier than walking for her. She had clasped his fingers around the spray can and told him to draw whatever he wanted and make it as big as possible. Lifting him up into the air with her, they levitated to a portion of the bridge that would have otherwise been unreachable. The bridge, he noticed, was void of traffic and the concrete was empty. Bare, as she had described it. Naomi said they should get to work. And then the dream began to slip away, today's morning filling the tiny room, inserting itself between him and the false reality. He kept trying to grab it back but it was slippery and moving. What should he paint? Riverside as he saw it, lonely and wanting? Naomi as he saw her, still dancing midair?

And that was how he knew it was too late. To accommodate all that thinking he was already too conscious. The dream had left him.

Squirming out of the beaming light reflected from his mirror, Saint glanced around his bedroom. He fished his phone out from under him and tried switching the screen on but it was dead. He must have fallen asleep last night texting Naomi and forgotten to plug it in. He reached for his charger and did that now. Similarly, everything else was just as he had left it. His sketch pad was flipped open to a fresh page, but he hadn't gotten a chance to begin a new piece because Naomi had texted him at that exact moment. Last night's shoes were kicked off at the foot of his bed. Leaning up, he noticed he hadn't changed his clothes either.

Glancing over his shoulder, he saw that it didn't smell like it, but it was raining. But on closer inspection, actually, it didn't even look like it was raining either. There wasn't a cloud in the sky. Saint crawled closer to his windowsill and peered out the glass. Cheerful screams and shouts echoed from the sidewalk, and he noticed the water wasn't coming from above, but below. A fire hydrant had been hit hard enough to shower the entire block. Children were racing around in its discharge; some were in their bathing suits, others in their pajamas or what looked like the first things they could pull on. There was nothing to indicate what had caused the artificial rain, but the kids couldn't care less. Neither did the adults who were watching gleefully just out of the splash zone. This summer, they all needed this, Saint thought. If Mother Nature wasn't going to give them rain to help beat the heat, they'd make their own.

Getting out of bed fully, Saint changed into his pajamas and followed the smell of fried eggs to the kitchen. His father was standing there. He had his back turned, slipping the eggs from the frying pan onto a plate when Saint exited his room. Sully was reading at the dining table, though Saint knew his brother was only pretending to read. He never read there. No one used that dining table. The boy was really sitting that close to the kitchen because their father hadn't made breakfast in two years. Saint examined the back of his father. Passing his younger brother, Saint gave him a light push on the shoulders. *Morning, loser* in their language.

He groaned back annoyingly. *Morning.*

"Welcome to the land of the living," Richard Owens commented from by the stove.

"You should be in bed."

"I feel fine." He turned off the stove and slid a plate of eggs over to him. They were scrambled, it turned out, just slightly burned. "Grab some bread and give that to Sully."

Saint did as he said, but grabbing the butter out of the fridge he also buttered the two slices of bread and hid the burned eggs in between them. He sliced the sandwich in two. "I'm serious. The doctor said not to strain yourself if you don't need to. If you want some fresh air, we can go to the park—"

"Where are my cigarettes?"

Saint looked up. His father's tone lost all its morning pleas-antness and dipped a few octaves down. Two nights ago he had asked Saint to pick up cigarettes for him on his way to the supermarket, but Saint hadn't gone to the supermarket at all yesterday. The boy realized now that the breakfast was a test. There were no groceries in the house, and Richard Owens, in making breakfast, had to have known this now. Saint delivered the egg sandwich to Sully saying, "You shouldn't be smoking anyway."

"Where did you go?"

"I went for a drive."

"Bullshit," the man boomed, "and you couldn't pick up a pack for me?! Where the hell were you?!"

Saint was more than awake now. "Dad, I'm not picking up a pack for you. Are you crazy?!"

The man left the stove altogether and came to loom over Saint by the kitchen counter. Quietly, he seethed, "Don't you ever talk to me like that, boy."

Saint's eyes found the wall behind his father. He let his breathing even out. "I'm not buying you any more cigarettes," he said.

Richard laughed. It was light, but it cracked into coughs and wheezing anyway. Saint was still looking at the wall. "I'm a grown-ass man," he finally said when he regained enough control, "and you're not the man of this house yet. Not until I'm dead."

Saint gritted his teeth.

Richard continued, "Take the damn eggs."

"I'm not hungry." Saint turned around. "Sully, do you

wanna play outside? The fire hydrant's broken, and kids are on the sidewalk."

The little boy was looking between Saint and Richard. It took him a second to find his voice. "Dad said I couldn't go."

Saint turned around. "Why would you say that?"

"What?" Richard shrugged, biting into a slice of bread. "He's reading. He loves reading."

"He's nine!" If Richard was awake throughout the day for long enough, he would know that Sully wasn't even reading anyway. Sully was watching his father. Waiting to see if the breakfast making meant that his father was finally doing better and in a good mood. A good enough mood to take him out and play with him. "Sully, go change. Let's go outside."

There was a moment of silence at first, and when Richard didn't protest, Sully got up and ran into his room to get changed. Richard shook his head. "The kid was fine reading. I don't know why you feel the need to do all this. What are you trying to prove? That you can raise him better than me? I'm his father. I'm your father."

"You don't care about him reading, don't pretend. You just didn't want him to go outside because you couldn't be bothered to go out the door and watch him."

Richard took another bite. "And you feel big because you'll do that."

Someone has to. When Sully came back into the dining room Saint fully turned away from his father. He attempted to shed Richard from his mind. Be lighter. For Sully. "Ready?" he asked.

Sully was in his swim trunks decorated with cartoon sharks, and holding swimming goggles in his right hand and a cheap water gun in the other. He was biting back a huge grin. The boy nodded.

Saint almost laughed. "Don't know what this getup is, but okay, let's go."

"I don't want the water to get in my eyes!"

"Do you wear those in the shower too then?" he teased.

"No!"

"Yeah, you do. Don't lie. You're scared of water."

"I don't! *I'm* not!"

Richard chuckled. Saint said, "Sure thing, scaredy-cat. Let's go."

"Wait, are you going like that?" Sully said, pointing at Saint's pajamas.

He hadn't even noticed. Saint just wanted to get out of this house and away from his father as quickly as possible. He decided against changing. This was for Sully, anyway, and he'd be dry standing on the adjacent sidewalk. He told his brother, walking to the door, "Yeah, I'm not afraid of water."

"I'm not afraid of water!"

Saint pushed his feet into his slides and opened the door, and the boy ran out. Before he went after him, though, he walked back inside, just far enough so that his father could see him coming out from the corridor. He said to him, "Get someone else to fetch your cigarettes. I'm not doing it. Think about Sully, for once."

The man hardly moved, pursing his lips in annoyance. Saint left before he could reply. He grabbed the house keys and locked the door behind him. Then he followed Sully outside where it was artificially raining. It was hard not to wonder if this would be his life forever. These days it felt as if he was living in a purgatory, stuck in their little home because he couldn't leave his father and his brother alone, nor together. Somehow that ruled out college, and moving out, and letting his inspiration take him too far. He stole these moments when he was important because of that. For the briefest of moments he could step away and not think about all the responsibilities that awaited him. He could just stand here under a tree, or paint a cityscape, or draw a beautiful girl, and he would forget all about it.

The kids were still there, their joy unaffected by the fighting that had just taken place inside Saint's house. Sully ran to join them, and Saint shouted that he'd be watching from under the shade of a tree across the street. Sully shouted back that he understood, and when he made it to the rest of the playing children, he was caught up right away. A few of them came over to him in no time, asking how his water gun worked. Sully demonstrated by catching water in it from the fire hydrant. He turned it on the kids and shot a stream at them. They screamed playfully and chased him. Running, laughing, Sully became a howling wind.

Naomi had found an artist who cussed over the melodies of a piano. The music backdropped the memories of all the things she had done with Saint yesterday. There were pieces of her soaked and dried onto the architecture of Riverside now and she thought that made her permanent. If, one day, she decided to leave this town and go elsewhere, in a way she would always still be right here, and there wasn't a single person who could displace her. Not even she herself. That might have been the most comforting thing she had experienced in weeks. The concept that although she was bedridden in this moment, at the same time she was also at the Riverside Bridge watching the sun rise in the sky over water as lazy cars zipped by.

At first the music was a little jarring. It sounded nothing like the old, composed sounds she had spent hours dancing to. But eventually she came to understand it. The lyrics didn't sound like they were written for the classical instrument but what is music if not self-expression? And what is more expressive than exactly those kinds of lyrics? Her head bopped along to the rhythm and that, helped by the feeling of still being by the edge of town, made her feel a little invincible. She wondered if this was the kind of music that Saint found himself listening to as well. She hoped it wasn't. Just so that their journey would last a little longer and there was still more road for him to take her on, more bridges for them to see, more places to paint their souls onto.

The door opened but Naomi recognized that it was too hesitant for it to be her mom. She paused the playing track and heard a hushed voice call her name. For a brief, frightening moment she thought it might be her father visiting again. Maybe after last night he had finally figured out that she was avoiding him. Or that he was the real reason she had asked her mother to bring her dinner up to her room, not actually because she was in pain. Or maybe he had finally come to tell her that he was being too distant and he wanted permanency in her life.

But then she saw Aspen step inside. Naomi watched her slowly enter. Her hair was down and she clutched a bouquet of flowers, while disgust painted her face. She looked around at Naomi's room, clothes left on the floor, the desk halfway to the wall. Things still looked missing. Then she turned and saw Naomi on the bed.

She jumped. "Oh my god!" she breathed. "You scared me. What are you doing just lying there?"

Naomi didn't move. "This is my room." Those were the first words she'd uttered since she'd spoken to Saint the night before.

After she had turned her phone on and saved his number, she'd texted him and realized quickly that he preferred communicating via audio messages and short videos of a tiger modified to speak with his voice. She responded using the lion character, and somehow, they'd made it an unspoken rule to talk to each other solely like that for the rest of the night.

"Well." Aspen's eye caught the half-eaten breakfast on her night table. "Your room smells horrible. You need to throw that out." Her shoulders fell as she looked up and down the naked walls and back at the girl covered to her neck in bed-sheets. "I have to admit, this is not at all what I was expecting from you, Naomi."

"What were you expecting?"

"A life-size cutout of Diana Vishneva over there, maybe your ten-year collection of pointe shoes strung up on a wall right there."

Naomi smiled at the irony. "I prefer Misty Copeland, and the pointe shoes are actually in my closet. You're not that far off."

Aspen shook her head but Naomi saw the smile flicker across her lips. "You seem pretty chipper for an injured dancer."

Naomi's heart raced like the engine of a car. *Is it that obvious?* Had Saint already left that much of a noticeable impression on her? "That's good. I didn't want . . . I just thought I'd come see how you were doing."

Naomi sat up in her bed. Aspen seemed sincere, although it was a little ironic given the fact that she was the one who could still stand on her own two feet and that meant, at least for Prix, she had beaten Naomi. It was interesting to think that Aspen was able to feel some of the things Naomi did. "Thank you," Naomi answered. Then she looked at the bouquet of purple flowers in her hands. "Are those for me?"

Aspen's attention snapped to her own hands. "Yes." She held them up. "These are orchids. They're very stubborn flowers. You can forget to water them for days and they'll still look this bright. At least, that's what the florist told me. I thought it would do you some good to see something trying as hard to keep going as you are."

Naomi couldn't find the words to reply. She watched as Aspen avoided eye contact and instead was looking out the bedroom window. Naomi wondered if all it took was her, nothing else, to pull Aspen all the way across town to her bedroom. Just to see how she was doing.

Aspen rested the flowers on top of Naomi's dresser. "Your mom said she'd bring a vase to put these in. Who—speaking of—I just had to lie to through my teeth." Naomi's head tilted in confusion. Aspen walked closer to Naomi's bed and set her handbag on the free space on top of the night table next to the plate of food. She whispered, "Why does your mom think you came to the academy yesterday when I haven't seen you in days?"

Naomi lurched forward. "What did she say? Wait, what did you tell her?!"

"Don't worry. I covered for you. It caught me off guard, but I told her you had a rough time watching us all dance while you had to sit in a corner. That's what you told her, right?" Naomi let out a breath. She fell back onto her bed, a pillow flopping off and onto the floor. Aspen picked it up and set it back next to her. "Naomi, what's going on? If you weren't at the academy yesterday, where were you?"

Naomi bit her bottom lip. She had to be more careful. But in her defense, she hadn't known that Aspen would show up at her house. Maybe she shouldn't have been lying at all. "I was out."

Aspen narrowed her eyes. "Yes, I know that. But where?"

"Riverside Bridge."

"Riverside Bridge?" Aspen repeated.

"I went with a friend." She tongued the sharp bits of the top row of her teeth. "His name's Saint and we just kind of . . . went to see the water."

The weight in the room shifted. "Who? Who's Saint?"

Naomi sat straight up now. She realized her own hair was not straight and long the way Aspen was probably used to seeing it. But she didn't care. If Aspen wanted to get to know her, this was her. She was a person outside of the ballet tights and the Riverside Performing Arts Theater. Albeit, a different person. If Aspen was to get to know her, she would have to know both sides of her.

Naomi told Aspen everything. She spoke about the boy, and how they had met late at night at the theater when she was probably at her lowest. How they met again at Evergreen

Memorial Park, and he didn't even seem to notice the ankle brace or the crutches when he saw her. How she felt free around him, and she never knew she could feel that way around anyone except Jessica. Halfway though, Aspen had to take a seat on the edge of the bed just to take it all in. Naomi continued on about the spray paint, and how good it felt to do something and have no one watch or care.

When she was finished Aspen said, "Wow." Naomi wondered what Aspen thought of her now that she knew Naomi was seeing a boy when she should be in the dance studio. She then wondered if Aspen herself would ever take that risk, but then remembered quite vividly the speed with which her father's hand had sliced across her cheek.

Aspen said to her, "That's—that's something." There was a longer pause. "I'm glad you're having fun."

"You don't like it," Naomi said flatly.

Aspen put her hands up. "No, no, I'm happy for you. I'm glad you're exploring Riverside and having fun, as long as you're not doing anything stupid. But I guess I just thought you'd be focused on getting back in shape for Prix?"

Naomi thought for a moment. "What if I don't heal in time?"

"What if you do?"

What if I don't want to? Naomi looked back at the orchids abandoned on top of the dresser.

"Does it hurt? Do you feel any pain?"

Naomi shrugged. "As long as I keep it elevated, not really. I just can't stand to stay in here all day. It gets so depressing."

Aspen told her that while she might be bedridden right now, she could still think. Perhaps she should really use this time to think about what she wanted from the academy now, and what her future in ballet looked like.

The air grew heavy. Naomi looked straight ahead. "I really don't want to talk about that."

Aspen nodded. "Yeah, of course. I get it." Neither of them said anything.

A few beats passed during which Naomi watched the flowers. Aspen looked at them, too, because Naomi was, and fiddled with her acrylic nails before finally exhaling. Then she saw them. She pointed at Naomi's dresser. "Valentino's keys. You were the one who took them."

Naomi slumped in her bed. "You can give those back to him. I don't need them anymore."

Aspen turned to her. "Why'd you take them in the first place?"

"You know why."

Aspen's eyes narrowed at her. "Naomi, I don't think I do."

Naomi was exasperated. "Because I needed to rehearse, okay? Like, I needed to be perfect because I've lost so much already and I couldn't lose anything else and I needed the extra rehearsal time to make sure that didn't happen. I needed them." Aspen looked away from her. Naomi's heart was still hammering in her chest when under her breath she finished, "Jessica didn't give me a choice."

"God, I feel so stupid." The words fell out of Aspen's mouth like a ball that was too heavy for her to keep carrying. "All of us do. I think we knew that after Jessica passed something was going on with you, but we thought it was grief, you know? Normal grief. I guess none of us took you seriously enough in the way we should have. But now that I look back at it, your best friend died. That's a lot for one person to bear. I guess I just don't want you to feel that alone again?" Somewhere in there Naomi was sure she heard Aspen's voice crack. "I should have noticed and helped you, or something. I'm sorry. All of us at the academy feel like absolute shit. We almost dropped out of Prix after what happened last week."

Naomi's eyes popped. "What?! Why?!"

Aspen looked at her incredulously. Then she said slowly with concern, "Naomi, look at you. You're—"

"Broken? Losing?" she finished for her.

"Injured," Aspen corrected.

Naomi flopped backward against the headboard. "Yeah, well, I'd assume some of you would be happy about that. You get to dance Odette." She looked at Aspen pointedly. "Isn't that what you wanted?

The words went right though Aspen. "Naomi, I didn't take your routine." She scoffed. "And to think I did it in honor of your ungrateful ass."

"Well, that's your loss. It's an iconic variation and if you wanted first position you should have grabbed it," Naomi grumbled. She inhaled and exhaled like an active volcano. Burning silence fell between them but neither of them left. Then, after a moment, Naomi asked, "Who took it then?"

"No one." Aspen was looking away now too. "Valentino didn't offer it up, and no one asked."

At the mention of his name, Naomi realized Aspen should have been dancing right then. It was a weekday, and it was still pretty early in the afternoon. Except Aspen was here in a black crop top, jeans, and sneakers. She wondered how much convincing it took for Valentino to give her a day off. Or if she had even told him at all. Would she have done that for Aspen?

"Hi, girls." Aja entered the room carrying a vase, and Aspen pointed her to the flowers. "Naomi, isn't it nice of your friend to come visit you?" Naomi didn't answer. She kept the inside of her cheek between her teeth.

"Aspen, dear, are you staying for lunch?"

Before Aspen could answer, Naomi spoke. "Well, she just got here, so I think if you're already making it, she might as well stay and have some." Aspen turned to look at Naomi but Naomi didn't meet her gaze. Usually, Naomi wouldn't answer on anyone's behalf like that. Saint was already changing her, she realized. And this new trait she'd just exercised was one she thought she could start getting used to.

Aja clasped her hands. "Well, okay then. I'll go make us all lunch." She left, announcing that she'd be back with plates. The room door closed halfway. Aspen turned around.

"So," Naomi said testing the atmosphere, "how have you been?" Would the other girl understand this as an attempt at an apology? Her own way of saying, *Stay, I'm sorry. Don't leave.*

Aspen smiled. "I've been okay. Thank you for asking, finally!"

"Oh, shut up."

"I swear all you do is talk about yourself." Naomi laughed. "Do you realize that? My cat could've died today and you would have just now known. I've been here for twenty minutes, Naomi." She burst out laughing.

CHAPTER SIXTEEN

Saint felt sick. His father was out of medication so he had to drive down to the pharmacy to get more—spending money he'd been thinking of using to buy himself another sketch pad. Even then, Richard had asked him to buy more cigarettes. Saint told him no, and his father responded by asking who the hell Saint thought he was talking to him like that. The slam of doors. The hiss of teeth. Then, again, silence.

It was only nine in the morning. Saint leaned against the other side of his father's bedroom door. He attempted to catch his breath but it was determined to leave him one way or the other. He just couldn't help but think that if he wasn't the one to bring Richard the cigarettes then his murderer would probably go unknown and unidentified. Which was worse? At the back of his mind was the realization that the end of summer was nearing and the new school year would be coming. Should he even go? Would it be irresponsible of him to get an education when their house had zero income earners? The thoughts concentrated between his throat and his chest. He was about to burst, or pass out, or pass out because he had burst. When Saint's body finally hit the ground, he tried to feel every single fiber of the carpeted flooring.

When that didn't work, he tried to feel himself. He grabbed the outside of his hand, the one that was still scarring over, and pinched as tightly as he could, twisting and twisting the skin until that was the only part of himself that he could feel. His breath stopped sputtering for a moment, and that's all it took for him to wrangle it back under his control again. He choked it into submission.

"Saint?"

Raising his head, Saint saw Sully standing a few feet away watching him. He too was breathing unevenly. Saint scrambled up.

"Are you okay?" his little brother asked as Saint rushed to close the space between them, pulling the younger boy in for a hug before he even finished his sentence.

"I'm okay." He kissed Sully's forehead. "I'm okay, I promise." Sully waited for his brother to release him so he could look him in the eye. His chest was still pulsating. "Do you want breakfast?"

Saint was releasing the hug and dipping into the kitchen before his brother could reply. He turned on the stove and tried not to wonder what his little brother must have been thinking as he couldn't hear his brother's footsteps immediately following him. But when Saint turned around to finally confront his brother, he saw Sully sitting on the couch, refusing to turn around. Sully reached forward and flipped the television on.

The eggs Saint made were runny and undercooked. It

meant he was in a rush to leave again, and Sully was about to watch him go. Sully kept his eyes on the television as Saint slipped on his slides and sauntered out the door, still in his pajama bottoms and plain white T-shirt. Briefly, Saint felt grateful they had started reading *Macbeth*. Maybe his little brother could pick the book up now on his own. Exercise his imagination.

The fresh air hit Saint's unwashed face as he wiped the remaining crust out of his eyes. On days like this there was only one place Saint could rely on to be unchanging for him: Elizabeth Park. Thankfully, the walk there wasn't too far, and his bench remained unoccupied too. Only a few dog walkers and joggers were scattered around the park at this hour. One woman with her baby in a stroller jogged right by Saint as he plopped down on the wooden bench. Saint started to seriously consider what dropping out would mean for him. If he got a job, where would he work? Would it be enough? Would Sully be okay? Sully. Even if Saint couldn't get an education, what mattered most was that his brother could. What would senior year teach him that the rest of high school hadn't anyway?

A shadow loomed over him. He didn't have to look up to recognize who it was. Saint could smell the man first, then he noticed the tattered shoes and mismatched socks. The man took a seat next to Saint.

"Sky falling got you down?"

"Yep," Saint answered. Mr. Blythe nodded knowingly, as if he knew exactly what that felt like, and he was feeling it now too. He did that often with Saint during their conversations in the park. When they had first met, Saint had really thought that maybe the man did know. Perhaps in a life before this, living in a tent on the grass in the park, Mr. Blythe had gone through something similar in his youth, and flashes of that past replayed in his mind when he and Saint spoke. Now though, Saint knew the old man well enough to recognize that his eyes were always that glossed over, and he was never reminiscing. He was constantly looking forward, if anything, and you couldn't be nostalgic about the future.

The man said, "Don't be sad. When the sky finally hits, you won't even feel it. None of us will." He propped both his arms up against the back of the bench.

Saint looked up now and met his gaze. "Did you ever run away?"

The man cocked his head. He seemed puzzled. "You're not talking about the sky?"

Saint redirected his focus. "How far did you make it before you ended up here?"

He laughed. "I ran, sure. We all ran. And running sounds nice until you realize you'll get tired. And you're forgetting something. It's not all it's cut out to be." Blythe had stopped looking at him now.

Saint leaned back with him, letting his back touch the bench. "Okay, but you weren't always here, right? You were on the road at some point. What was that like?" If he was honest with himself, the questions were pointless. He couldn't run away no matter how badly he wanted to. Sully and Richard couldn't take care of themselves, much less each other. Saint had to be in that small home or else all their lives would get worse. But right now, Saint didn't want to be honest. For one small moment in the past two years, he wanted to think about what life would be like if he got what he wanted, for himself, with no one else to think about.

Mr. Blythe said, "You can only run for so long. By the time you look back, you'll realize you haven't made it that far at all. What you were running from is still there, and it hasn't been swallowed up by the sky yet."

Saint cocked his head. "You're not talking about the sky."

The man smiled. "You're not worried about that. You want to escape something else."

Saint said nothing.

Mr. Blythe didn't stop there. He told Saint, "Sometimes I say to myself, I wish I could run away from the sky. Sometimes people ask me why I don't leave if I know it will kill me. Well, that's because I can't really run from it. Not really. Even if I steal a spaceship and move to a different planet like Zenon, the sky will still fall, and everything I've ever loved will be gone. I don't want to run. I want the sky to stop falling altogether."

Saint ignored the reference to a planet he was positive did not exist and the urge to ask Mr. Blythe to list the things he loved and instead asked, "But you can't stop it from falling, right?"

"You tell me."

Saint looked back at the people passing by in the park. "But then what do you do?"

Mr. Blythe laughed. "My boy, you better find a way to make the most of it." Then he became suddenly solemn and quiet. "Say, you got any spare change?"

Saint ended up purchasing a pack of cigarettes for his father. Richard was asleep when he came back home so he simply left it on the nightstand. His father would wake up to it sometime today, and he would whisper a thank-you to the universe and grab the lighter next to it. For at least the next week, he and Saint would not be shouting at each other anymore.

In the living room, Saint read the rest of *Macbeth* to his little brother, and they each promised to read specific characters. Saint's Lady Macbeth was loud and prudish. Sully's Macduff had a deep rumbling voice that was close to shouting. Neither of them liked the ending but they knew they had to get there. They had grown attached to Macbeth, despite the death and pain he had caused. They still wanted to him to prevail. After all, all he wanted was the crown and security for his family. The choices he made weren't the best, but they were for good reasons most of the time.

That evening, Saint texted Naomi and asked her to join him for a second trip. He had plans for a bowling alley he used to go to as a child, but she told him this late in the day she couldn't leave home; their adventures needed to be earlier. Tomorrow, however, she could see him, and even though her bowling skills were subpar, she'd attempt her best for him.

Saint told her that, like the bridge, the bowling alley wasn't just a bowling alley, or at least it wouldn't be when they were done with it. As he waited for a response he wondered if she'd changed her mind about the way he expressed himself. Maybe vandalism, as she had described it, was the last thing she wanted to be a part of. Reasonably, going from dancing ballet to what they were doing was a drastic change. He watched the small indicator showing that she was typing pop up on his phone. If she said no, he told himself he'd go anyway.

I was hoping you'd say that, was her response.

Who was he kidding? If she had said no, he didn't know what he'd do.

The next day Naomi remembered to bring the first aid kit she used for ballet and treated the cuts on the back of Saint's right hand. When he asked how she knew what everything in that box did and how to wrap a rolled bandage so well, she told him the truth: ballet wasn't easy.

The next few days were more or less the same—driving through the most boring parts of Riverside and turning them into little kingdoms with spray paint and words they would never otherwise get the chance to say out loud. With Saint, Naomi's worst thoughts didn't come for her. She didn't have to rethink ballet or her future; she could just sit next to him, and they could both hold Riverside by the ears, ride it into the ground.

CHAPTER SEVENTEEN

Pulling up to the Riverside Performing Arts Theater for the fifth day in a row, Aja put her car in Park and watched Naomi pull over her crutches from the backseat. Even this close to downtown, at this time of day on a Sunday the roads were nearly empty. No one was going to work. People were at home spending time with their families. Naomi could not remember the last time her family had dinner together at the dining table. It might have been sometime before she got injured. After she broke, she realized, other things followed suit. She was sure her mother knew this, too, when she watched Naomi exercise her ankle daily to regain her strength. But nothing else was being repaired. In the absence of ballet, where did the rest of their family go?

"Are you sure Valentino's holding rehearsals today?" Naomi had told her that Valentino had extended class hours but the academy had never been open on Sundays before. They were still two months out from Prix too.

"Yes, Mom," Naomi answered thoughtlessly.

Aja forced her thoughts into submission. When the crutches were with her, Naomi checked outside and opened the door. "Wait," Aja said. "Talk to me, how is everything going in there? Has it been helpful?"

Naomi repositioned herself in the passenger seat and closed the car door. After it clicked shut, she waited ten extra seconds to think. "It's good. I mean, it's different for sure but I'm glad to be back."

"What do you do all day? Do you just watch them dance?"

Naomi thought again. "Yeah, and I study them. Sometimes I imagine myself dancing with them too. It's nice to just enjoy ballet from like a third perspective."

Aja smiled. Even Naomi believed herself a little. She realized that this was how all intricate webs of lies began.

Aja asked, "I was thinking, sometime this week, we should have dinner together, as a family again. It would be nice."

Naomi's lips sealed themselves. So her mother had been thinking the same thing as her. Naomi swallowed and nodded.

"Great," Aja continued. "How's next Sunday night? I can make jerk chicken."

Naomi licked her bottom lip. "Yeah, no, that sounds great." She opened her door. "Can't wait."

Naomi exited the car and didn't think twice about her quick departure. She waited for her mother to drive off before she collapsed against the wall of the theater. She took a deep breath. It felt as if there was a bomb ticking, timed for a week from now when she would have to sit at her family dining table and pretend her father didn't make her sick. Face-to-face with her mother sitting next to her, would she be able to keep up the ruse?

Even out here where there were no walls she could still feel the pressure building. She had thought she'd escaped this feeling. Battled it and won, but it had come back to haunt her, it seemed. And the narrowing feeling felt so familiar it was as if it had never left her.

This afternoon, Saint had left behind his spray paint. When they met in Evergreen Memorial Park among all the graves and dancing trees, he told Naomi he had a different plan for them. He asked her, "Do you want to see a place that's already alive and waiting?"

Of course, Naomi told him yes. She hadn't told that boy no since the day they met.

In reality, Saint had not brought his backpack and the usual equipment because the paint was getting low and buying a new can so soon was a waste of money. His father's money. At this rate, Richard Owens would certainly realize money was missing and the groceries were thinning, and then he'd ask Saint, and Saint would lie, and Richard wouldn't believe him, and before the day was over, they'd be shouting.

So as Naomi and Saint climbed into the front seats of the Silverado, Saint made the ultimate decision that today they would just have to do something else. "Are you hungry?"

Naomi tore her gaze from outside. Suddenly, the leather seats felt hot. Saint wasn't looking back at her; his eyes were steady on the road. Something told Naomi that he already knew what she would say, and he was just waiting for her to say it. Like every other day, Naomi had already eaten a heavy breakfast. Aja had prepared an açai bowl with yogurt, berries, and granola, and so she still felt quite full. But lunch, maybe, couldn't hurt. Not if it meant they got to see somewhere new. Not if it meant they were still exploring Riverside together. "I could eat," she told him.

Saint grinned. "Good. See, there's this Mexican place near my house, and when I tell you their nachos are the closest thing we have to heaven on earth . . ." Naomi laughed. "I don't know what they put in that cheese, but I promise you, it'll change your life." She knew he was only joking, but if she was really honest, Naomi wanted to tell him her life had already changed the moment they stood under the Riverside Bridge. And it had been changing every day since, all because of him.

The sky branched out in front of them, with the clouds surfing the wind. Naomi was looking out the window again, trying to take in all the places it seemed like she had missed in this city when she heard the radio get louder. She turned around to Saint's hand vigorously putting up the volume. He didn't stop until it was loud enough to make her armrest vibrate.

Saint threw his head along with the blasting drums. When she didn't follow along, he gave her a confused look. "Don't tell me you don't know this song!" he shouted.

She would have told him he was right except she wasn't sure her voice could go much louder than the music. She made a face instead. "Are you kidding?!" He bopped his head harder. Then he began shouting the lyrics, "*And nothing ever stays the same!*" He was a little off-key but he was singing his heart out anyway. Naomi laughed. "Join in! Join in! Come on! *No, nothing every stays . . .*"

". . . *the same*," she echoed sheepishly. And she was right. Her voice really could not be heard over the speakers. This did not even seem like the kind of song you would scream at the top of your lungs in a car. The drums weren't that heavy, the lyrics were slow, kind. Saint, however, was smiling as if it was a grand anthem. *"Oh, nothing ever stays the same!"* When the verse came in, he said to her, "Come on, Naomi. You have to give me more than that. This is an iconic track, do you realize that?!" She was laughing at him. When the tempo built up again and the chorus restarted, he sang along with the lyrics, *"Oh, nothing ever stays the same!"*

Now he was slamming his palms onto the steering wheel. Laughing too. She watched him attempt to dance while driving. He was giving her permission to do the same. She looked ahead of her into the sun. Naomi shouted with him, *"Oh, nothing ever stays the same!"*

"No, nothing ever stays the same!"

He put his left hand out the window.

She put hers out the right. She looked at him once more, his mouth wide open.

"No, nothing ever stays the same!"

They could drive straight into forever like this. The breeze outside tickled her, but she realized that if she screamed loud enough, she couldn't feel it at all. If she screamed loud enough nothing on earth could take away this feeling ever again. After the car in front of them made a right turn and made room for them on the open road, she shut her eyes tight and allowed herself to feel the sun on her. She let her voice burst from her chest. Naomi was screaming, and this time it was because of a good thing. She didn't realize it, but every person that they drove by stopped to watch their scream-singing, wishing silently that they could be half as loud and unapologetic as them.

When the song ended, Naomi and Saint turned to each other breathlessly. Saint flung his head back, still laughing, but this time it was made audible as the track ended. Naomi leaned forward and hit Replay on the song. She readied herself one more time. For a while, it really did feel as though they were headed into a forever and like yesterday's problems belonged to the past. Today was new and fresh, and they were healed and free.

They went for their second round of the song.

The restaurant Saint had in mind was Tio's Tacos, and it was an open concept building, not only by nature of the hibachi grill–style kitchen, but the dining area itself, which was also wall-less, with tables scattered outside on gravel under wooden gazebos. When they parked, they were essentially right next to a couple eating. Naomi could see them only a few feet away feeding each other at their table. They seemed old enough to be married but young enough not to have any children. At their life's peak perhaps. All Naomi could think about as she watched them was that she had only ever imagined herself dancing in the New York City Ballet at that age. No marriage. No one feeding her. No dates on the outskirts of a small town. She glanced over at Saint to read what he might be thinking, but the boy hadn't noticed the couple at all. He was already jumping out of the truck.

Naomi followed him to a spot that he claimed was the best seat in the house. It was a booth made out of dark wood located right next to the kitchen. Close enough, Naomi noticed, that she could hear the meat sizzling on the grill and cooks shouting commands back and forth. The head chef standing by the massive grill near their table was midflip when he saw Saint. His eyes widened. "Saint! Back so soon?"

"Can't stay away, Tio. You know that."

The burly man laughed heartily as Naomi and Saint sat. There were various dishes scattered across his grill, and he seemed to be completely aware of what was freshly put there and what was cooked, including how long it had to be there for. Every time he flipped something the food looked more and more ready, never burned. The moment she relaxed in her seat, Naomi could see why Saint considered this place alive and waiting. There were simply no walls holding anything back and the smell from the grill tricked you into thinking you weren't in Riverside at all, but somewhere else entirely. "Hey," he shouted again. "How's your dad doing? He all right?"

Saint didn't hesitate. "Yep. He's doing great."

Tio said, "Tell that old man I owe him a meal. On me."

Saint wasn't about to tell Tio that his father didn't leave the house for anything anymore, not even food. Or that the better route would probably be for Tio to offer a pack of cigarettes instead. And he was definitely not going to say any of this in front of Naomi. She still didn't know how sick his father was, and he was planning on keeping it that way for as long as possible. Instead, he joked, "What about me? I'm your most loyal customer, and I never get a free meal."

"That's because you keep coming back anyway."

Saint frowned. "I don't think that's how customer appreciation works."

They laughed at each other before Saint introduced Naomi and confirmed they were here for his usual: Tio's famous nachos. Tio laughed evilly. "Your wish is my command."

"You ready for this?" Saint asked, turning to Naomi.

She put both elbows on their table. "Born ready, baby."

Saint chuckled. He'd never heard her speak like that before. He liked it. "Good," he affirmed. Then he launched into a story about how his father had been the one to introduce their entire family to Tio's Tacos years ago. Saint wasn't sure how Tio and his dad knew each other exactly, but he vividly remembered the day Tio came over for dinner when he was a little boy, and from then on Tio was just sort of always there. Just as his name described, he had become sort of like an uncle. Naomi told Saint that her family didn't have anyone like that. It was Ethan, Aja, and Naomi; no one else. At least in Riverside the three of them were all they had.

"Small," Saint commented.

"Suffocating," Naomi corrected without thinking.

The next question came naturally. "Why's it like that? Do you guys not have people over or . . . ?"

Naomi shrugged. "I don't know. My dad and my mom both moved to Riverside, they didn't grow up here, so they don't really know anyone. And since then, my dad's always been working, and my mom, well, her entire life has become ballet at this point because of me."

"But you're not dancing anymore. So what's she doing now?"

Naomi wiped her sweaty palms on her jeans. "Actually, she thinks I'm still dancing, sort of." Saint leaned forward in the booth. She said softly enough that Tio wouldn't hear, "My mom doesn't know I'm here with you, okay? She thinks I'm at the theater still. Doing . . . I don't even know, watching them, I guess. As if I could bear to see that right now."

It explained why she insisted on hanging out at a certain time of day and only allowed him to pick her up and drop her off at the same location, but Saint didn't press her on it. He could already see something dark pushing at her seams. Instead, he redirected their conversation to Tio. He told him that Naomi was homeschooled, and thus might be able to give him some advice about whether or not Tio should homeschool his own child. It was his first child, Tio was explaining, and he didn't want his learning disability to "other" him in traditional school. Naomi looked back at Saint, who gave her an encouraging nod. She said the first things that came to mind about her experience at home, avoiding ballet where necessary.

Saint didn't think he'd ever heard Naomi say so much, for so long, so freely. While they waited for the nachos, Saint briefly left to use the bathroom. On his way back, he noticed Naomi's feet under the table. Even with the ankle brace, there was a clear pattern and rhythm to them. She was dancing. It wasn't quite the swan Saint had seen onstage at the Riverside Performing Arts Theater but it was close. Above the table, the girl was flipping through a menu as if she was only idly shaking her leg. If he was Naomi's mother, he imagined, he'd believe Naomi if she told him she wanted to spend her free time at the academy. She seemed as if dancing was all she was ever meant to do. He didn't bring it up when he sat back down. But he noticed it more frequently in the days after when they waited for the stoplights to turn green in the Silverado, or whenever they idly stood at intersections. Naomi was, whether she knew it or not, still onstage, still dancing. She had never truly come off.

CHAPTER EIGHTEEN

The first thing Naomi realized about Saint Owens when she sat next to him in the shared space of the 2002 Chevrolet Silverado was that his hair was no longer in twists. Now it was all out and free, but without a lineup it looked unlike him. This afternoon, Saint was taking Naomi to the community library. He said that a little after four in the afternoon on a weekday the building usually began to empty out and they could probably get away with going up on the roof, where the most spectacular view of Riverside would be waiting for them. She asked him if he had been on the roof before. He told her it was one of the oldest and tallest buildings on this side of town. So, naturally, he had seen it before and, naturally, he wanted her to see it as well. With him.

"It's so tall that people used to jump off it." She turned to him. After a moment, he clarified, "Suicide pandemic. Right here in Riverside."

All Naomi could ask was, "Why?"

"For the same reason we're on our way to see it right now, I guess." Naomi glanced back at his hair. She thought it looked unkempt more than it looked free. She preferred the twists. He said, "To see what all the excitement's about."

Inside the Riverside Community Library, it was just as Saint had said it would be. Empty. There were a few librarians sitting around the front desk, clicking away at the computers in front of them and patrons sitting at desks, but outside of that, nothing moved. In the quiet, one of the librarians looked up and saw them. She waved happily. Saint and Naomi waved back. Upon realizing just how big her smile got, Naomi turned to the boy. "You know her?"

He shrugged. "Yeah, that's Shanel." Under his breath he said, "We like Shanel. She's the nice one." When he had told Naomi that he frequented the library she hadn't thought to imagine it was so often that he would know the full-time staff's names. How many visits did it take to befriend the people who worked here?

Saint motioned for Naomi to follow him deeper into the building. In his wake, she asked, "How often do you come here?"

"Maybe once a week or so?" Shelves of books and display cases filled the building. Maps. Old movie posters. Rolled-up architectural blueprints. "My brother loves it here."

Naomi stopped. "You have a brother?"

Saint nodded. "Yeah, that guy loves to read. It's all he does." He glanced back at her. "That and watch TV."

Saint still hadn't realized how strangely Naomi was looking at him. They had been doing this together for almost three weeks now, and he had never brought up the fact that he had a brother. "Why don't you ever talk about him?"

"I don't?"

"No, you don't. I promise, if you had mentioned that you had a brother, I'd remember. How old is he?" Naomi tried to imagine a smaller version of the boy in front of her running around this library, looking for books and whatever else he could find to entertain himself. The same way Saint drove around Riverside looking for the places that were alive and waiting, so he could paint himself there.

"A whole nine years old. It's crazy to think I've known him since he was the size of my forearm."

Naomi was still trying to picture his sibling—a smaller more innocent version of Saint—but all she could see was Saint just as he was now. Or how she thought he was before she noticed he was letting his hair grow unruly and was no longer looking at her for what felt like hours at a time. Glancing around the library, Naomi noticed that most of the bookshelves were wooden and brown. In fact, most things here were wooden and brown. "What types of books does he like to read?"

"Mystery, mostly," Saint said, trying to recall the stacks of books in his brother's room. "He really likes mystery. Although a few weeks ago I read him *Macbeth* and he seemed to like that, so maybe he'll go through a Shakespeare phase now."

Naomi got as far as the very first syllable of her next question, *What's his name?*, when Saint cut her off. "Here it is. *The Flying Angels of Riverside.*"

He pointed to what appeared to be the most modern thing in the entire library. It stood around eight feet tall, and was located past the front desk and in the center of the building, where the library hall met the stacks. It was a large, dull, metallic statue. Naomi got closer to it. The statue depicted what must have been dozens of miniature people free-falling through the air at various heights from the ground with their clothes and hair frozen in wind and with large wings sprouting out of their backs. They were all smiling too. Some even looked like they were letting out a mad laugh. But, Naomi noticed, despite the wings they were still falling.

Saint looked the whole thing up and down, admiring it. Every time, no matter how long he had stared the time before, he always found something new to appreciate about the metal statue. This time, it was a little baby wrapped in cloth, its wings proportional to its small body and its face turned up to the sky, smiling. It was the only one not looking at the ground, yet it was so small it was easy to miss it among all the adult-like figures. Saint's eyes flicked to Naomi. She was watching the statue in the exact same way he had when he first came here years ago. "Remember the people I told you about who jumped from the roof?" he asked her. "This is them. All of them. The library and the city built it as a memorial."

Naomi let out a breath. As her eyes traveled downward, she realized the statue portrayed the ground as clouds. The angel-people were falling without risks. She read the plaque on it: TO ALL THE ANGELS WE'VE LOST HERE, WE HOPE THE NEXT TIME YOU FLY, YOU NEVER HIT THE GROUND. Naomi didn't know why she'd thought Saint was kidding. "I had no idea this happened. How many people died?" The list of names under the quote on the plaque were too many to count.

"I can't remember, twenty-something?" He watched confusion take hold of her. "Yeah, no one really talks about it anymore, but my mom said that when she was a little girl all this was still happening."

Naomi wanted to ask what it was about Riverside, really, that drove so many people to kill themselves. To make sure that they found the absolute highest building to use to do it. To know that once they leaped there was no rope to be cut or pills to be thrown up. Saint turned to her. "Wanna see where it happened?"

Before she could tell him no, he took off. With her ankle brace, she had to awkwardly jog to catch up with him at the end of the stacks. Saint looked both ways before finding a staircase and pulling Naomi along the corridor toward it. He knew that Shanel usually walked back and forth between the stacks here so he took quieter steps all the way to the second floor, where a door opened onto a back concrete staircase.

"Saint, wait."

As he flew up the steps, he kept on describing how magnificent the view was from that high. "You can see the whole town, really. Actually, I think you can even see Clearview Falls. Just the edge of it, but still. And you can see all the other roofs of Riverside. You wouldn't believe how dirty they are. A lot of them have soda cans and, like, old backpacks up there. I don't think anyone really cares about being on the roof but, damn. They don't know what they're missing."

The whole way up Naomi realized Saint had not carried his bag of spray paint and she wanted to ask him exactly what their business was on the roof of the library. The question lodged in the back of her throat as she struggled to keep up in her ankle brace and crutches. Instead, she asked an easier question. "But won't it be locked?" *Considering all the people that used it to end their lives.*

"They can't lock it. It's one of the only things that makes this town special."

That didn't sound like an answer to her. "I thought we were seeing the things that were alive and waiting?"

"And we are." At the top of the staircase Saint pushed open the rooftop door and light flooded in. Naomi didn't want to think about it, but the thoughts kept spiraling in her mind. *If all the way up here we're the only things that are alive, what would we be waiting on?* Saint stepped through the door.

Naomi hurried to catch up with him. She came up the stairs little by little until she was able to take the thing one foot at a time. When she got to the top, she pushed open the door like Saint had and immediately understood what he was talking about. She really could see the very top of almost every building in Riverside. They must have been six stories up. Saint was standing not too far away from her, in the center of the roof. Next to him was another statue, identical to *The Flying Angels of Riverside* on the first floor of the library. Except, in this depiction, instead of falling, all the people were flying. The angels had their eyes turned skyward.

Saint looked up with them. Naomi followed his gaze. She realized they were much closer to the sun this high. It was still miles and miles away, and Naomi knew that, but up here she couldn't help but feel that the bright ball of light was just close enough to touch. And she wasn't wrong. She thought about the myth she had heard once about a god, or a man, who had flown so close to the sun that he eventually burned up.

Naomi turned to the sound of quick footsteps. Her eyes grew wide. "Saint!"

The boy was dashing forward. Running to the point where

the building stopped. He jumped onto the ledge. "Saint! What are you doing?!" He turned around, smiling at her. "Get down!"

His smile got wider. Couldn't he hear her? Why wasn't he listening? Her hands went cold.

Naomi clenched her teeth and stepped closer to him. She only made it about three steps when Saint jumped backward. His body dove over the side of the roof.

"Saint!"

In a flash, Naomi set off. She threw the crutches away and put all the weight she could manage onto her ankle. She went as fast as she could, her heart hammering against her chest, and when she got to the ledge her palms slapped the waist-high concrete. She peered over. Saint was smiling up at her. He was maybe six feet down from where she was standing, on a secondary ledge. Another roof. At the end of it, instead of another concrete ledge, there was an entire wall made up of only barbed wire curving upward. "You idiot! Why would you do that?!" She paused to take breath. "I thought you jumped!"

Saint was still smiling. "But I did jump." He spun around proudly, pointing to the barbed wire. "They built this so people couldn't jump off the roof anymore. You can't scale this ledge and you can't climb it, either, with the barbed—"

"You know what I mean!" Her voice cracked. "I thought you had *jumped*." She looked up, wiping her face.

His smile fell completely. His face turned confused. "You really thought I was going to kill myself."

Naomi leaned up off the ledge. "You jumped off a building, Saint! What did you want me to think?!"

After saying nothing for a long time and looking back

and forth between Naomi and the second metallic ledge he was standing on, he answered, "You're right." Naomi breathed. "That was stupid of me."

Her breath finally began to slow. She wanted to tell him that stupid didn't begin to describe what he'd just done. It was reckless. The way he planted that imagery in her head of all those people on their suicide mission and then brought her all the way up here, only to jump where dozens had already died, as if he was paying forward their legacy. This would have been the second death of a friend she'd witnessed in the span of only a few months. It was unfair. It was cruel. And fed up, she said this all to him. By the time she was done, Saint had turned his back to her. He was looking right at the barbed wired separating himself and the rest of Riverside. Naomi asked him, "Why would you do that?"

He turned back around. "I thought we could jump together." Together? He'd lost his mind. "I wasn't thinking."

Naomi made sure her eyes were dry. Then she noticed that even though she had just run on it, her ankle wasn't hurting. She looked down and examined it closely, testing the range of motion, and felt the whole thing twist easily. She hardly felt anything at all. Still, she didn't want to jump six feet down like he had in order to meet him. She examined the rooftop for an easier way and noticed a ladder nailed into the side of the building. She maneuvered herself down it.

Saint was sitting on the second ledge now. He touched the metal beneath him and said, "I didn't want to tell you this was here because I thought it would take the thrill away. I'm sorry I frightened you."

She looked out next to him. She didn't realize she was still out of breath until she started speaking again. "It's fine, just don't do that again."

Saint thought for a moment. Then he said, "I wouldn't have killed myself, you know." Naomi suddenly became acutely aware of the fact that the only thing keeping them here was the barbed wire, rising and curling so high into the air that even if Naomi had stood on Saint's shoulders and jumped off, her body would get tangled in the blades, pinning her and her bleeding parts up for all of Riverside to see.

She sat next to him. "Saint, why are we really here?"

Saint had never known anyone for this long who didn't know about his father, and he knew he would be giving that away. But he thought of Naomi out on the stage of the Riverside Performing Arts Theater, and the girl in front of him now—how different they were. Maybe this was another sort of jump he was to make. "My dad's sick. Like, really sick. He started coughing up blood yesterday."

Guiltily, she noticed she'd never thought of his father before. "I'm sorry to hear that. What's he sick with?"

Saint pronounced it as if he was spelling it out. "Chronic obstructive pulmonary disease." His voice darkened. "Basically, it means he'll die if he doesn't stop smoking. The blood means it's close."

"But he does it anyway. Smoke, I mean."

Saint smiled bitterly. "He doesn't care."

She blinked. "And your brother?"

Saint was looking past the barbed wire now. "He used to be too young to know what's going on, but now I think he definitely knows his dad's dying right in front of him. I'm the one who has to take care of them both. They need me."

She could see it happening right in front of her. Saint was sinking. "I couldn't jump off this rooftop even if I wanted to."

She wanted to ask him why his father refused to stop smoking or if Saint ever confronted him, but then she remembered how far she took things with ballet, and how she never confronted her own father about his infidelity. It was never that easy, she knew. "Why don't you ever talk about him?"

When Saint met Naomi's gaze, she noticed tears building in his eyes. She had never imagined she would see him crying. She hadn't thought he could. When they first met, even the second, third, fourth time, he was always the opposite of her. He had a hunger for life. He never seemed like the type of person who could produce tears. Saint answered, "I'm not sure. I try not to think about it, if I'm honest. Especially when I'm out here with you; I just want to leave all that at home. Find a little peace."

Naomi rested her head on his shoulder. A little peace, she thought. After a few beats she said, "Tell me about your mother."

Saint smiled. He pulled Naomi into him and began with his best memory of Miranda Owens. "She's the reason I started art. Well, kind of. She never really got it, but she would buy me supplies, and when we'd go on walks she'd challenge me to pick one thing, memorize it, and then draw it when I got home. The reason I draw and paint all the time is because of her. She didn't know it at the time, I don't think, but even then, she was making me." He told Naomi that she was lactose intolerant so she never bought him ice cream because she would get jealous. He said all her bedtime stories were the same but he liked it that way. Sully was different, though; he wanted a different story each night. Saint described the way he had to learn how to tie a head wrap closer to her final days, when she had lost all her hair in chemotherapy, and that even then she still tried her best to smile in spite of everything, especially around Sully. Saint explained all the things he wished he was for his family. More specifically, that he was older and wiser, with a good-paying job and no regrets and a lot less selfish. He told her how he often wondered if he was making his mom proud like she said he would. Naomi assured him he was. Proud and then some.

Then she asked, "And who do you wish you were for you? Who would *you* like to be?"

Saint chuckled. "I never really thought about that." They sat in silence. Naomi didn't want to push him any further in case imagining a reality he could never truly make real was a painful step he would rather not take, but she could tell he was still thinking. She waited for him. "I suppose I'd want to graduate high school. Maybe go to a college out of state. Move to a place close to the ocean, like California or something, start a family out there and die a really boring death."

Naomi took her head off his shoulder and looked at him. She smiled. "That doesn't sound like you at all."

The way he could still surprise her after all this time made him smile. "What do you mean?"

"I thought you'd move to like a big city and be a full-time artist. I could see you in New York, running a gallery." As soon as she said it, she remembered she wanted to move to New York. Then she wondered if the only reason she could see him there was because she would be there too.

Saint laughed. "Nah, I think I'd get tired of a big city like that after a while. Plus, I don't want to make art my job. I only paint and draw when I need to escape, and I think I want stuff like that to be just for me, you know?"

Naomi looked out at the barbed wire. She assured him his mother would love him if that was what he wanted to do too. She would love him anyway, just based off of the way he talked about her. Saint just turned to smile at her. Even if she was just saying it to make him feel better, he wanted her to say it over and over again.

"Tell me about Jessica."

Now it was Naomi's turn to grin. After flipping through their memories, she tutted her name. "Jessica, I think, was the only person who understood me. She was brave and loyal, but also carefree. She didn't really care what anyone thought of her. I wish I was more like that." She told Saint how they were the only Black people in their academy and how isolated that made them feel, but also how it brought them together. As she spoke, Naomi noticed Jessica was still working; Miranda too. Their deaths, the proximity of their graves, ultimately put her and Saint in the same memorial park, and now on the same rooftop. She supposed they were still looking out for them. "You're going to think this sounds crazy, but after she died, I saw her. That's what I meant at the park. She came back to me all the time. It was this evil, twisted version of her that kept repeating back to me all my insecurities."

"Like what?" Saint sounded as if he was treading cautiously.

"Once she told me I couldn't play the White Swan in the way she'd be able to. That I'd have to play the evil, jealous alternate—the Black Swan. She told me it was already in the name."

"Oh, that's messed up. Wasn't she Black?"

"Light skinned," was all Naomi had to say. Saint nodded. "But that was my own insecurities, you know? She didn't come back to haunt me, they did. That's why I was in the park that day to visit her. To apologize."

As they sat on top of the metallic roof, they both noticed they were resting on the physical manifestation of a second chance. Saint watched the bustle of Riverside happening beneath them through the gridded metal. "Do you think you've recovered fully from that?"

Naomi ignored her father and Prix and dinner next Sunday and said, "I think so. Have you?"

He said, "I think so."

The two of them looked out to see where the sky met the concrete. They stayed like that until it got dark.

CHAPTER NINETEEN

With Saint, Riverside used to seem so much smaller. So much more achievable. It was as though the city was a thing in the palm of his hand. Naomi thought, by the way he had held, thrown, and caught it, that it was a light thing. More than manageable. Now, in the silence of his barely operable 2002 Chevrolet Silverado on another Wednesday afternoon, she was starting to understand that just because it looked light didn't mean it actually was.

When Saint picked her up from outside Evergreen Memorial Park, he had told her that there was another alive and waiting place he wanted to take her to.

She had asked him, "How many of these places are there?"

He'd shrugged. At the time, she had just assumed that he didn't know and was making it up as he went along. That was a comforting idea. But the more she thought about it, the more she wondered if he might have just been keeping it from her. It was like him, she was coming to know, to keep secrets and make it look unintentional. Like what he did with his father and his brother and everything turning sour in his life. She looked across the console at him. He caught her glance and smiled brightly at her. She saw it for what it really was: a wall.

On their way through Riverside, Naomi realized she was becoming more familiar with these streets. She was unraveling him, and she liked that. As they drove, Naomi knew when they were close to Gold Bloom Plaza, and she knew that in its parking lot there was an ice-cream truck; on Fridays they had the most customers. Out closer to the Riverside Bridge was a bus station that took you out of town, and depending on what time you went you'd either get to an empty bus or be the last to line up and have to wait for another bus altogether. Like Saint, Riverside was becoming more familiar to her too.

The pickup truck slowed down outside of a low building with fading paint. The roof looked rotten from the inside out, and a banner spanning the outside read A PEOPLE UNSHACK-LED FROM THEIR PAST. It was beginning to catch dust and cobwebs. They turned into the lot. Saint sighed. "Welcome, Naomi, to the pristine Riverside African American Historical Society."

There were no sounds, not even the faintest hint of a breeze as they took in the underwhelming block of cement. Saint added, "Where Black history sits with the roaches, and spiders put their cobwebs over us."

Naomi looked out at it. "I didn't even know Riverside had this."

Saint exhaled. "Me either. I found it a few weeks ago. When you were telling me about the academy and Jessica yesterday, I knew I had to bring you here. It looks like the city is responsible for its upkeep, but, as you can see, they're not even doing that."

The building had potential; it was obvious. If perhaps the banner was replaced with a real sign and the building was painted in a color that didn't blend in with the overgrown bushes and plants on either side it could look brand-new. It was a two-story structure with little personality. They got out and walked up to it. "I think it used to be a museum of sorts for Black artifacts," Saint was telling her. They opened the unlocked door easily, and Saint attempted to flip on the lights but nothing happened. "But Riverside doesn't care much. I think I'm the only person who actually remembers this place."

Inside were unlit pedestals and horizontal display cases. From what they could tell by the bits of sunlight that entered the building through the few windows, various pieces of artwork hung on the walls, and sculptures stood tall. Naomi stepped farther inside the room. "Where did all this stuff come from?"

Saint pointed to a low display case. "Well, the signs on some of these say they're tools slaves used that got lost over time and were only recovered in the last few decades. There are others that are more modern, too, like the late 1900s."

Naomi thought back to what Mrs. Norris had taught her in her history class. "I thought Riverside didn't have any slaves."

"Everywhere in this country had slaves," Saint said. "Maybe no plantations, but there were always slaves. Or ex-slaves, or descendants of slaves. It doesn't matter. We were everywhere. They just either pushed us out or convinced us that there was some imaginary line that separates one side of the country from the other."

Naomi couldn't believe she hadn't known that. "Did you learn that in high school?"

Saint laughed. He told her simply that they didn't teach this in high schools either. His father was the one who had told him years ago. Now he was telling her.

Naomi walked up to a vivid painting of dark-skinned women with head wraps catching water in buckets from a low pipe in the ground, while a group of children ran in the background. They were all smiling. In the bottom right of the painting was a signature: Keyona Williams. Below that, the plaque read COMING HOME, and it was dated 2007. "So, we were here all along?" She thought she was talking about the building but her mind wandered. Naomi wondered if all her old dance instructors knew a place like this existed. That there was a building, not far from their studios, where Black art lived. What would their words be in the face of a space where there was a Black person everywhere they turned to ruin their perfect rehearsal lineup?

Saint turned around in the building. "One day I'll get this place up and running again. Get the lights on. Get more artwork. It'll have a second grand opening, and I personally will make sure Riverside pays its dues." Saint was still looking across the room when Naomi turned to face him. She understood now that spray-painting wasn't rebellion for him, it was resistance. It was deliberate. He wanted to resist the world, this town, everything that stood in his way. And he was doing it in the only language he knew.

"All right," roared Saint. "Let's make our own art, shall we?" He dropped his bag to the floor and took out the cans of spray paint followed by huge sheets of white cartridge paper.

He moved to the nearest empty wall. He shook his paint can.

Naomi held up her hands. "What are you doing?"

Saint pointed to the bag, and another roll of white cartridge paper sticking out of it. "Aren't you going to start?"

"Saint, are we even allowed to do that?"

He looked around. "Who's going to stop us?" He stepped forward. "Look, when you said you felt like you didn't belong, I felt that. But look around, Naomi. We do belong. We've always belonged here; we just didn't know it. This is our space. We own it. It's one of the few things we have in this white town. Adding to it means keeping our legacy going."

She stared at the painting in front of her. All the smiling women. *Legacy*. He said that word a lot.

His voice echoed throughout the building. "This is us. I am Black art. You are Black art. We are that way without even trying. You want to know why? Because they've tried to wipe us out so many times and still we don't give up. Isn't there something artful in that?"

She could feel him even from the distance she stood. Naomi told him, "Show me."

Saint spread out four pieces of cartridge paper on the ground and placed them next to each other to make a larger piece. He began with wide arcs. He reached into his bag and took out a stencil. He switched out the nozzle, changed colors, and continued to work like that for the next few minutes. Naomi watched. At first she couldn't make out exactly what he was creating, but then she could see that there were eyes forming and a full mouth. Other facial features were slowly added. And all throughout she thought it was of a woman she did not know, up until the end when Saint finally stood up and stepped aside. The painting was of her.

"See? Art."

In the painting, Naomi's hair was much bigger. It was a full afro that took up most of the paper because of how alive and thick it was. And she was smiling happily too, midlaugh, at whoever was on the other side of the cartridge paper. In that moment, Naomi realized that other person would definitely have been Saint Owens.

The paintings Saint had done on the belly of the Riverside Bridge didn't compare to this. Those were only sketches; in fact, most of them were sentences. This was the opposite. It looked as though it really did deserve to be hung up in here. "This is incredible."

He looked up at her like it was obvious all along. "That's you."

She tried not to look directly at him. "No, but I mean the way you painted me. This is really good, Saint." She understood what he meant now when he called both of them art. She supposed he was right and they were artful without ever trying to be, but she wondered if he realized that he was the artist and that was so much more impressive. "I know you said you've been doing this for a while but I can't believe you got me that well. It looks just like me."

Of course, he didn't tell her that he'd been practicing drawing her for weeks now. That he had sketched her forehead and traced the outline of her lips so often that by now he was sure every woman he drew would be some version of her. He stood up and retrieved the other roll of paper and handed it to her. She looked at it and back at him. He reminded her, "It's not a competition."

It was the way he said it that reminded Naomi that she wasn't in the Riverside Dance Academy where people only said things like that to make themselves feel better. He was saying it, and he meant it. She took the paper from him and unrolled it next to his. Saint told her, "It can be whatever you want it to be." She thought for a moment about what she wanted to add here the most. She couldn't spray-paint something beautiful like Saint but she still wanted to add something. She didn't want it to be words either. There were no other words here. The only other art form she knew was ballet but even that was lost to her now. Then she remembered what Saint had said.

Naomi shook the spray paint can and fired it onto her own palm, coating her skin with a layer of fresh black paint. Then she pressed her hand against the white cartridge paper. Her lone handprint dried on the paper. Then she decided to keep doing it, overlapping fingers and palms with previously made stains until the paper was more black than white. When she was finished and Saint looked at her, she told him, "If we are art anyway, I want to be the kind of art that leaves a mark."

She held it up to the light coming in from one of the windows. Her handprints made shapes, Naomi realized as she inspected it. She was still becoming.

"I love it," Saint told her. He took the painting from her and took a stapler out of his backpack. He punched her artwork into the wall, then his next to it, and said, "This might just be my favorite place we've been yet." Which was like saying this was much better than any graffiti on any random wall in the city; here they didn't have to make a legacy from scratch but rather add to it.

But the pair had no idea that even despite the lack of

funding at the Riverside African American Historical Society, the building's silent alarm was still functioning. All over Riverside they had been leaving lawless trails of themselves on public and private property alike. Now they were breaking and entering too. One city could not take this much upending of its laws, and leaving a piece of artwork depicting Naomi's face so accurately in a town where she had been performing since she was a little girl was exactly what the men in power needed to do something about it. When the police officer saw the painting of her later that evening, he recognized Naomi immediately, and it was only a matter of time until he could recall from where exactly.

CHAPTER TWENTY

Today, Saint admitted that he didn't know any more alive and waiting places. They were out there somewhere but he was just one person, and this was Riverside. All the alive and waiting places were probably hiding miles and miles apart, etched behind storefronts or around the corner from little homes. So they decided that they would keep on driving until something stood out.

They were speeding past Mission Hill Hotel when Saint gagged at the high buildings and expensive cars driving in and out of the parking lot. He said to Naomi, "They have no idea what's really going on in Riverside. None. Or maybe they do, but they just don't care. Either way, it's evil for them to be living like that when there are still so many people out here on the street. Isn't that insane? What are they gonna do with all that money, anyway? They could feed my entire neighborhood, probably."

Naomi nodded. She omitted the fact that she herself had

stayed at the Mission Hill Hotel. That her father had attended dentistry conferences there, and sometimes they would pay for the entire family to stay at the all-inclusive hotel for a few days. She didn't tell Saint that inside the building all the counters were marble and the ceiling was so high you could hardly make out the intricate paintings decorating it. She avoided letting him know that they served you mimosas upon entry, and the rooms were so big you could fit a family in them, though they were designed for just one person. She didn't tell him any of this, not because she was afraid that he would get angry, but because she wasn't sure at whom his anger would be directed.

If she told him how much her pointe shoes cost and how many pairs she went through per month, would he look at her differently? After she realized that she was choosing not to go to university while he never had that option in the first place, and she had a personal physiotherapist while he was avoiding doctor fees, Naomi knew that they were different in ways she hadn't considered before. Maybe if she never mentioned it, they could keep being similar. The truth seemed so much easier to keep out of their safe little space in the old Chevrolet Silverado.

"Oh, this is it," Saint told her. "You'll like this spot."

Naomi followed his gaze out to the massive green space extending behind the sidewalk. Elizabeth Park wasn't as empty as all the other places they had been together. There were kids running in circles, kicking a ball despite there being no goalposts through which to score. People were making laps around the circumference of the park, too, earphones plugged in as they went.

Saint pulled up to the park's entrance. Naomi wasn't sure people were supposed to be parking here, but there was no sign indicating otherwise, so the cars lined up, and Saint rolled the Chevrolet in behind them. She imagined that a street just like this near the Riverside Performing Arts Theater or even in Downtown Riverside would have a sign stating parking times and a parking meter to charge people for their time there. Here, no one seemed too worried about how much time they had left, and the city was allowing them everything, all her amenities, for free. Bringing the car to a complete stop, Saint asked her, "What do you think?"

Naomi looked out her window at everyone she saw and none of them looked back. Preoccupied with eating food around a wooden picnic table or chasing their friends through the scattered trees, they didn't have the time to. The space didn't show them a purpling sky or a blinding sun; it held life in other ways. "It's beautiful here."

Saint said, "I come here all the time to think. This park is always the same. The same people doing the same thing at the same time of day, every week." The routine reminded Naomi of the Riverside Dance Academy. "It's nice," he finished.

They got out and Saint took her to his bench near one of the larger English oak trees. In the shade he sat on the bench, but Naomi thought twice and planted herself on the ground in her jeans. The buildings surrounding the park had a different, older architecture. They didn't reach very high to scrape the skies like the buildings downtown or the Riverside library. These were brick, and stout. "It doesn't even feel like Riverside out here."

"We're on the edge," Saint informed her. "Maybe about a mile that way is Clearwater."

Naomi gave him a quizzical look. "Do you live near here?"

He didn't answer right away. He was watching the boys play football on the grass. He nodded. "Not very far."

An elderly man rocked up to them. His salt-and-pepper beard was full and straggly, and his tattered clothing was so dirty and layered that he must have been hot in this weather. Naomi said, "Sorry, we don't have any change."

Mr. Blythe blinked at her. He turned to Saint. "Some company you got here."

Saint laughed. "I mean, can you blame her? Look at the way you're dressed, Blythe!"

The both of them laughed. Naomi slapped a hand over her mouth. "Oh my god, I am so sorry. I had no idea. I thought—"

The man smiled. "It's okay, kid. Frankly, you thought right. But I usually ask for change at the end of our conversations." He winked.

Saint reached into his pocket for two quarters and handed them to the man. "She's still a little new. Give her some time, she'll catch on soon enough."

The man took the quarters before he said anything else. When they were pocketed and secure, he said thank you a few times in between Saint telling him to stop acting so humble in front of his friend.

Saint fanned all the gratitude away like it was a pesky fly. "How's the sky looking today, Blythe?"

The man's head fell all the way back. He peered into the deep blue above them. "Closer," he said. "And faster. One day she'll come crashing down so fast none of us are gonna know what to do. On the day we finally meet her, we'll realize how vicious she truly is." All the color had drained from the man's face. The veins in his eyes were bright red and his hand was shaking.

Looking back and forth between them, Naomi asked, "When's that day?" She could tell Saint was trying to pull responses out of him too.

Blythe's eyes found her again, his head coming back down. He smiled. "Wouldn't you like to know? But that's the thing about her. She's unpredictable. She cares about herself and herself only."

Saint chuckled. Naomi said, "She sounds selfish."

"Oh, I wish I was that selfish. Do whatever I want and not give a damn about what other people think. That's the dream, little miss. Don't you want that?"

Naomi hummed to herself. She didn't know how to say no to that. She didn't want that at all. She wanted to care about the people around her and the way she affected them, even if that made her shrink herself in certain ways. She'd been selfish before, and she didn't like it. Blythe was still confident, though. He looked at her like a magician who was sure he had your card. Naomi settled on not saying anything at all.

Saint said, "I want that."

Naomi tuned to him. "See?" Blythe chirped. "Everyone wants to be more selfish. No shame in it."

Saint shrugged under Naomi's glance. He had already given so much of himself for so long. He deserved this. Saint got off the bench and sat next to her. "Why are you looking at me like that?"

She said to him, "Is that what you really want?"

"You already know what I want." Saint fell back onto the grass and watched the clouds float across the blue expanse.

Blythe said, "You better learn to be a little more selfish, little girl. More people are than you think." Naomi wanted to tell him that the people who mattered the most to you shouldn't be. She looked at Saint for a moment, his eyes cast skyward, then back to Blythe, but the man's attention had clicked onto something else. He was already rocking away, making his way toward a family sitting under another tree who appeared to be having a picnic, his palm open and outstretched.

"He's a character," Naomi commented.

"And he's always like that too."

She asked, "Are you guys like friends or . . . ?"

Saint laughed. "Something like that. After my mom died, I came here a lot. Mr. Blythe lives here in the park and so every time I was here, we'd see each other. One day he asked me if I ever looked up and noticed the sky was falling. Apparently, he asks everyone that question, but I was the only one stupid enough to say yes as a joke. And here we are."

Before she could ask a follow-up question he asked her, "What about you, Naomi Morgan? Have you ever looked up and noticed the sky was falling? Answer wisely." Naomi joined Saint flat on the grass. She brought her hands into her chest.

He was chuckling but she was still remembering how he had said he wanted to be more selfish. "They say if the sun burns out and the Earth falls out of space, we'll be dead before we even realize anything's going on."

Saint was watching the sky through the leaves now. "How do we fall out of space?"

Naomi shrugged. "Maybe we'll crash into another planet in another galaxy somewhere? Or maybe the drop is endless."

"No, you want to know what I think will take us out? A slow disaster first, like starvation or global warming. Definitely global warming."

"Can't believe I'm about to say this, but I'd prefer the sky falling to that." Before Saint got a chance to ask, she answered, "Because then there's no one to leave behind. I mean, no one to endure your funeral or learn to move on. Everyone just goes the same way at the same time, and there's no picking up the pieces. It's all over."

"Peaceful," the boy commented, chuckling. There was something about the way he didn't move that told her he was still thinking about it.

A football skidded by them in the grass. Naomi watched it go by followed by a group of young boys racing after it. "What if we're the ones who kill ourselves?" he asked.

"What do you mean?"

"What if we're the ones to end it all?" Saint watched the boys catch, juggle, and kick the ball away again. "It doesn't have to be a natural disaster. What if we go up in flames because of war? Or another disease we create?"

"Well then"—Naomi propped herself on her elbows—"who would be to blame?"

Saint sat up. "No one. Everyone?"

She watched him for a moment. "Well, if we can make the choice to end it, we can make the choice to not end it."

He narrowed her eyes. "What if it's not that easy? Who would even make that choice?"

"No one. Everyone?" she repeated. "As long as it's together."

Saint began plucking out the grass. "And if there is no choice? What then?"

"Then I'd hope we at least have the sense to go quickly. Put out the sun on our own, or something."

When she said that Naomi realized it wasn't long ago that they had met in a field just like this one. But instead of graves now there were living people running around and laughing. She wondered if he noticed this too. The difference between the things they were surrounded by back then and now. She was about to ask Saint if this was a deliberate choice he had made when she saw him with his phone to his ear. A concerned expression clouded his face. She swallowed the words. Then she watched his eyes go wide and his jaw slack.

She grabbed his shoulder. "What's wrong?"

Saint was already standing up. "Yes, yes, okay, stay there. Don't call an ambulance. I'll be there in a few minutes. Keep trying to wake him up."

As she watched him hang the phone up, Naomi stood. "Saint! What's going on?"

"It's my dad." Time stopped. "He's not moving."

Saint put his phone back into his pocket and cast a glance to the spot in the grass where they had just been lying. Then his gaze shifted to the park bench. The speed at which his chest was expanding and deflating was picking up. Naomi reached out and squeezed his hand. When he looked at her, she was urgently looking back. Saint squeezed Naomi's hand in return and they took off running out of the park.

They dashed back onto the sidewalk and skidded to the Chevrolet, dirt lifting up to make way. After pulling open the truck doors and jumping in, Saint pushed the key into the ignition and gave it a turn. When it sputtered in fatigue he tried again. In between the futile sounds of the engine and his begging, "*Please, please, please,*" Naomi wanted to tell him it would be okay. That he should try to stay calm and breathe, but the words were lodged in her throat.

Saint was slamming his fist against the steering wheel now. On his fifth try, the Silverado finally came to life. He gripped the wheel tightly and shifted the gear into Reverse. Naomi watched Saint frantically maneuver through the Riverside evening traffic and tried to be the sturdier friend. "This can't be happening. This can't be happening. This can't be happening," he was muttering.

She didn't know what to say to him except that she really hoped his father would be okay. She couldn't imagine losing both parents. Saint and his little brother would be orphans if their dad passed. Only a few days ago Saint had told her that his father was coughing up blood. She knew that could not be a good sign, and he had to have known it too. She reached across the console and put her hand on his forearm.

He shut his eyes for a moment when he felt her touch.

The drive to Saint's house was shorter than she expected it to be. It dawned on Naomi that when Saint had told her he didn't live far away, he'd meant it. These buildings comprised his community. This was his home. They jumped out of the car and ran up the doorstep. Saint practically busted the door open with his shoulder. Naomi saw his little brother standing in the hallway, crying. He croaked, "I—I didn't do anything. I just heard a crash and he was just lying there and I—"

Saint dashed right by him. Naomi's chest heaved. She didn't move off as quickly. Instead, she watched the boy in the hallway fight to hold back his tears. He didn't know her, but he was looking up at her as if he was begging her for mercy.

Naomi fell to her knees and pulled him in. She gave him the tightest embrace she could, and she immediately felt him give way into her, like a wet, eager landslide.

"I don't want him to die," he whispered.

"He won't. He won't. He won't."

Saint's voice came loudly through the house. "William! Come help me get him in the car." The boy separated from Naomi and wiped his tears. In a split second, she saw the Saint in him—the way he was one thing this moment and something else the next. He looked changed, older. The boy ran off to help his big brother, and Naomi pushed herself off the ground so she could follow him. Looking around now, she realized the home was crammed. There were dishes in the sink and a litter of books across the living room couch. Even the air was humid and thick.

When she got to the bedroom door she had seen the boys sprint through, Naomi saw them lifting their father. There were bedsheets on the floor. Broken glass in a corner. A bin filled with paper towels turned over and spilling out its contents.

The boys heaved up the man who looked more like their grandfather. She went to help them but Saint stopped her. "It's okay, we got this." Immediately, Naomi knew what was coded under his refusal of her help. She glanced down at her ankle brace.

"I'm okay," she told him. "It doesn't even hurt anymore." She was telling the truth. She didn't even need the crutches anymore. She usually left at least one of them at home these days.

The pair of brothers got to moving, gripping the parts of the man that that they could manage. "Naomi, please," Saint interrupted, shuffling out of the room holding his father's life-less torso. "Get the door. And get the car running. The keys are on the counter."

She spun. Naomi sped outside, grabbing the car keys on her way. The driver's door was easy. It opened on the first pull of her wrist. But as she got in the truck and put herself in the front seat, her hand was shaking. She gripped the small metal key as hard as she could and pushed it into the ignition. Tears were trying to escape from her eyes. She held the steering wheel to steady herself. Then she turned the key. The truck came alive. Saint and Sully practically ran out of the house a few seconds later. Naomi reached behind her and unlocked the backseat door, pushing it open so by the time they made it across the street, they only had to heave the man in. Sully jumped in next and Saint had run to the front seat by the time Naomi slid into the passenger. Naomi clicked on her seat belt. Saint locked all the doors and clenched his teeth. With a brief exhale he shot them down the road.

The radio wasn't playing on their way to the hospital, even though it had played everywhere Saint and Naomi had gone before this. This time the track list was the sound of Sully cry-ing in the backseat. His whimpers were soft and painful in the confined space.

Saint looked at his brother in the rearview mirror. "Hey, hey, everything's going to be okay, okay?"

Naomi turned around to look at him. His father's head was lolling in his lap, drool coming out his empty mouth, and the boy was sitting so still. It was as if he was afraid moving even an inch would kill his dad.

Naomi turned around. Tears came to her eyes. "Saint."

"Hey, Sully? Sully? Is he breathing? Check if he's breathing."

Saint used the rearview mirror to watch his little brother. He nodded at him. "You got this."

Sully put his ear close to his father's nose and mouth. Then his ear to the limp man's chest. "He's breathing."

"Good. Now be strong for Dad, okay? We're going to get through this. He won't die on us. Not if we help him by being strong too."

Naomi glanced at Saint and knew that not even he believed what he was saying.

At the hospital Saint told Sully and Naomi to stay in the car while he ran in. A few minutes later, a group of nurses rushed to them with a stretcher. They put the man on it and wheeled him inside the building. Naomi tried to keep up with the brothers and the nurses who were peppering the two boys with questions, but she was too far behind with her brace. She still couldn't walk that quickly yet.

Then they dipped into a room, and a nurse stopped her. "I'm sorry, are you family?"

Naomi exhaled. She looked at Saint and Sully. "No, but I was there."

"I'm sorry, ma'am, you're going to have to wait in the waiting room."

She paused. Saint found her at the door. He said to her, "It's fine, Naomi. I'll be right out."

She stopped in her tracks. He pulled her into his arms. "Thank you," he whispered.

She put her face into his shoulder. "I'm here for you no matter what happens. I'll be waiting for you."

When he pulled away, he nodded. Saint grabbed her face

and smacked his lips on her forehead before spinning away and ducking into the room. The door shut.

Naomi finally let the air out of her lungs and walked back where she came from in an effort to find the waiting room. The whole place smelled more like death and sickness than it did alcohol or drugs. Naomi imagined what that meant for the patients here. She asked a nearby nurse where she could find the waiting room and continued in the direction she was pointed in. Arriving there, Naomi took a seat. She didn't want to give her mind the chance to start predicting outcomes, and there was nothing here to keep her occupied either. Eventually, she decided on taking out her phone and earphones and playing an album that could take her away. She started by searching for the song she and Saint had screamed in the car that day. She typed in the only line she knew and hit Play on the first result.

Naomi stayed like that for around an hour, and silenced her notifications so the song would take her away uninterrupted. She had to restart the album twice but that was okay with her. And when there was no one else in this waiting room she eventually began singing along to it:

Nothing ever stays the same . . .

Saint came in from the hallway and saw Naomi lying across three chairs pulled together. He walked over. He gently shook her awake and Naomi's eyes flew open. She took out her earphones. "Is he going to be okay?"

Saint took the seat next to hers, slumping all the way down. "They think so, yeah. He should be waking up soon."

Naomi glanced at him. It didn't look like he planned to get up. She thought of all the reasons Saint might not want to be sitting next to his father when he woke up. She looked around in the empty waiting room. "Where's Sully?"

"Vending machine," Saint whispered. His eyes were on the polished hospital floor and his dark figure mirrored on the reflective tiles was distorted and obscure. He watched himself for a few more moments.

He nodded. "Naomi, he wasn't moving. He looked like he was already—"

She cut him off. "But he's not." She grabbed his hand and squeezed it as tightly as she could. She reminded him, "But he's not."

He looked at her. "But for how long?"

Maybe she was right. In a few minutes Saint's father would open his eyes, and he'd smile up at everyone, and the nurses would discharge him and tomorrow all of this would feel like a bad dream. But what about the next time when they weren't so lucky?

"Then we'll face that day if it ever comes," she answered.

He didn't answer right away. Saint put his face into his hands. "What time is it?" he mumbled. Naomi took her phone out of her pocket to check and told him it was seven o'clock. Then she took her phone off of Do Not Disturb to check what she'd missed and the thing began to erupt in her hand. The first was a text from her mother followed by ten more asking where she was and if she knew what time it was. "Shit," she breathed. "I have to go home."

Saint said, "I'll drive you back."

She looked up at him. There was no way she could ask that of him. "Are you sure?"

"Please," he begged. "I need to move. I need to get out of here." He stood up. "I'll take you."

She wasn't about to refuse him anything. They in silence waited for Sully to return. When the boy came around the corner with an open bag of M&M's, he looked back and forth between Naomi and Saint. Before he could ask what was happening or where they were going, Saint simply told him to follow.

The moon rose over them in the Silverado, and Naomi watched the boy sitting across from her. It felt as though there was no language to accurately communicate all that had happened tonight. She knew he was thinking the same thing.

Even though they were both familiar with death, she didn't want his mind to go there, so she told Saint, "He'll get through this."

Saint glanced at Sully in the rearview mirror. He glanced back at her. "I know."

And Naomi knew he was lying again. They both were. It was pointless.

As they drove deeper into Riverside, Saint was taking notice of the way the brand of cars changed and how the grass was cut indicated that they were on a different side of the city now. These streets were completely peaceful, with no one aimlessly walking about or selling things they shouldn't to put food on the table. Out here, sprinklers were going off to keep grass green.

Naomi said, "I'm sorry."

He smiled but there were tears in his eyes now too. "Stop apologizing."

"I'm not apologizing," she said. "I'm letting you know I'm here for you—both of you."

Sully chirped, "Wait a minute! Now I recognize you!" He was standing in the truck, popping his head between the two front seats. "You're the ballerina! The Swan Princess!"

Naomi turned and found his starry gaze. The words wouldn't leave her at first. Saint flinched in his seat. "Well, technically I'm not a ballerina just yet. That takes a lot more practice, but Swan Princess?"

"Sully, sit back down!" Saint reprimanded his brother.

She turned to Saint. "Swan Princess? Like the White Swan?"

Saint's eyes were trained on the road. "Please, don't ask."

Naomi chuckled.

All of a sudden, the Silverado felt safe again. They were recovering. Saint's father was all right and they had less to worry about. Tomorrow, Naomi imagined things could start returning to normal. When she pointed out her house, and Saint pulled into the driveway, she told him, "No, now I have to know."

Saint let out a breath. He shut off the lights and switched the engine off. Glancing into his rearview mirror, he made eye contact with his younger brother. "Nice going."

Sully shrugged. "My bad."

In the dark, Saint turned to Naomi and cleared his throat. He began, "You see, when we met that time at the theater—"

"Naomi!"

They spun. Aja Morgan was out on the porch, the front

door open wide behind her, and all its light shooting out onto the lawn. "Naomi!"

Naomi cursed under her breath then pushed open the car door and hopped out. Saint was next, jogging around the old Chevrolet. "Hey, Mrs. Morgan! I'm sorry about Naomi coming home late, it was my fault. We lost track of time, and—"

"Naomi, where the hell have you been?!" Her mom's arms were straight at her sides, as if they were the only things keeping her inside her body. "And who the hell is this?!"

The girl walked quickly up to her mother, and when she was close enough to whisper, she said to her, "He's a friend, Mom."

Her mother looked at the boy confusedly. "What friend?!" She turned to her daughter again. "Is this who you've been going out with when you said you were going to the academy?"

Naomi stopped.

"Yes, we know. And do you have any idea what time it is?!"

"Please, it's my fault, really," Saint said hurriedly. "I'm sorry I kept your daughter out so late, Mrs. Morgan."

She narrowed her eyes at him. His sweat-soaked shirt and tired eyes. "Naomi, go inside," she seethed.

"Mom, please let me explain—"

"Naomi!"

Naomi grabbed her mother's hand but Aja broke from her grip. She stepped around her daughter and went straight for Saint. She glared at the boy. "Stay away from my daughter."

"I'm sorry I was just trying to—"

Her eyes narrowed. "If you know what's good for you you'll leave. Right now."

Saint stepped back.

"Saint," Naomi said. She was trying to catch his eyes with hers. So she could say she was sorry, and her mother was overreacting, and she would explain what they had just gone through, but the boy was deadlocked in Aja's fiery stare. He nodded soberly.

"Sorry again for the trouble." Saint packed himself up and turned away, heading back to the truck wordlessly. He would be either going home to a house void of anyone to lean on, or a hospital where everything would remind him that tonight his father had almost died. And he couldn't be weak in the face of either because he had a nine-year-old brother in the backseat who needed him.

"Mom! Why would you do that?!"

"Don't you ever scream at me! You've been lying to me for weeks!" Naomi stared at her speechlessly. "Get inside right now!"

By now, Saint's Chevrolet had started and he was already reversing out of their driveway, his headlights meeting them on the lawn.

"Now, Naomi!"

She bit her tongue until blood dripped out. She could already hear Saint's car going off into the distance now, farther and farther away from her. She huffed inside, kicked off her shoes, and balled her fists. She'd have to think of a new lie now. A stronger one. She might need Aspen's help for it. All she knew was that she just needed to see Saint again so she could explain and apologize. Her mother came in behind her. Naomi turned to glare at her.

Aja slammed the door shut and watched her daughter, daring her to say something out of order again. But Ethan called Naomi's name from the living room. "Naomi, come in here."

Aja motioned for her to get going. Naomi kept her teeth tight on her tongue and obeyed, for now. In the living room, her father was sitting on the couch with his elbows on his knees. Valentino Beaumont was sitting next to him. Naomi stopped in the doorway. Strangely, Aja's wish to have family dinner this Sunday came back to Naomi's mind. That seemed so small now. So unlikely to happen. It really felt as though that was not a thing this family did anymore.

"Naomi, where have you been?" She wanted to laugh. The audacity her father had to be confronting her about lying about her whereabouts was comical. Ethan said, "Naomi, the police and Valentino came to see us today."

"What?"

Aja repeated, "The police came to our house! Looking for you!"

As much as she didn't want to, Naomi had to look her father in the eye instead of her mother. He was always the more lenient one. The one she could rely on to speak in her favor. But the thought of Saint unable to look at either of his parents tonight, much less have the luxury of choosing, disoriented her for a moment.

Ethan continued, "The police say they have a large painting of you linking you to a series of crimes in Riverside. Vandalism? Breaking and entering? We thought there was no way. It wasn't possible for you to have done any of this because you were at the academy." Naomi glanced at Valentino sitting on the opposite end of the couch. She knew where this was heading. "But that's when Valentino told us what he told the police when they contacted him today. He hasn't seen you in weeks!"

Aja came into the living room and stood next to her husband. "I hope you know what this means, young lady."

Naomi's chest began to tighten. She could feel something dark and malicious bubbling up inside of her.

"You're grounded. And this time you really won't be going anywhere except the academy. And you will dance!"

"But my ankle!"

Aja Morgan was a syllable ahead of her. "Your ankle nothing!" she exploded.

Valentino stood up now. "Look, Naomi, I don't know why you haven't been to the academy when you said you would, but after the police came to the theater I volunteered to bring them here so your parents and I could testify to your character and talent. With that being said, I think we should talk about you coming back. For real this time."

Naomi huffed. They still didn't get it.

A small smile started on Valentino's face. "And I have some good news. Naomi, the School of American Ballet is interested in you. They want to see you dance at Grand Prix."

"What?"

"They saw your application and were impressed with all the first positions and medals you've received. They think you're a true top contender." Naomi glanced at her mother. "Your ankle is only sprained. I've worked with that before. If we take it slow I can get you back on your feet in time for Prix. We still have a little over a month."

Naomi shook her head. She looked at all of them. She still stood a chance?

Saint was so far gone now that she couldn't hear the rusted engine of his Chevrolet Silverado. Instead, she was hearing pointe shoes and pianos. The sound of theater lights clicking on so brightly they burned.

CHAPTER TWENTY-ONE

Naomi stirred under her sheets and forced her eyes open against the blazing brightness of the sun. It was sitting in its lush sea of blue, unmoving and unchanged. She'd spent all of last night trying to call Saint but he never picked up. The hardest part was not knowing exactly why. Was it because her mom had run him off the lawn as if he was the worst type of stray animal one could find (the kind that got attached immediately after you fed it once), or was the reason more sinister? When he made it back to the hospital, did his father refuse to open his eyes ever again? Being left in the dark was just as awful as it sounded. Shadows looked just as evil as the things creating them.

Her bedroom door opened.

When Aja saw Naomi was awake, she sang, "Good morning," and came in to sit next to her. Naomi looked away. She could smell something like pancakes and eggs following her mother, but she refused to give her the satisfaction of looking.

She hoped her grumbling stomach wouldn't betray her. "I know you're mad at me right now, but this is for your own good, Naomi. One day you'll realize that," Aja said, setting a plate on her night table. She stood up and opened Naomi's curtains all the way. The ball of light screamed in laughter. "We're going to see Dr. Gonzales today."

Aja tuned around, smiling. Naomi didn't respond. Dr. Gonzales and whatever she had to say didn't seem nearly as important as it had before she'd watched two sons struggle to carry the lifeless body of their father out of their small home. Despite the flashes of her competing in the Youth America Grand Prix. Extending herself across a stage over music. Arriving in New York.

Naomi squirmed. Aja came close enough to make out the dry cracks in Naomi's bottom lip. "Did you hear me?" she said. "We're going to work to get you back on your feet, Naomi. It's not over for you." She wasn't even mentioning him. She didn't care. "Naomi, if this is about your friend, he wasn't a good influence. Think about it, he had the police knocking at our door. People like him don't deserve to be in our lives. I'm sure he'll be fine. But right now, you need to focus on ballet. Remember what we said about how important this was?"

People like him?

Naomi wished it was the bone, not the ligaments, in her ankle that had shattered. "Naomi, please."

The overhead fan continued to spin, and tears began to form in the edges of her eyes. Although she was denying her mother a direct look, Naomi was watching her in her periphery. They were still noticing each other. Naomi's eyes found the orchids Aspen had given her weeks ago. They were wilting, and Naomi remembered that she hadn't watered them once.

Suddenly, Aja's lips set. She walked back over to Naomi's bed, took a fistful of the fluffy purple blanket, and pulled. "Get up," she demanded. "Get up right now."

Naomi grabbed for the blanket but its end was already out of reach, thrown far off the bed. Aja dragged and dragged until all of it was on the floor. Naomi didn't attempt to catch it anymore. She was still in yesterday's clothes, motionless and exposed. Aja's jaw dropped, and she looked at her daughter lying there, helpless—for the second time this summer.

Aja closed her mouth and gritted her teeth. Naomi looked back at her mother with rebellion in her eyes. Spite.

This time, Aja's hands moved a lot swifter, and her voice raised as if it was spilling out of a bubbling-over pot. "Get up!" Her hands latched onto all the sheets and pillows that she could reach and she pulled them all away. Naomi scrambled after her, but they were all flying before she could grab them. Frustration made Naomi's bottom lip tremble, but when everything had been tossed on the floor, and there was nothing left to fight over, they were only left with each other. Aja grabbed Naomi's arm. Their eyes caught one another. Then, they both pulled.

As everything came to a peak, it was self-evident that Naomi doing ballet was not only about her or the ballet for Aja Morgan. In large, it had to do with Aja herself. Because she had been her daughter's support system for so many years, and she had invested almost as much time and energy into ballet as Naomi had; somewhere along those years of sitting quietly in the living room sewing and dyeing Naomi's costumes, ballet had become her dream too. She too had dreamed of the New

York City Ballet and driving there with the windows down.

"Get up! Get up! Get up!" her mother screamed, planting her feet on the floorboards and fighting with all her strength. The pair of them pulled with every ounce of anything they could muster until it was a war between fits of shouting and frantic kicking. When their strengths finally matched, Aja started doing heavier tugs one by one. Naomi struggled and kicked, and she thought another tsunami was about to rush out of her eyes, but it wasn't. This time, it was a thunderstorm.

The thunder rolled when her throat opened. "No!" she screamed. Perhaps the loudest word ever uttered in the Morgan home.

And the lightning came afterward when her palm cut right across her mother's face.

Then the rain began; it poured from her eyes.

Struck silent, Aja stared. Her eyes froze over as she exhaled a slither of some incoherent word. Then her hand came next. And harder.

Naomi's head spun with its force, and the impact rang in her ears like church bells. They were both breathing heavily. Naomi gave way first, crumbling onto the mattress. The bed was naked now. It felt as though she was trying to let out of her something that had already made itself at home and refused to leave. Naomi writhed in tears.

She wasn't sure exactly when her mother left her, but there was an unmistakable moment when she felt loneliness reenter her room. She almost called after her. She wanted to ask Aja if she could feed her again, like she had weeks ago. She wanted her to return and pull Naomi into her lap, rock her, slice her pancakes for her.

Aja didn't see her daughter again until Naomi got in the car next to her later that afternoon. For Naomi, walking down the stairs and out the door was a lot easier than she'd expected. She imagined that her fight with her mother had startled her body awake, or perhaps it was the very act of leaving the Morgan house that she gravitated toward. In her heart, she knew which of the two was right.

Neither of them said anything. Naomi wondered if her mother wanted to apologize as much as she did right now. Naomi looked out the window and when Aja clicked on the air-conditioning and they drove off in silence, Naomi found herself missing the way cool air didn't work in Saint's Chevrolet and they had to keep the windows down in order to not swelter in the summer heat.

In contrast to everything Naomi felt, Dr. Gonzales ultimately said that Naomi was fine. It was time to take the ankle brace off. She would be strong enough to go back to the Riverside Dance Academy and compete in the Youth America Grand Prix, just nothing too excessive. She said it as a congratulations, and Aja was practically cheering, but Naomi couldn't figure out what there was to celebrate. It felt absurd. She slumped lower on the stiff physio table when the doctor started talking about her diet and a two-week–long, in-house recovery regimen they'd need to begin. Dr. Gonzales unstrapped Naomi's brace. For the rest of the visit, Naomi watched the ceiling.

CHAPTER TWENTY-TWO

On the first day of her recovery regimen, Naomi decided she would start watching one of the television series Saint had once told her could take your mind off anything. Today, she needed that. She needed to keep her thoughts from drifting back to what had happened two nights before, and she needed Saint to be the one to help her do it. Maybe this way she could also pretend that he was still here and willing to help her.

She didn't blame him for not answering her calls. She knew how hard returning to familiar things could be, especially after all she'd put him through. But didn't he know that she needed him too? Didn't he know that the only reason she was not there with him right now was because everything had fallen apart? They'd both already lost the people closest to them; how could he bear to lose another?

From the corner of her eye, Naomi caught movement. She looked up. Aja was standing in the doorway, her lips moving but none of the sound making it to Naomi. She paused the episode playing on her laptop and removed her headphones.

"What?" she asked.

"You need to turn that down."

Aja, just like her daughter, had a knack for ignoring the elephant in the room. After both their hands had connected with one another's cheeks, her mother was doing an excellent job of pretending like it never happened. She didn't punish Naomi or address the malicious silence when they were confined in the same space. Instead, she made an effort to not bring it up. Naomi thought about what her mother told her in her bedroom that night, about how she had to leave her country to escape her wicked things. Her mother had always been a strong woman, she supposed, but looking at her now she seemed worked to the bone. Naomi wondered if power was always this temporary. First with her mother, now with her. A curse laid upon the Morgan women.

"I was saying," she continued, "in a few minutes you need to come downstairs. Dinner is almost ready." *Or perhaps she's waiting for an apology.* Naomi's mind continued to wander. *Even taking all her sick and vacation days from work just to hear you say it.*

The spoken words began to register. "This early?" From her window, the Riverside sun was still taking its turn jeering at her before the moon swapped in.

Naomi's mother turned to exit. "Dr. Gonzales said you should eat earlier, remember?" she said over her shoulder, a plea slipping into the syllables of her following words. "Please, come downstairs, Naomi."

Naomi grunted, looking back at her laptop screen. "Can't you bring it up?"

Aja wouldn't entertain the idea. She left the room. "Come downstairs." Naomi slumped farther down into the mattress. She wanted to plant herself here in case Aja was calling her down to have dinner with her father today. Maybe if she was going back to the academy, Aja wanted them all to go back to other things too. The thought made Naomi sick to her stomach. But she also knew that she couldn't sit here. They still hadn't recovered from the last time she'd told her mother she didn't want to leave her bed.

Naomi threw the sheets off but didn't bother taking the bonnet off her head. Instead, she pulled her loose pajama pants up to her stomach and stomped down the stairs. Stuck in her own miserable thoughts about her father and her mother and how they called themselves parents, Naomi missed a few key things. The farther she descended, the clearer the whispering voices became, and as her feet greeted each step there was a heavy shuffling somewhere in the house. In hindsight, she should have noticed all these things, run back upstairs, and locked her bedroom door, too, just for good measure. But when she thought of her father, nothing else had the room to thrive in her own mind. He consumed her, and she'd never really paid the price for that, until now.

Naomi got to the last few steps and saw that there were people waiting for her downstairs. Only she didn't realize the number of people until she got to the landing. She stopped. The entire Riverside Dance Academy was looking back at her.

"Surprise!"

They were still in compression shirts and tights, smiling wide. Hands were up in the air, and some people even jumped. Naomi searched the crowd but her eyes kept drifting to the same people. Alex, the boy who could laugh while he danced and made jokes no matter how exhausted he was (everyone always laughed with him too); across the room was Samantha, who didn't even like ballet. Then there was Lucas, lazy yet talented. Bethany, chatty yet smart. They all flooded her vision in a way that she couldn't ignore. The Riverside Dance Academy was here, looking up at her, waiting, smiling, expecting.

But she had nothing left to offer them.

"Naomi?" a voice called.

Her bottom lip trembled. Not again.

"Naomi, are you okay?" Scattered smiles fell one after the other, so slowly she never realized it was happening until they were all gone. Emerging out of the huddled bodies was Valentino, standing just below her at the foot of the steps. He was still smiling.

He put out his hand to meet her. "Naomi, come on."

Her eyes flashed back to the crowd, switching between the strange faces again even though she was afraid of what they would tell her.

She saw Aspen closer to the back, her arms folded but a smile on her face anyway. Their eyes settled on one another, and the room dipped into oblivion.

When Naomi felt the tears coming, she clenched her teeth and blinked until she was seeing everything through flashes. "Get out."

"Naomi—" Valentino started, but she never saw him.

Her eyes were too busy bouncing around the room, searching for some explanation or cause for her embarrassment. Then it was there. Closer to the kitchen was her mother, looking aghast, a plate full of sandwiches in her raised right hand. Naomi's nose flared. She looked back at the crowd. "I don't want any of you here," Naomi said, shoving every amount of authority and strength into her voice as she possibly could. "Get out."

When no one moved, she decided to let them know just how serious she was. She took one step back up the stairs, then two before wholly spinning her body away from them and leaving completely.

A hand stopped her. "Naomi, all these people are here for you," Aja said urgently, holding on to her. "You can't leave."

"I don't want them here."

"They care about you."

Naomi felt the ironic humor building in the air between them. "No, you care about parading me around." She pulled back her arm, an apology glinting in her eyes before she continued up the stairs.

"Naomi," a familiar voice called.

When Naomi reached the top of the staircase she turned around to find Aspen coming halfway up to meet her.

Her voice trembled. "Aspen, I can't—"

"Let me come with you," she said.

But Aspen was in her tights, and she had also come with the rest of them, and Naomi wasn't sure if she wanted to see any of that. Not yet. "I just . . . I need to be alone."

Wounded, Aspen took a step back and watched as Naomi headed for her room without another word. She turned to Naomi's mother, who already had her head down. Aspen descended the stairs and began telling everyone it was time they started packing up and going. Naomi didn't feel well enough to come downstairs.

That night, Naomi didn't cry. She lay awake and wondered if Valentino would forgive her for what she had done today. Would any of them? She was half expecting her mother to come through the door any second now. Or maybe Aspen would block her number finally. Maybe they all were going to realize she was much worse than what they had initially thought. But these things didn't hurt like they once did. One thing was certain, however—she could not return to the academy. Not, at least, as she was now.

CHAPTER TWENTY-THREE

On Naomi's second week into her recovery regimen, she flung her phone across the room. All day yesterday she had stopped herself from texting Saint, thinking that maybe he needed more space or time, or whatever it was people told themselves they required before they texted someone back. She'd told herself twenty-four hours was enough. But today, when she checked, their chat was still all blue. He was still not answering her.

Naomi buried her face in her knees. He probably hadn't even noticed that this was the first day in two weeks that she'd gone without texting him. Or considered how much willpower it took for her to let him go. Naomi's phone skipped across the bed, all the way to the edge before halting just enough to prevent its demolition. It went unnoticed, however. Naomi's back was already turned.

If she was sitting with him on the grass of Elizabeth Park next to his favorite bench again, which was to say, if she had another chance to return to their peak, this time she'd hold on to his phone for a moment before it rang. Naomi was certain she would. Only for a few minutes, though. Only long enough to imprint that moment a little more firmly in her mind so that the memory would be fresher in the haunting weeks to come. Then, when she was satisfied, however long that took, she'd hand him his phone finally and he'd look at it, see the missed call, call back, answer. Then she'd watch everything wilt on his face for the second time.

Naomi launched herself off the bed and made her way to the door, thinking only to leave this room for a moment. Or just get up and walk. Walk away and leave the memories of Saint and her phone here. The kitchen, she decided as she pulled her bedroom door open, would be her temporary safe house in the meantime. But what Naomi hadn't considered was that it was Sunday and the sun was shining brightly still. That meant both, not one, of her parents were home. Perhaps, if she had taken a moment and scraped Saint from her mind properly, she might have remembered. But to her detriment, Naomi only realized the fact when it was already too late.

Right there in the hallway on that Sunday afternoon, Naomi saw her father. Ethan was coming up the stairs with his head down and his hair ruffled. His tall frame was seemingly more hunched over than what she was accustomed to, and she could now plainly make out his sins strolling in behind him. In the shape of some brunet in high heels. When he looked up and saw her, he took a single step toward her. "How are you feeling?"

About two months ago, he'd carried her up these steps after picking her up out of a wheelchair. A decade before that, he was doing it also. She hadn't prepared herself to see him so suddenly. Naomi found walls to make eye contact with instead. They were looking back at her, too, daring to keep up their tradition. "Fine. Just hungry."

"Do your feet feel stronger? Dr. Gonzales said you've been making really great progress."

Naomi tucked her chin into her chest. The ankle brace had been off for a few days now, and if she was being honest, she didn't feel the pain at all anymore. "I suppose she's right," Naomi answered.

Two beats passed. Three. "I know you're still upset, but we did what we did for your safety. For your future. If the cops hadn't—"

—listened to her mother's pleas, decided not to convict her, realized her father was a white man . . . "I know. I already got the speech from Mom."

Ethan nodded. "I just want you to recognize how serious that situation was, Naomi." After waiting a few more seconds for his daughter to raise her head and look at him again, he came to terms with the fact that she was deliberately choosing not to. He sidestepped her. "Well, go get something to eat. You'll need it for Tuesday. Big day . . ."

Naomi slipped past him as he finished speaking, muttering something even she didn't fully hear. Behind her, his footsteps departed in rhythm with hers. When Naomi had first seen her father kiss another woman, she hadn't wanted to confront him. That night, as their whole family was sitting at the dining table, all she could think to do was what she always did: stay silent. But now, despite the pain it might cause her mom, and how it might affect their family, Naomi wasn't sure the lie was any better. At least confronting him would release the force pressing down on her chest every time she saw her dad. At best, it would set them all free.

When she got to the kitchen Aja was already there. Naomi's palm tingled with the memory. Telling her that her husband was cheating on her would be another slap, Naomi knew. Clearly, this was the type of daughter she was. The type of daughter, perhaps, she had always been. Otherwise, what kind of girl would abuse, neglect, hurt, run from, run toward, destroy, tear away, tear up, tear, tear, tear . . .

"I already made you lunch. It's in the microwave," Aja told her.

Naomi muttered a form of a thank-you and opened the microwave. Pasta. She shut the door and set it to heat for a minute. Neither of the Morgan women addressed each other until the timer beep interrupted their silence. "You should start doing some stretches to get you ready for Tuesday. Did you take your antibiotics last night?"

Naomi grabbed the steaming food. "Yes."

"Good, I just want to make sure that you're keeping up with your recovery. Valentino said Tuesday will be like normal for you again. You'll need your strength."

Naomi chose not to tell her mother that the type of strength that had fortified her for her entire life had now been properly shattered and could not be regained overnight.

The doorbell rang. Neither of them, it seemed from their expressions, had an answer for whom it might be. Until they remembered. Saint. It could be him; he knew where they lived now. Maybe he had seen Naomi's texts after all, and he was here to pick her up so they could go somewhere else that felt like them. Alive and waiting. But if this was the case, Aja could not be the one to answer the door. Naomi hurried to answer it, but her mother moved faster. She launched herself at the door, successfully getting there first and pulling it wide open.

"Hi, delivery for Aja Morgan?" the boy said. He brought in a box with a clipboard and pen on top.

"Oh." Aja breathed after a half beat. "I completely forgot I ordered these."

The boy held out a pen and a paper for her to sign, and she quickly scribbled her signature. They exchanged thank-yous, and Aja and Naomi watched him retreat back to his truck. Slowly, Aja closed the front door. Even if it wasn't Saint, Naomi guiltily thought that, maybe, if she wasn't alone in expecting him, the chances of him actually showing up and ringing their doorbell were even more likely. Her chest tightened.

Aja turned around with the box in hand. "Your new pointe shoes are here," she announced.

Naomi blinked. She had almost forgotten that in ballet she wasn't the primary thing to be broken in.

CHAPTER TWENTY-FOUR

On the last day of Naomi's recovery regimen, the day before she was to officially reenter the Riverside Dance Academy, Naomi took a pair of the newly purchased pointe shoes and broke the things in. The practice came back to her easily, like riding a bicycle. Bending them back and forth in her hands, carving the bottoms of them with a sharp knife, sewing on the ribbons, burning their ends, it was all muscle memory. She put the pointe shoes under her knives, needles, and fire until they looked like they were supposed to. Then she packed all her equipment (tape, numbing gels, ibuprofen, tights) into her bag and placed it in a corner.

Next, Naomi entered her bathroom and looked at herself in the mirror. She plugged her hair straightener into the wall and allowed it the time it needed to get hot enough so it could burn. Divided into sections with clips, Naomi's curls were stretched and ready to be set between the hot clamps. She frowned at herself in the mirror. She put the straightener down.

What kind of dancer would she be, what kind of performance would she give, if her body and ballet were continuing to reject each other like this? She might not be able to control how darkly she stuck out in class but she could redefine sticking out for herself. Perhaps it was a good thing she stuck out like this. Perhaps she should do it more often. She was reminded briefly of the way Saint's eyes had lit up when she'd worn her hair like this. And the way the real Jessica never gave a second thought to people's opinions of her. Naomi pulled the straightener plug out of the outlet entirely.

When she was a little girl, Naomi could never have imagined all the effects ballet would have on her today. All she cared about then was the way dancing made her feel. How the music could often transport her away, and she would simply let it. Nothing else ever came so naturally to her. Even now, looking in her bathroom mirror, nothing ever did. She could not picture a world with her in it not dancing ballet. And she didn't want to. Only, if this world was inevitable, she wanted it to be sustainable too. Not perfect. Naomi could still remember the first time she danced for an audience, and she wanted to get that little girl back.

Reentering her room Naomi decided it was time to put things in order. She spent the rest of the night hauling the desk back to where it was supposed to be. She moved the rolled carpet under her bed so she'd have easy access to unfurl it once the time came. She mounted the television again. The truth was, Naomi didn't doze off into sleep until the late hours of the night. She was too busy redesigning what she wanted her bedroom to look like from now on. And what was more, she no longer felt afraid of waking up late and missing rehearsals.

There was something authentic in showing up later.

The next morning Aja delivered her daughter to the Riverside Dance Academy a little late. Aja wasn't used to waking up this early on a Monday morning because she didn't work those days. She usually trusted Naomi to make her own breakfast and take the bus to the theater, using the rest of the day to sew and stitch Naomi's costumes. Because of it, her movements were unfamiliar and weak. Nevertheless, she insisted on taking her daughter herself. Naomi knew why. She wanted to follow her inside and speak to Valentino. Make sure she was, in fact, dancing and not off with Saint again.

The Riverside Performing Arts Theater didn't look like it had missed Naomi. It was the same as she'd left it a month and a half ago, miserable. The last time Naomi had seen this building was in a dream and, back then, it was locked away and she had permission to simply sit outside and watch Riverside walk by. But when Aja tugged on the door now it came open easily. For a brief moment, Naomi felt as though this must then be whatever the opposite of a dream was. But then she reminded herself of who she was dancing for. And that unlocked doors were blessings. And this was a second chance, just like the metallic second roof at the Riverside library.

Backstage, Aja told Naomi that the first day back she shouldn't worry about performing but simply try to do her best. That it might not be easy and that was okay. Then, as if she was just now noticing it, Aja said to her, "You didn't straighten your hair."

"You think I should have," Naomi answered, the question hanging between them.

"Actually, I like this." She looked at the way Naomi's curls were already beginning to escape the afro-puff. "It looks more like you. Meet me in the studio when you're finished changing? I want to talk to Valentino."

Aja hugged Naomi tightly—a good sign, Naomi convinced herself. Even despite all the pain she had caused her mother this summer, Aja could still be burdened to love her.

When Naomi got to the dressing room there was no one else there. She sat in her spot farthest from any form of vanity and began to change. Gently, she pulled her tights up her legs. She wrapped athletic tape in the spots where it needed to be. Opted out of ibuprofen and Tiger Balm. She gathered herself with a few exhales, and then finally left for the dance studio.

As she pulled the door open all eyes landed on her. Her mother was the first to smile. Valentino wasn't far behind. Aspen was next. And like wildfire, it spread. Out from the silence someone began to clap, and suddenly applause ensued. It roared and echoed, crumbling all the walls. She wanted to believe her mother had come here and warned them all to start cheering for her, to make her feel welcomed for the second time. But Aja seemed startled herself and was one of the last people to join in. The Riverside Dance Academy did not hate Naomi. Maybe it never had. Maybe they had all showed up to her house and refused to dance the White Swan variation because she had a real place here. Naomi was taken aback by the fact that for the first time this summer she was not bracing herself to face them. The academy, even after everything, had not given up on her.

"Thank you," Naomi said to all of them, hearing the way their clapping was beginning to sound a lot like laughing.

"Welcome back," said Valentino. "Glad you'll be joining

us after all. Why don't you get started with some stretches and then I'll see you over at the barre soon?"

Naomi nodded. Everyone was still looking at her until Valentino recalled their attention. He restarted their count.

Normal in the Riverside Dance Academy looked different today, like a home she'd already outgrown. But a home is still a home as long as you make the beds, turn the lights on, and remember to keep paying the bills.

ACT THREE

CHAPTER TWENTY-FIVE

When Saint Owens returned home on the night his father almost died, he and his little brother slept on the living room sofa. There wasn't enough space to fit the pair of them but neither wanted to be in their rooms that night. Or, more precisely, neither of the boys wanted to be even farther away from family. So they opted for the tiny, uncomfortable couch. They never said it aloud but they knew they shared a reason for staying together that night.

Later, when Saint first saw Naomi's missed texts and calls, it was already the next day. He woke up to all the notifications on his phone and read them to himself. She was saying things like *Sorry, can we talk?* and *I miss talking to you.* Saint toyed with his phone for a moment. If he was to call her back, what would he say? Should he tell her he'd never been humiliated like that before? Or that he was pretty sure his father would die soon so maybe humiliation was the least of his worries? Or maybe she needed to hear how he had always known that Naomi came from the things he'd secretly wanted, like two caring parents, money, and a big house, and after last night he could no longer ignore the way that she threw all those good things back in the face of the universe. Just the image of her mother shouting at him, standing on her perfectly mowed lawn, across from her shiny Audi, in a community he didn't even know existed. It was clear he didn't belong there, and Naomi's mom knew it too. He belonged here in the darker, spottier side of Riverside. When she was casting him out, she was really telling him to return to a place like this.

Sully stirred awake next to him. He frowned and rubbed his eyes. "What's for breakfast?"

Glancing over at his little brother, Saint thought finally that maybe the thing that Naomi needed to hear the most was that he could no longer visit alive and waiting places with her. Nowhere in Riverside could need him more than this house right now. No one in Riverside could need him more than this little man.

"No good morning?"

Sully groaned. "Good morning. What's for breakfast?"

Saint remembered that among everything, they hadn't eaten last night. "What would you like?"

Sully gave his older a brother an incredulous look. *Really?* Saint nodded. "Omelets! And pancakes! With lots and lots of syrup!"

Saint sat up straight on the couch and yawned. "Well, to make all that we're going to need to get groceries." They had a consistent schedule for when they got groceries; usually twice a month on Saturdays, and Sully knew this. It was Monday. But before Sully's smile could fade away completely, Saint told him, "Go get dressed."

Under his breath the boy cheered. He stood and gave a big, long stretch. Watching him leave to get changed, Saint was reminded of the very last experience in the truck. Him crying at the steering wheel, trying to get them to a hospital. Sully holding up the head of their unconscious father in the backseat. But he was not going to keep them in this house. He knew the sooner they set foot inside the Chevrolet again, the sooner they could give it new, better memories. Similar to what he and Naomi had done to the wall under the Riverside Bridge and the paintings at the Riverside African American Historical Society and the back wall of the bowling alley.

After they'd both gotten dressed and picked up everything they needed from the supermarket, Saint and Sully made their omelets and pancakes together in the kitchen. Sully also said he wanted chocolate-flavored cereal, and even though Saint knew that his brother wouldn't finish it, he gave it to him anyway.

"I'm going to the hospital today to check on Dad," Saint told Sully after flipping his omelet. Sully, who was halfway through his cereal, looked up.

"Oh," he said.

Originally, Saint wanted to tell Sully to come with him, but he realized he really wanted to give the boy a chance to ask for himself. He wanted to give him the option to choose because Saint thought that perhaps if he was at his age, watching his father die, and having few memories of his mother, the hospital would be the last place he'd voluntarily want to go. What if he just wanted his father to die as far away as possible from him? So Saint only offered the idea and waited, but Sully never took it a step further. He watched his older brother and said good-bye when he took up the car keys and went to the door.

Saint saw his father in a hospital bed that the doctor had suggested he likely would not be able to leave within the next two weeks. After having passed out from a lack of air circulation, Richard was still coughing up blood and having chills, the disease and his addiction combining into a greater problem.

"Dad, how are you feeling?"

The man turned to look up at him, fire in his eyes, and said nothing.

"I'll give you two a minute," the doctor said, exiting the hospital room.

"Dad—" Saint began again.

"Why did you bring me here?" The man's eyes narrowed and sharpened. He was in a hospital bed, weak and barely breathing, but Saint felt as though his father's hand was around his neck.

"What—what do you mean?"

"Why the hell did you bring me here, boy? Don't you know we can't afford these hospital bills?" *You were about to die.* "Tell them to let me out. We're going home." *Should I have let you die? Do you want to die?*

How could there be an IV in his arm, and he was still this angry?

"I couldn't just leave you there. I had to do something."

Richard was shaking his head. "There's a clinic right on—"

Air left Saint's lungs. "A clinic?"

"Well, who's going to pay for this, Saint? I can't, and I know it won't be you." The blinds were open, a grassy parking lot just beyond them, but Saint felt as though there was no escape from this room aside from the single door beyond his father.

On the fourth day Saint's father stayed in the hospital, Saint decided to get a job. He walked up and down the corner of Lambton and Oxford, going into every small store he could find and asking if they had any positions open. He couldn't do anything too skilled, so any restaurant or retail outlet was his target. But after hours, when he hadn't booked a single interview, he went to the park before going home. He lay there for a moment, wanting the sun to set on him.

He couldn't help but think back to the last time he was here. Naomi and him talking about the end of the world as if it would never happen. It was almost cruel, how funny it seemed now. He reminded himself he couldn't stay here long; Sully was alone at home and he was probably getting hungry.

Blythe sauntered over and wordlessly lay next to him. When he asked what was the matter, Saint simply told him that he would be joining him soon. They'd both be out here begging for change with nothing but the clothes on their backs. Blythe, of course, said over his dead body. If Saint joined him out here, where would he get his change from? They'd both suffer. Saint turned in the grass and watched the man. He knew Blythe was trying to pull him up with humor, but it sounded too much like he, too, was another person who was dependent on him. Saint didn't answer. Instead, he fantasized about exactly what would happen if he disappeared tomorrow.

Two weeks passed, and Saint brought his father back home. Sully was still putting things away and making the final touches to his room when Saint rolled his father inside in his wheelchair. For the first time in months the room didn't smell like cigarettes. The air was lighter, crisper, and Saint made it his mission to keep it this way for as long as possible. He'd keep the window open in here.

CHAPTER TWENTY-SIX

As Naomi now knew well, this side of Riverside at midday was small huddles of friends laughing on sidewalks and people on lunch breaks rushing out of coffeehouses and restaurants. In the car, Aspen bopped her head to meaningless pop music, going as far as to mumble lyrics she clearly didn't know all the way.

"Best cupcakes in Riverside, hands down," Aspen was telling Naomi as they found their booth in the Symphony's Safehouse café. Naomi couldn't say she'd expect that, considering the lonely parking lot and the starving lights. The inside was thick with the scent of fried food and sugar concealing cheap disinfectant. Beanbags were scattered across the floor and low tables were paired with even lower chairs. The ceiling felt dangerously close too; it couldn't have been more than eight feet high. The poorly painted building with dirty glass windows did not look like a place where Aspen would spend her free time. Even from the outside, if you looked through the glass, you could see the scanty seating and the idle staff leaning on counters while lonely people on their laptops hardly paid attention to their food.

The girls seemed like giants when moving past the furniture, awkward and lanky big things. But the moment they sat, they seemed to shrink to fit the rest of the café. They were so close to the floor Naomi wondered what was even the point of having seats at all. Unlocking her phone, Aspen told her, "Some of us girls in the academy come here after rehearsals. You should come."

Naomi didn't say anything for a moment. For so long she'd thought all the other girls went home and did exactly what she did: eat what they could manage, study routines on YouTube, and rehearse again in their standing mirrors. She almost never considered the reality that when they left the academy, they packed ballet up until the next the day. She'd never have imagined a group of them would eat cupcakes here. Then Naomi said, "I'd really like that. Thank you."

"Hi, ladies." An average-looking woman hovered above them. She clearly had a few years over the girls, yet somehow, Naomi couldn't help but notice that she didn't sound or move like she was that much older than them. Aspen smiled at her, and a conversation quickly bounced back and forth between the pair. They seemed already well acquainted. Naomi leaned back in her seat and, as a precaution to any inside jokes she'd have to grimace through, stared pointedly at the laminated menu on the table.

Outside, behind the glass windows, Naomi felt as though she was watching Riverside and all its people smile, laugh, and cry from a separate space. She'd participated in that once.

Saint had showed her that Riverside was always this way, and she hadn't known because she was just stuck in the Riverside Performing Arts Theater for too long to notice or get close enough to it. How quickly she'd found herself watching from afar again. Naomi's attention snapped back to the table at the call of her name. Aspen repeated, "What are you ordering?"

She glanced down at the menu, but ultimately, she felt their eyes silently watching her, so she simply said, "I'll have whatever she's having."

The lady muttered, "So, that's two waters?"

Naomi looked at Aspen, puzzled, and said, "You're only having water?"

"I'm not hungry."

Naomi cleared her throat. She told the waitress, "I'll have your most popular cupcake and a glass of chocolate milk, please."

When the waitress left their table Aspen said, "Don't give me that look."

"What look?" Naomi asked. "There is no look." She defended herself.

Aspen rolled her eyes. "You know I can't overeat."

"It's not overeating, Aspen. It's just eating."

"You know what I mean." She followed up with, "How often do you eat?"

Naomi pursed her lips. "Not as much as I should. I can say that now."

"Well, maybe if I don't get into a company or a ballet school, I'll buy myself the nastiest cheeseburger money can buy."

Naomi looked at her. "You don't think you'll get in?"

The only sound was the overhead fan whirling above them. "I don't know. Grand Prix makes the difference between actually making it big and whatever plan B is. That's a crazy thin line."

"What's your plan B?" Naomi kept her eyes on Aspen, her words coming easier that way since there was no one for her to be mad at, except her own vaguely translucent reflection sitting expectantly in the glass window in her periphery.

"College, I guess. Any one that'll take me, and then I'll figure something out from there."

"Would you be happy?"

"If I gave up ballet and got a nine-to-five like everyone else? God, no. At least with ballet I get to do something I actually love."

Naomi was thinking it, but hadn't realized the thought had actually been spoken aloud. "You keep dancing even though you think there's a chance you might not make it?"

Aspen cocked her head at her. "Isn't that what we all do?"

Naomi shook her head. "I don't have a plan B."

The waitress came back and rested one cold glass of water in front of Aspen. The girl thanked her and began drinking. "What do you mean you don't have one? We all have a plan B."

"I don't. I always thought if I worked hard enough and sacrificed enough, I'd make it."

"Naomi, you know that's not how—" Aspen told her.

"I know, but I wanted to believe it, you know? I never even thought about college, if I'm honest. And now I'm back in the academy, and I have a shot at Prix again . . ."

Aspen set the now empty glass down. "Is this about that boy?"

That boy. Wasn't it all?

Naomi didn't answer her. She couldn't. When the waitress returned with her cupcake and chocolate milk, Naomi stared down at them and, without ever opening her mouth, felt as though she was choking on something she had bitten off that was proving to be more than she could swallow.

She heard Aspen shuffle across from her. "Naomi, you're one of the most talented dancers I've ever seen. So if you don't get into a ballet school, accept that maybe, this time, it was out of your hands. You've sacrificed enough."

Naomi didn't say anything, but she thought of Jessica, and her ankle, and Saint, and her father, and took a large, obnoxious bite of the cupcake. She nodded, holding it up. Still chewing she told Aspen, "You're right. These are really good."

When Naomi returned home that evening, she took a glass from the kitchen and filled it with tap water. Then she went up the stairs, into her room, and watered the dried orchids that Aspen had given to her earlier that summer. She did it for two reasons: one, she really couldn't bear for anything else to die around her. And two, because she wanted to do something for herself now, too, and this felt like agency. Keeping water in the vase would be a habit she'd uphold for the months to come.

CHAPTER TWENTY-SEVEN

Naomi could hear her mother calling from downstairs. She imagined the dining table was probably already set for dinner by this hour and Aja was distributing plates. Therefore, Aja was really asking Naomi to return to the dining table in the same fashion her daughter had been returning to the Riverside Dance Academy: with hope. But Naomi didn't shout anything back. She could not go back to looking at her father because it would gut her, and she had been spending all this time patching herself up from the last time.

The lack of a response lured Aja up to her bedroom, where she opened the door. She said loudly, "Dinner is ready, honey."

"Mom, wait." Aja turned back. At first, Naomi wanted to say that she wasn't hungry, but she was. Then she wanted to ask if her mother could bring the food up to her, but Aja had stopped doing that weeks ago and likely wouldn't again. Then, Naomi wanted to just blurt everything out and confess what she'd seen that evening on Sixth Street and how she felt her chest cave in and collapse, and how she'd been a little hollow since. She cleared her throat. "Can I talk to you?"

Aja smiled, stepping inside. "I thought you'd ignore me forever."

"Forever is a long time."

Naomi looked at her mom, not sure where she should even start. When she set herself in front of walls with Saint, she did whatever came to her first. Her instincts weren't always right, but that was never the point.

Naomi said, "I'm sorry for hitting you. I just, I felt like you weren't listening to me. I don't know what came over me."

Aja came to sit on Naomi's bed next to her. "I'm sorry too."

Naomi searched her mother's eyes. Now that she'd gotten the easy part out of the way, she asked, "Can you do my hair?" It was the first type of loudness she wanted to practice. To ready herself for all the things she had left to say tonight. Naomi still had ballet tomorrow and the day after and, hopefully, hundreds of days after that. But she did not want to do it dishonestly any longer. She didn't want to keep quiet. When her hair was out, she felt so much more like who she was supposed to be all along, and she needed to draw on that bravery right now.

And anyway, if the white dancers got to wear their hair naturally, and Jessica got to wear her hair naturally, why shouldn't she? Naomi never wanted to enter the dance studio with her crown melted down ever again. All she needed was for Aja to say yes.

It was the easiest thing her mother had ever agreed to. The women stood and gathered all they needed to begin on Naomi's hair. They rinsed it out under the cold water from the sink and Aja squeezed pools of shampoo into her hand. The whole bathroom smelled of sweet fruits by the time all the shampoo was out of Naomi's hair. They had been silent for the cleaning process but Naomi knew there was further for her to go. "Do you still love Dad?"

Aja's hands paused in Naomi's hair. "Naomi, what are you asking me?"

Naomi told herself although she would be speaking this time instead of spray-painting, it was the same, just as permanent and necessary. All she had to do was open her mouth and say it. Speak.

"I have something to tell you."

Naomi slowly raised her dripping head from the sink and looked directly at her mother. Water ran down her face. "I saw Dad. Downtown. With another woman." When Aja didn't say anything immediately, Naomi just came out with it. "They kissed. Mom, he's cheating on you."

She watched as her mother's expression contort from worry to sadness, until it struck pain. Tears escaped her eyes. Naomi blinked strangely. She noticed something odd. Among all the emotions circling on her mother's face, there was never a hint of shock. Then, agonizingly, it slipped out. "You knew."

Aja put the towel up on Naomi's forehead to stop the downpour on her face. Her chest was uncontrollably heaving.

Naomi shook her head. "Then why are you still with him?"

When Naomi's forehead was dry, Aja squirted some product from a bottle into her hands and lathered them. She gently pushed Naomi's head back into the sink and continued conditioning Naomi's hair. She set her fingers deep into her scalp and raked her hands all the way through to get rid of any knots. "It isn't that simple."

Naomi gripped the sink and stood tall. "Then explain it to me."

Aja looked into the bathroom mirror next to them. Naomi followed suit and they both saw the women looking back at them. Tall, impatient, tired. She said, "He's your father, Naomi. I can't just leave him. He means something to me."

Naomi looked into her mother's reflection in the mirror and frowned. Then, agonizingly, she said, "Mom, he's cheating on you."

"He said he'll cut it off. He doesn't want our family to suffer just as much as you and I don't want that either." Naomi wanted to ask her mother's reflection if he had told Aja that before or after Naomi witnessed him kissing a stranger. Aja continued, "Our family will fall apart if I leave."

Naomi's voice was lower than a whisper. "It's falling apart anyway."

Aja turned to look at the Naomi in front of her. She cleared her throat and, looking down at her hands, asked, "So, what do you think I should do?"

"Whatever you want, just not at your own expense." Naomi lowered her head back into the sink.

Aja angled her body to better stand over Naomi but she didn't resume conditioning just yet. "And what about you? He's still your father."

For half a minute Naomi didn't have an answer to that. He'd raised her. He took care of her. He'd been there for every single major event of her life, even though he likely didn't even know what was going on half the time. There was no time of her life that did not include her father. Her voice echoed off the porcelain bathroom sink when she told her mother, "Yes, but he's not yours."

Aja pulled her daughter out of the sink. Naomi's eyes locked with her mother's teary ones. Behind her, Naomi saw the bathroom wall retreat, as if it was being pushed on wheels. As if it finally knew its place now, no longer directly behind her, crowding and crushing her, but instead farther back to allow room for all the big things she would continue to do from here on. Naomi pulled Aja in for a deep hug.

CHAPTER TWENTY-EIGHT

Three days before the Youth America Grand Prix was set to begin Naomi was now not only performing her solo as the White Swan in *Swan Lake* but also a pas de deux with Aspen and a group ensemble with everyone in the academy. While she was recovering, the ensemble had been rehearsed a number of times, but Valentino told everyone that Naomi could not be back and be back halfway. If she was here, win or lose, she would dance with everyone. And Aspen and Naomi had only decided to do a pas de deux the previous week. For one thing, more performances usually meant better odds, but also because Naomi was the one to suggest it and that was really all it ever took for Aspen these days.

The academy worked another eight-hour day. However, Naomi never stayed back to rehearse for longer or attempted to continue her routine in her bedroom mirror. In fact, she was given three five-minute breaks. During that time at the back of the studio she could see Lucas whispering something to the boy behind him, and the two of them stifling a chuckle. Samantha, even when nothing was playing, continued to hum the tune from the piano. When Naomi noticed that, she vaguely began to remember the sound of her voice singing in the dressing room when they got changed. And the intern, Eli, Naomi noticed, had been the same intern for years. He only dyed his hair a different color occasionally.

Alive, then dead, then alive again, Jessica Kingsley had taken up so much space in the academy that Naomi hadn't had the energy to notice these little things. Naomi secretly wished Jessica was here again. Only this time it would be Naomi, not her, pointing out things they should be giving their attention to in the studio. Naomi imagined that Jessica would gladly turn her eyes toward whatever thing Naomi pointed at and they'd make fun of it together before maybe even joining in themselves.

Two days before the Youth America Grand Prix Naomi brought a fresh bouquet of flowers to Evergreen Memorial Park. These would replace the old, dried flowers still sitting on Jessica's grave. She put them right next to her headstone and took a seat. She pulled a sandwich out of her bag and took a bite. The first thing Naomi told Jessica was that since she'd last visited things had, much to her luck, gotten marginally worse. But better also.

"Also, Aspen and I are like, friends now? Can you believe that?

"Valentino said Bethany has a good chance of getting into Idyllwild.

"Yesterday, my mom asked me how'd I feel if she divorced my dad."

It felt good that no one was replying back.

Naomi took another bite of her sandwich, and let Jessica know that she was still doing everything in her power to get into the School of American Ballet, and from there, the New York City Ballet. Their plans were still in effect, and Naomi would get there for the both of them.

When Naomi was taking the bus back home from the theater, she was imagining what tomorrow would look like at the Youth America Grand Prix. As of right now, she didn't feel shy or nervous but she was sure tomorrow before she stepped onstage her stomach would be flipping. She tried to convince herself that it was only another dance competition, and she should see it that way, but even that was too incredible a lie. This entire summer had led up to this point. After tomorrow everything would change, depending on whether she got an offer or not.

Watching Riverside go by her through the window Naomi saw the ice-cream truck out by Gold Bloom Plaza. Today, the line was longer than usual. Naomi pulled herself back from falling into old habits. She quickly reminded herself that everything had already changed. She was already different, and she didn't need an offer from a ballet school to justify that.

She liked that who she had become, this sort of resilience, had nothing to do with ballet.

On the sidewalk now, nearing her home, Naomi immediately noticed the truck sitting two blocks down the street from her house. The 2002 Chevrolet never stood a chance of being incognito. She would recognize it in a sea of 2002 Chevrolets. Naomi walked over to it. Saint was sitting in the front seat, flipping through his phone so attentively he hadn't noticed that she was standing right by his window. When she moved her hand to knock, her shadow startled him. He jumped and looked up at her, as if he had been caught doing something he shouldn't be. Realizing who it was, Saint took a slow, measured breath, watching her.

The way Naomi had imagined Saint's return was a little different, a little happier, from this. She thought he would be the one knocking, on her front door, or maybe her bedroom door if Aja allowed him to get that far, and that they'd be smiling and one of them would suggest picking up where they left off and the other would say yes because that was their tradition, but now she guessed it was all the opposite. Naomi indicated for him to lower the window but instead he opened the door altogether and stood out on the sidewalk in front of her.

He confessed. "Sorry for lurking. I didn't know what I would say when I saw you."

"Did you figure it out?" Naomi asked. Saint shook his head. Naomi could see that he'd been to the barber since the last time she'd seen him. He looked a little more like the boy she had first met in the theater that night. Nothing, she thought, could ever bring that boy back all the way but maybe that wasn't the point. Neither for Saint nor the younger version of herself. As long as they kept close the most important fragments of the people they used to be they could keep growing and still honor them. "Did you get my texts?" It felt right to kick things off with honesty after all this time. Maybe, with every card laid flat on the table, things might go a little differently. Maybe, if they actually let each other in fully, not halfway, they stood a real chance.

"Yes." When Naomi didn't say anything else it was because she was still taking him in. He was standing here now, for real this time, which meant he had come back after all, which meant he was thinking of her, too, even if it was a few weeks too late, and he was a few feet shy of her actual house. Looking him in the eye, she didn't have to ask why he was so far from her lawn or why it had taken him this long. Saint, however, assumed she was looking at him that way because she was waiting for him to continue. "My father got released from the hospital, and things haven't really been the same since."

"You don't have to apologize."

"But I do."

"If we both started apologizing, we would be here for hours." She didn't really believe that but in some ways it was true.

"I see your ankle brace is off."

Naomi didn't remember him actually looking down at her feet long enough to take notice of that. It was just like that time they met in Evergreen Memorial Park and he'd looked at her without looking at her feet, and for the first time Naomi felt like her identity was not attached to the things she used for ballet. She said, "Yeah, it's all better now."

Saint nodded. "Which means . . ."

"Which means I'm dancing again. The Youth America Grand Prix is tomorrow, actually." Naomi wanted to tell Saint the rest of her good news. That her mother was divorcing her father and their home didn't feel so weighted down anymore, but then she remembered that she had never told him about the infidelity in the first place. It had never come up. Or perhaps she had been deliberately avoiding the subject. Naomi wondered about all the other things they hadn't had a chance to tell each other. Almost like how she might never have known Saint had a brother or how extremely sick his father was if it wasn't for the pure coincidence of their circumstances. They never really spoke about the things that mattered. A large portion of their friendship was spent running, not talking. Albeit for different reasons, they had fallen together into a Riverside dreamscape of their own making, but it wasn't real all the way, and for that reason it couldn't last.

Saint's eyes widened. "Wow. I mean, congratulations. That's huge." He smiled at her bitterly. Naomi imagined he was probably thinking how she had the privilege of going back to her life as if it waited for her patiently to return while he was nursing a sick father and trying to keep a roof over the head of his little brother.

"I'm sorry," she blurted.

He laughed. "I thought we weren't doing that."

"I couldn't help myself." Saint continued to laugh and Naomi could tell by now that it was a substitute for the sadder, much more desperate thing he wanted to do. But she humored him.

"I have a question," she began. Saint hummed. "What was Sully talking about in the car? Swan Princess?"

He winced. Falling against the door of his truck he said, "Oh god. You don't make this easy, do you?"

Naomi shrugged. Why should she? She had learned that from him, after all.

"The first time we met, that night I was walking around Riverside looking for inspiration for a new art piece I wanted to make. I wasn't sure what I would find until I found you. I went inside the theater and I saw you, and something struck. I think it had to do with the loneliness of it all. You were kind of in this huge theater completely alone, dancing in the middle of the night, and there was something about that I could relate to. I don't know exactly why, but even then, you spoke to me. So I went home and I drew it. Drew you. Then painted you. I wanted to make you appear less lonely." Naomi was about to ask if she could see it but bit her tongue. She remembered what he had told her on the roof of the library about how he loved keeping the art to himself. "Saying it out loud, I'm starting to realize how creepy and weird it sounds."

"I don't think it's creepy or weird." Naomi looked at the pavement.

"So are you excited to move to the big city?"

"*If* I get into the School of American Ballet, then yes, of course. I've never been to New York, but I think I'll like it. I think it'll be good for me." Saint was smiling.

"What?" she asked.

"Nothing," he answered. Naomi looked at him pointedly. The boy laughed. "I just think it's funny that you really believe, even now, after everything, that you might not get in. If I'm honest, when summer's over I don't see you anywhere else."

Was that his way of telling her he wasn't sure if he would ever see her again? Was that the reason Saint had shown up outside her house? To say a final good-bye? Naomi steered their conversation away from herself and ballet. "And how are you? With everything."

Saint grimaced. "Hanging in there."

"I wish I could have been there for you," she told him sadly.

"He's alive. It's just—"

"There's a lot on your plate."

Saint told her she was right. His father's health was deteriorating, and he had to brace himself for what would soon come. He needed to brace Sully as well but he had no idea how to even go about doing that. For now, he was just gifting him more mature books from the library so that when the time came, it wouldn't be his first interaction with such pain. Saint said he knew it sounded cruel. Naomi didn't think it sounded cruel at all. When she asked him what he would do when it all happened, that was when he told her that he was going to drop out to get a job full-time and keep his and Sully's lives afloat. Naomi didn't say anything at first, then she whispered, "Please call me if you need anything."

He smiled. Teasingly he said, "You're gonna come all the way from New York just to comfort me?"

"Yes."

Naomi imagined even if he wanted to, not even Saint could give a proper explanation for the way he reacted next. The tears came out of nowhere. All of sudden, the boy's head was buried in her neck. It was the opposite of his panic attacks. The inverse of gasping for air on a sidewalk and bleeding out. It was life making its way back to him. He apologized. She told him to not be stupid. Out of all the traditions they had made together, this was the best.

When they pulled apart, the two of them slumped against the old truck. The evening was turning dark. "Don't leave," Naomi said. She invited Saint inside.

He cleared his throat. "Your mom might not like that."

"She'll get over it. Just be sure to tell her how good her cooking is."

And he did. Saint walked into the Morgan home and greeted Aja in the kitchen, mentioning how good it smelled in there. Naomi stood between them at first, but before she could say much, Aja was telling him the recipe. Over dinner they realized Saint's mom had been Jamaican, too, and although Saint had never been to the country, it was on his bucket list. Naomi made a mental note to invite him on their next trip back. They passed the plates of food between the three of them as if it was second nature, and when Saint asked if Aja was excited to bring her daughter to the Big Apple, Naomi realized Saint had a truck.

She could already picture them driving there, windows down. She already knew what song would be playing.

CHAPTER TWENTY-NINE

The Riverside Dance Academy was in chaos.

At first, it was hard to tell because the Riverside Performing Arts Theater was quiet, and bright lights were the only things occupying the stage. But the deeper inside one went, the clearer the faint shuffle of feet and shouts became. Every so often a panicked dancer would dash through the basement corridors to collect something from their family waiting in the audience or a member of the orchestra would escape from their pit when it was most convenient to use the bathroom or grab water down here. Naomi sat in the corner of the dressing room. Her mother had already done her makeup at home so she didn't have to get in front of a mirror like everyone else and apply more. But Aspen insisted.

It was, after all, the night of the Youth America Grand Prix. She said that some dancers could get away with sloppy techniques because of how beautiful they were, not that Naomi's technique needed the distraction, but it couldn't hurt. Naomi knew she was lying. Aspen only wanted to grab her and pull her onto the ottoman in front of the vanity so they could look at themselves in the mirror to truly see themselves for all that they were tonight. Outside of the competition and the dancing.

Valentino Beaumont's voice could be heard carrying through the basement. "Fifteen minutes!" he shouted. Bodies started for the door. All the girls, including Naomi and Aspen, rushed out, dropping everything they had been holding on to and making their way to the corridors that would eventually lead them backstage.

Naomi and Aspen stood at the back of the line, thinking. Aspen told Naomi that no matter what, they were to do their best and have fun. That was what mattered. That was something a judge from a ballet school could not take away from them. Naomi had, of course, already known this. In the White Swan costume her mother had finished sewing, Naomi told Aspen that even more importantly, they could do their worst and that would be okay too. Wordlessly, Naomi reached out and held her hand. They could hear the announcer begin, *"Welcome, ladies and gentlemen, to the Youth America Grand Prix . . ."* The girls started shaking.

Valentino ushered his dancers up the stairs. Their pointe shoes clacked all the way until they got behind the curtains on the main stage.

After a head count Valentino told his dancers, "Don't be nervous. We've rehearsed for this. I'm proud of every single one of you." The Riverside academy held on to each other since there were no waist-high metallic barres here. "Solos go first, so if you're doing a solo, be ready." Valentino looked at each of them.

Aspen squeezed Naomi's hand a little tighter. Briefly, Naomi regretted her decision to come out here without taking any ibuprofen. And she'd left her Tiger Balm and athletic tape at home. The decision was made in an effort to dance authentically. But she had forgotten all too soon how many people would be watching her, and that she was not only dancing for herself, but for Jessica as well. Maybe she hadn't been as ready as she'd claimed she was. Perhaps if she'd rehearsed for a little longer in the dance studio, she'd be more ready. Naomi was still battling with her thoughts of running to the bathroom to grab a fistful of the paper towels and stuffing her pointe shoes to cushion them as she and Jessica used to do when they were thirteen when she heard Aspen calling her name.

"Naomi, Naomi, you're on." The announcer came over the speakers to repeat Naomi's name. "You got this." Aspen hugged her. Valentino came over to gently push her onto the stage. The flooring was crisp Marley, the stage lights reflecting so hard off it she had to squint and look away.

Naomi tried to contain what was in her chest, and walked to the center of the stage like she'd rehearsed for years. She realized, as she looked out into the crowd, that there was no one out here with her. Her hands felt dry and clammy. The music for her variation began.

Naomi Morgan did not move. Her pointe shoes just felt a little too tight. And those damn lights. The audience hushed even more. Naomi told herself that she could do this. Just dance. She knew the moves. She knew the variation. The walls were far apart and she could look people in their eyes. Breathe.

"You can do this, Naomi!" A child's voice cried out from the audience.

Naomi looked farther back to see a child fist pumping among the still crowd. A father, it looked like, was attempting to get him to sit down, whisper-shouting at him to hush up. Naomi squinted her eyes.

When Saint could not quite get Sully to sit back down, he turned to look at Naomi. He was laughing, and so was Aja, who was seated next to them. He shouted, "You got this, Naomi!"

Immediately, she was back at the hospital with him. She was sitting in the waiting room and praying the boy's father hadn't died because there was no way he could recover from that with his little brother. Suddenly, they were screaming song lyrics over the booming stereo in the Silverado they never got around to naming. Finally, they were here again in the empty Riverside Performing Arts Theater in the middle of the night, and he'd never seen ballet before in person, and he was the first friend she'd met who was like that.

She cocked her head. "Really? There wasn't anything you thought I could improve on or I should change?"

Saint thought for a moment. "No." He came up short. "To me, it was perfect the way you just did it."

Naomi smiled.

The man at the piano told her from across the stage, "Let me know when you'd like to begin."

Naomi undid her bun, freeing her afro. The theater walls fell away. "I am ready," she told him.

Two long arms transformed into giant black wings, twisting and flapping downward as Naomi lowered her body to her feet. The music began. Then she rose.

ACKNOWLEDGMENTS

This novel took a village; it would not have been possible without a support system that stood behind me and cheered me on all the way. Firstly, I'd like to thank Wattpad for allowing me a platform to start my writing journey and helping me grow an incredible readership. I'd like to thank Deanna McFadden and Grace Kabeya for seeing something special in this story and taking a chance on me. You gave me the opportunity of a lifetime and I can never repay that. I also would like to thank my meticulous and thought-provoking editor, Fiona Simpson, and my amazing, ride-or-die agent, Léonicka Valcius.

I must also take the time to thank all my readers who have stuck by me for years and continued to read my work. So many of you have sent me thoughtful messages and comments that have pushed me on the days I felt as though I had nothing. I definitely would not have made it this far if it was not for every single one of you.

I'd also like to thank my family, friends, and teachers/professors who saw my writing as something meaningful and encouraged me to be something greater.

And last, but not least, I owe this book to sixteen-year-old me. We had nothing but passion and a dream, and still somehow made it happen for us. I am so proud of us, Matthew.

ABOUT THE AUTHOR

Matthew Dawkins is a Jamaican-born Watty award-winning author and poet whose works have amassed close to half a million reads. Matthew attends Western University in London, Ontario, where he is pursuing a BA in the School for Advanced Studies in Arts and Humanities and English literature.

Turn the page for a preview of

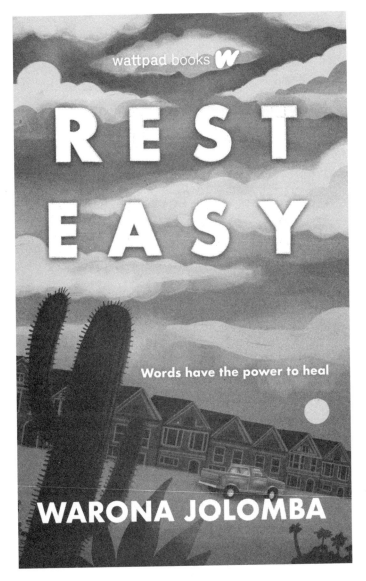

wattpad books

REST EASY

Words have the power to heal

WARONA JOLOMBA

Available now, wherever books are sold.

1

THE RESTLESS

Dee Warrington could not sleep. And he felt like letting his ex-girlfriend, Vanessa, know about it. He was itching to fill up the emptiness inside his chest, the cavity that grew mercilessly, a black hole feasting on light. He hadn't wanted her so much since the last time they were together. So at 3:22 a.m., while his heart refused to drum a lax cadence, he scrolled down through his phone's contacts until he saw her name. His thumb hovered over the Call button as he held his breath. Before he could talk himself out of his decision, he pressed it. To his surprise, she answered the phone.

"Hey, Dee. What's up? Is everything okay?"

"You're still awake?" he asked, trying hard to mask his triumph at the sound of her voice.

"Yeah. I have a Spanish final tomorrow. Cramming, you know. I was just about to sleep. What's going on? Are you okay?"

"I'm fine. Uh, actually . . . I—I'm just having trouble sleeping."

"I gathered that. Did something happen? Is Dylan home?"

"No. He went out. I've been studying for the history final. I know I'm going to fuck it up, though. Mrs. Meyers' voice is so whiny. I just zone out."

"I don't think you can really blame Mrs. Meyers' voice for your grades."

"No shit, Vanessa." He gulped another shot of his brother's whiskey as he sat upright in bed, looking out his open window. There was not even a slither of a breeze, and the air felt stifling.

"Sorry. Um . . . why are you calling me? We haven't spoken in weeks."

"I don't know. I can't sleep. It's been really bad lately. I'm scared." He paused, sighing, trying to keep himself together. "This house is so empty. I can't handle it. I don't like it. I don't know who else to talk to. I just knew you'd understand."

"Of course I understand. Yeah, I do." She spoke as though she was convincing herself. He sensed hesitance.

"I really miss you," he mumbled. Their relationship had ended just after their one-year anniversary. The cavity in him was taunting him as it grew, and he thought he might just die. He knew he'd feel better in a few months, but that didn't matter in that moment. Hopelessness never pointed you to the future.

"Okay. I'll come over," Vanessa said. Another surprise. Dee wasn't expecting such a statement from her, but then he didn't know *what* he'd expected.

"You sure? It's dark out."

"It's a five-minute drive. I'm a big girl. I'll bring my bag and my toothbrush so we can just leave for class in the morning."

"What are we gonna do?" he found himself asking.

"I don't know. What do you *want* to do?"

"Uh . . . I don't know. I mean . . . wait, no. There's something I have to talk to you about."

"There is?"

"Yeah. Something I think you really ought to know."

"Right, okay . . ." Vanessa responded, her voice thick with intrigue and suspicion. "I'll see you in ten, then?"

"Sure. Sure. I'll see you soon."

His palms were instantly clammy once she hung up. He didn't know if he was ready to see her up close, even though he thought he was. He had started off pathetic around her when they first met—a skittish mess, hiding his nerves behind flirtation and cheap jokes. Now he was feeling skittish again, but on a whole new level. In the worst way.

A half hour later, he got a text from Vanessa, who was waiting at the front door. He had been hastily tidying his room, shoving stray clothes under his bed and into his closet, clearing his desk, switching on his bedroom fan to dispel the warm stuffiness in the air. He finished the whiskey and drank a glass of water to compensate for his ever-intensifying intoxication. Vanessa knew he wasn't sober the second she saw him. She smiled softly, taking a deep breath before planting a kiss on his cheek. He led her into the living room, where cans of beer littered the coffee table.

"Dylan pregamed with some of his friends. Do you want a beer or something?"

"It's nearly four in the morning, Dee. We have class at nine."

"One drink won't kill you."

Vanessa shook her head. "I said I can't. God, you're like the devil on my shoulder."

"Okay, okay, whatever. How about a smoke?"

She looked to the floor, then back to him. Tilting her head back, she sighed. "I guess. Just a little bit."

Dee smiled. "That's more like it. Let's go upstairs. The stuff's in my room."

Once they got there, Vanessa sat on his bed and he went to his desk to roll up. His lamp was situated in front of him, silhouetting the back of his head in a soft incandescence. He played music on his speaker, something hushed and melodic.

"Did you join the pregame?" she asked him.

"No, I didn't. I just stayed in my room. Listened to some music until they left for Phoenix. I know he won't be back until, like, tomorrow evening."

"You mean *this* evening?"

"Tomayto, tomahto."

"So you've just been by yourself, huh?"

"Yeah. Lonely." He turned to look at her, licking the joint closed. He sealed the end up and shook it, not once unlocking his gaze from hers. Her stomach flipped. He was beautiful, and that was what she hated the most. He had always looked like a girl, with hair three times longer than her own, so long it almost reached his waist. She remembered the times she used to braid it, on quiet nights in. "Shall we?" he asked, getting off his chair and sitting next to Vanessa on the bed.

"What was it that you wanted to tell me?" She watched him take a long toke. He held it in for a few seconds, furrowing his brows at the heaviness in his chest, before blowing out a cough.

"Uh . . . I can't remember."

"You can't remember? It sounded important."

"It probably wasn't if I can't remember it."

"Come on, Dee. You're holding back, I can tell."

"I just wanted you to come over. I didn't want you to change your mind." He passed the joint to her, then picked up his phone to change the song. "Freudian" by Daniel Caesar started playing.

"You don't have to lie to get me to come over. I said I would."

"Remember how much we loved this album?" he said, lying back on his pillow. "How we'd make out to it, like, all the time?" He looked at her, smiling.

"I remember. It was nice." She killed the joint after taking a few puffs, leaving it on an ashtray on the bedside table. Then she lay on her back and turned her head to face him, their eyes level. Her heart was hammering ferociously, and she could hear the blood rushing in her ears. She turned on her side and placed a hand on his cheek. They were kissing each other before they could even register it.

Their hands slid all over, fingers slinking and climbing under T-shirt, bra, boxer shorts, panties, like they were desperately clawing for something within each other, holding onto skin and fabric like it was keeping them from falling over a precipice. The last time they were together felt like eons ago, but it also felt like it was just yesterday. Their love existed outside of the confines of time, or space, or rationality.

Each kiss carried a sprinkle of hatred. Hatred toward one another for taking advantage of the other's vulnerabilities; hatred of themselves for letting themselves be taken advantage of. Still, Vanessa held onto Dee, kissing his neck, kissing his shoulders, draping her leg over his, holding his chest against hers. He had shattered her heart, yet he still got to have her, whenever he wanted.

All he had to do was call her at stupid-o'-clock in the morning, and she'd be there. She resented him for it. He knew it was easy for her to come to his aid. He had been through a lot the past few months. He had been through a lot his whole *life*. She was the lucky one, the one with the functional family and the money and the opportunities in life. He wasn't. There had to be a compromise, and it was right there, in each other's arms.

Vanessa got on top of him, gazing into his eyes. She leaned down and kissed him again, and he suddenly froze. Something had changed; the mood had shifted. His grip had softened, and he wasn't moving.

"Are you okay?" she asked, her breathing heavy.

"Wait, wait—stop. Please get off."

"What's wrong?" She moved away, a wave of mortification crashing over her.

He sat up with eyes watering, lips creased into a frown. He was crying. "I can't do this. I'm sorry."

"What the fuck, Dee?"

He sat up, staring into nothingness. The silence cloaked the room for what felt like an eternity. "This isn't your fault. You *know* it isn't."

"This is about Karina, isn't it?" Vanessa's voice wavered. "That's why you can't sleep with me. God, I feel disgusting." Holding back tears, she moved to the end of the bed and grabbed her sweatpants.

"Vanessa, I . . ."

"It *is* about her? Fuck. I'm such an idiot."

"No, you're not. I'm the stupid one. You did nothing wrong."

"Why didn't you just call *her* over instead? Maybe you would actually have enjoyed yourself."

"Vanessa. It . . . it didn't happen. I'm telling you. She made it up."

"Oh yeah? Tell that to all of junior year, who found out before I did. Tell that to Karina, who literally *told* me it happened. I'm sick of this bullshit."

Dee sighed, defeated. "This wasn't a good idea."

"Exactly. I need to go."

"No—don't. I meant . . . us making out and shit—*that* was a bad idea. But I don't want you to leave me here alone. I can't sleep. I don't know what to do."

"I'm not going to sing you a lullaby or rub your back. You need to learn to deal with this. I can't always come to the rescue." He watched her put the rest of her clothes on and slide into her sneakers. She'd normally steal his hoodie, but she didn't this time.

He got out of bed and searched for his pants in the dim light. "You're right. I'm sorry."

"Stop saying sorry. I'm leaving now. It's ten past four. I'll see you tomorrow." She sniffed, wiping her wet eyes.

"You mean today." He smiled pathetically. She didn't react. Just grabbed her phone, slung her bag over her shoulder, and left his bedroom. Dee got an hour of sleep before his alarm went off.

Dee walked into his first class half an hour late. Vanessa was sitting on the left side of the room, as she always did. She looked up, sinking into her seat. He glanced toward her for a millisecond before traipsing to his desk in the newfound silence that saturated the room. His teacher called him out, asking him why he was late.

"I missed my alarm clock. My bad." He shrugged.

"That's not good enough. You should have informed the school before you got here."

"Well, I didn't," he said, rubbing his eyes, still burning from lack of sleep.

"Do you want to pass this class? Do you actually *want* to make it to senior year?"

"Oh my God. I said I was sorry I'm late. Can we just get on with the lesson?"

"That's my call to make."

"Okay. I guess we won't, then."

"Is that another detention you're asking for?"

Dee threw his head back, frustrated. "*Yes*, Mr. Bernardo. I would *love* another detention. It would be my *honor*." A couple of students snickered at his remark. Vanessa looked down at her desk, wishing she could dematerialize.

"You're not helping yourself out here," the teacher responded, pulling out a slip from his desk and writing on it. "I know you're much better than this. *You* know you are. Please start acting like it."

Dee spent most of the lesson with his head on the desk, somewhere between reality and a dream state. He could see Vanessa from where he sat, and he could tell she was trying to avoid looking at him. Still, when everyone emptied out into the hallway after class, she stayed and waited outside for him.

"Mr. Bernardo giving you another speech in there?" she said when he entered the hallway.

"As per usual. Next Tuesday I have to spend lunch in his office. Exciting times."

"You'll survive." Vanessa shrugged sympathetically.

"I hope so. He also made me sign up for this dumb volunteer

program over the summer. I'd rather blow my brains out than do that, if I'm honest."

"You're so dramatic. It wouldn't be the worst thing in the world."

"Not until the worst thing in the world ceases to exist." Dee smirked, then looked at the ground. "Aren't you gonna be late for second period?"

"Ohh . . . yeah. I wanted to ask if we could talk at lunch? Just for a second." She looked at him, crossing her arms.

Dee stared at her. "Yeah, sure." Kids in the hallway stared at them; this was the one thing he hated about dating Vanessa Bailey. Everyone knew, and everyone cared. Everyone talked. He treated the gossip as static noise, but when it got too loud, all he wanted to do was hide. So when he met her later, they found a discreet place on the school grounds to try and hash things out.

"You good?" Vanessa asked.

"I'm fine. Kinda hungover. It was worse in the morning."

"Yeah, I felt cruddy this morning too." Vanessa looked at the ground. "Sleep deprivation isn't ideal."

"Tell me about it. And hunger. Damn, I could murder a burger at Benno's right now. Think I'm gonna head there soon."

"Can't even wait until you're a senior for an off-campus pass, can you?" She shook her head.

"When have I ever waited for anything?" he responded, grinning. They both looked out into the distance. Then Dee crouched beside the brick wall of the school gymnasium and lit a cigarette—they were still on school grounds and he couldn't afford to get caught. He offered one to her, and she accepted, sitting next to him. He helped her light her cigarette as they leaned back on the wall. They both took long drags.

"I didn't last long, trying to quit," she said.

"Just be like me. Don't quit. Then you won't disappoint yourself when you cave."

"Good one." It seemed like they were trying to avoid the real reason they needed to speak. It was easier pretending small talk was the right way forward. But it wasn't; it never was. A group of girls walked past, ogling the couple like they'd just witnessed something scandalous. Dee wiped rhinestones of sweat off his forehead.

Vanessa sighed, looking at him. "Look, Dee. We need some time apart. For real this time. No more calling me up in the middle of the night. It kind of defeats the purpose of a breakup."

"Okay. Cool."

"I want you to be all right. I want to know you're handling things well. You know, without your . . . with everything at home. I still care about you."

"I don't need you to. I know shit's hard for me right now, but I really don't need your pity."

She frowned. "*Pity*? That's what you think this is? I care about you, and you think it's pity?"

"Whatever it is. Care, pity, worry, I don't know. I don't need it."

"I just want you to be happy! To be at peace. It's just you and Dylan. You have your friends. You'll always have me, as a friend. But right now . . . it's too soon. We need time to move on. But I don't want you to head for a downward spiral."

"Okay."

"Okay? That's it?"

"The fuck do you want me to say?"

"Oh forget it." She stood up and crushed the rest of her cigarette with the sole of her shoe. "Just get back to me when you've gotten your shit together, okay?"

He rose, looking out past the football field. In the distance, he could see someone he recognized—a girl from his math class. The girl briefly looked at them as she strode past, her frizzy blond hair bouncing along with her gait.

"Thanks for the pep talk," he muttered cynically. "I guess I'll see you around, then."

"Bye, Dee," she responded. As she walked away, the cavity in his chest throbbed. He was certain that nothing would ever shrink it. It would grow to immeasurable dimensions, and one day, he'd be swallowed whole.